MW01125545

The Rise of Magic
Book One
Restriction

CM Raymond & Le Barbant
Michael Anderle

COPYRIGHT

DEDICATION

To Family, Friends and
Those Who Love
To Read.
May We All Enjoy Grace
To Live The Life We Are
Called.

RESTRICTION

JIT Beta Readers

John Findlay
Alex Wilson
Jed Moulton
Warren Wheeler
Sherry Foster
Keith Verret
Kimberly Boyer
Bruce Loving
Micky Cocker
Doreen Johnson
Diane Velasquez

If we missed anyone, please let me know!

Editor
Candy Crum
Lynne Stiegler

⊰ IRTH ⊱
THE ARCADIAN VALLEY

THE FROZEN NORTH

Cella

THE DARK
FOREST

River Wren

The Tower

Arcadia

Craigston

Temple of the Mystics

THE MADLANDS

THE HEIGHTS

N

PROLOGUE

---◆---

The Far Future, Irth (Earth)

Catherine smoothed her white skirt over her long, slender legs as she prepared to enter the classroom. She was about to give the most important lecture of her life, and she needed to look the part.

Five years working in the Ministry of Education, and she still got butterflies before she walked into the room. She had a great amount of respect for the vocation of teacher so some anxiety was natural, but Catherine hoped someday she would feel comfortable amongst the students. She swallowed one last time and stepped through the door.

The classroom was abuzz with its normal electricity. The students were curious and even excited to learn. She knew that joy in schooling wasn't typical for students of this age, but she was lucky to have been given the honor students—the best in New Arcadia. And she also knew that many of them, if she did her job well, would advance far beyond their teacher.

It was not unlike the story she was about to tell—the story of the girl who changed the world.

"Take your seats," Catherine called out over the hubbub in a cheerful tone. "Settle down everybody!"

After what seemed like an eternity, the students complied.

She stood at the podium and shuffled her notes. "Good. Right. Who remembers what we were talking about last class?" Catherine asked.

Francis, whose parents were both teachers at the University, raised his hand. She nodded in his direction. "You had just introduced a new topic—the Age of Magic."

"That's right, Francis. We had finally finished going over the Age of Madness. Someone give us a quick recap into what the Age of Madness was. Remember," she looked over her audience, "it will be on the final exam."

All the students stirred in their seats. It was the kind of question that was too easy to want to answer, so they all waited for the others.

Finally, Randall, a boy whose parents were both manual laborers, raised his hand. "The Age of Madness was a time of chaos. Empress Bethany Anne had left Earth to travel the stars some time before. And in her absence war broke out, plunging humanity into the Second Dark Ages.

"It was after she left that the Kurtherian nanocytes affected most of humanity. It took generations, but they changed the world forever. Humans, for the most part, weren't prepared to handle the mutations introduced by the nanocytes' programming. In the meantime, Michael had returned and stopped an effort by several mutated humans from taking over large areas of Earth.

"Bethany Anne came back to Earth to pick up Michael after stopping the M'nassa and other tribes from attacking

Earth. She then emplaced the Planetary Orbital Defenses so that we could never be attacked again."

The boy paused, then continued. "However, Bethany Anne and Michael left without understanding the issues surrounding the changes to humanity. So instead of giving humans the gift that the Kurtherian Tribe Essiehkor had envisioned—allowing people the ability to tap into the Etheric—the nanocytes transformed many into monsters. Ravenous creatures who looked like humans, but lacked logic and empathy.

"The Mad, as those creatures were called, desired only to consume human blood to get Etheric energy it imparted. Their ravages significantly decreased an already low population and plunged the world from the Second Dark Ages into the Age of Madness."

"Good," Catherine said. "And how did the Age of Madness come to an end?" she asked.

Melissa, a girl in the front row, looked up and spoke without raising her hand. "The Founder appeared. He was a man of great power who could cure humanity of the Madness. He taught them how to control the desires within them, and in doing so, he showed them how to tap into the Etheric and produce magic."

Catherine felt a chill run down her spine upon hearing her student's words. She had taught them well, and they were now ready to push into harder lessons.

"That's right. And today, we pick up where that story ends. The Founder was only the beginning of the Age of Magic. He had an important role to play, but his gift was just the Genesis of our world. In the end, *he* would not be nearly as important as the one who came after him."

All the students leaned in. She was blessed to have such a hungry group. They'd been waiting all year for the good stuff. It was time for Catherine to give it to them.

And that was exactly what she intended to do.

"I'm sure all of you have heard the legends, but today we are going to learn the true story of the Heroine of Magic. How she rose from nothing to become the most powerful magician the world had ever known to that point, and, more importantly, how she used that magic to vanquish evil from our land. She led us out of darkness into the time of peace that we now know.

"It is time to tell you the truth about Hannah."

Chapter 1

———— ◆ ————

Hannah didn't know it, but in just a few more minutes her future would be changed.

Forever.

And how could she have known? It was a day like any other. She and her brother William were on their way to the park in uptown Arcadia, the one clean place they could enjoy themselves in this crowded, sweaty city. Their weekly trip to the beautiful grounds was the only thing she had to look forward to in her long, hard days.

Being with her fifteen-year-old brother was in many ways the only time she truly felt human. He was five years younger than she, and William was her purpose. All that she did day-to-day was for him.

Turning the corner onto the Street of the Patriarch, William suddenly stopped.

Hannah turned, allowing a little impatience to color her

voice. "Let's go, Will. We don't have much time."

Her brother stared into the distance, his small face ashen, sweat breaking out on his forehead. "Go ahead, Hannah. I…I don't feel so good. I'll catch up. I think I might need some—"

Her brother dropped to the ground mid-sentence. Hannah scrambled back to his side. His eyes rolled back in his head and he started to tremble.

"William?" As she checked over his body, her voice rushed out, "Will, this isn't funny."

His trembling turned to shaking, which transformed into full-body spasms. William's arms tightened against his chest, and his legs kicked like wild beasts. Drool leaked from the side of his mouth.

"William? *William!*"

But her screams were accomplishing nothing. His ashen color started to turn, not back to his usual pink, but to blue.

Heart pounding in her ears, Hannah fought back fear and tried to think. Pulling him into her arms, rocking him, she desperately whispered, "Breathe, William, *breathe!*"

She looked around frantically. "Help me. Somebody help me!" All around the bustling square, the early evening market goers streamed right by them noticing nothing amiss. Hannah wasn't surprised—this city had little room to care for people like them—but their indifference made her angry nonetheless.

Unable to hold herself together, Hannah shouted into the empty sky. Anger swept through her body, electrifying her hands as people continued stepping around her and her shuddering brother.

Sweat broke out across her forehead and spread across her limbs as her body grew hot. Hannah felt like there was something inside her that was trying to escape the confines of her skin. She looked down at her brother, but then a slight movement caught her attention.

A tiny white lizard crawled out from behind a vendor's barrel. It walked over, scrambled up her brother's arm, and sat on top of her brother's convulsing body. The creature stared her in the face and cocked its head.

Her brother lay dying in her arms and all she could focus on was this damned lizard!

As she watched the slimy little reptile, the pent-up fear and panic rushed out of her; every muscle in her body tensed and then released at once. Green light emanated from her, and in that moment the lizard grew to the size of a cat. Tiny spikes pushed through its skin, and it turned from white to dark green.

It blinked at her twice, then scurried out of sight.

What the hell?

Hannah looked down at her brother lying quietly in her arms, his breathing less erratic.

Thank the Matriarch and the Patriarch!

"What happened?" he asked. His color returned to normal, and his breathing fell back to a regular pace.

Hannah slumped, pulling her brother against her body. Life in Arcadia without him would be pointless.

"Hell if I know," Hannah said, looking at him. "You OK?"

"I think—" he started to answer.

A commotion across the street cut her brother's response short.

A street vendor was talking to a man with a head the size of an ox and a body to match. The vendor stopped arguing and pointed in Hannah's direction. The large man stared right at her, yelling, "Get her!" Two smaller men followed as he pushed people out of his way, heading toward her and her brother.

Hannah's eyes opened wide. Their chests were emblazoned with the sign of the Hunter; they were mercenaries hired to kill or capture anyone using magic unlawfully within the walls of Arcadia. They were licensed to use magic themselves, and while many in the community held them in high esteem, folks from Hannah's quarter generally despised the preferential treatment they were given.

All they had to do was flex their magical muscles and people would scramble to accommodate them. What choice did they have? Hunters could wield their magic with impunity. But while these men were a terror for the Unlawfuls, they had little to do with Hannah's life.

She was just a common girl.

Hannah glanced behind her looking for their target—an Unlawful brave enough to use magic in the market square. Her face scrunched up in confusion; there was no one there. A sick realization fell over the young woman, her eyes opening in fear.

The green light. The strange lizard, she thought. The Hunters were heading straight for William and her.

She was their target.

Scrambling up, she yanked William to his feet. She pushed him in the direction of their home, his safety her only concern.

"Go. *Run!*" she hissed at him.

Sweat beaded her forehead again, and her stomach flipped. Holding her ground, she waited for the men until they were a few yards off.

She reached into her cloak. The men froze, eyes wide. If they thought she was some sort of magician, caution would be called for. After all, she could be preparing some sort of a spell. She slowly pulled out her middle finger like it was a wand and waved it at them. "Screw you, douche nuggets!" Hannah yelled, a smirk on her face as she turned and ran for the nearest alley.

She had given William time to make his escape, and that was all that mattered.

———— ♦ ————

"Humph," Ezekiel snorted, leaning on his staff in front of Jones', his old favorite watering hole. The boards across its windows and door were rotted, indicating how long it had been closed. The sight of the abandoned pub soured even further what was turning out to be an altogether disorienting homecoming.

The old man had been absent for nearly half a century, but it seemed as if he had been gone an eternity.

He looked around, scratching his bearded cheek. Apparently, a lot could happen to a city Arcadia's size in four decades. His city had been transformed into a bustling trade center; the heart and some would say soul, of Irth. He turned from the abandoned bar and ambled on, taking in the few places which had stayed the same and the many that were as different as a lifetime could make them. But each cobblestone still felt familiar under his feet.

Rounding the corner, he was nearly knocked over by a shirtless man covered in body art. The tattooed man rode a contraption that looked like a cart cut in half down the middle. The rider cut close as he zoomed past. Ezekiel tripped and fell on his ass as he stepped back.

Mumbling under his breath, he noticed a hand extend into his view, offering to help him up. Ezekiel took the hand, which belonged to a kid with a smile that reminded him of the old days; proof that there was still good in Arcadia.

"OK, pops?" the kid asked.

Forcing a grin through his beard, Ezekiel nodded as the boy pulled him to his feet. "Will be. Not as agile as I once was."

"Well, those damn magitech speeders are a danger to all of us. Mostly just the rich ride them. Not sure how that guy got one." He nodded down the road in the direction the vehicle had gone, musing to himself, "Probably stolen."

"What's a—"

Shouts from a block away cut him short. A young woman with a convulsing boy in her lap was screaming and looking in every direction. Zeke's eyes widened as he saw the green light flow from her into a tiny lizard. His jaw dropped as the creature suddenly grew.

It was magic, there was no doubt about it. But that power was unlike anything he had ever witnessed. Following the disappearance of the green light, the boy's tremors ceased and color came back to his face.

A toothy grin cut across the kid's face, which lasted until a group of men rushed the boy and the woman. In a beat, they were running in opposite directions.

"What the hell was that all about?" Ezekiel pointed to the action down the block.

The young man was watching the action as well. "Hell's got nothing to do with it. They're Hunters. If they catch her, they get a bounty. Pretty lucrative position if you can get it."

"Hunters?"

"Sure. To catch the illegal magic users; unrestricted use of magic is outlawed here. Hunters bring in the Unlawfuls, dead or alive."

"That's monstrous," the old man's eyes narrowed and a flicker of anger flashed across his face. When he had left Arcadia, anyone with the will to handle magic was free to use it. Although one needed a mentor to tame their powers, of course.

But restrictions were unheard of when he was here last.

"You must've been gone a while, old-timer. That's how things are run here in Arcadia. Have to control the magic, that's what we're told. It's too dangerous if just anyone uses it. I'm sure it's for the best." The kid turned to watch the three men rush after the girl. "She should know better. Those guys are gonna do a number on her."

The boy shrugged and looked back at the old man.

But he had disappeared.

———— ♦ ————

Glancing over her shoulder, Hannah saw the men gaining. The three goons were faster than they looked. She turned right, then left, then right again. She popped out of the alley and into the heart of the bazaar. Her legs moved as if a new sense of life flowed through her body.

She hopped over a cart filled with apples and grabbed the handle, halfway dislocating her arm from the momentum. However, she was able to flip it and sent the green orbs rolling across the cobblestones.

She prayed the obstacles would gain her a few steps.

The grocer hurled curses behind her. Ignoring him, she ducked through a stall selling fine silken scarves that she could never have afforded. Hannah pushed through the crowd toward safety, but the shouts behind her indicated she had not yet lost the Hunters.

Her eyes cut around the square, flicking from exit to exit, now alive with the excitement of a chase. She spied an alley she thought she knew and broke for it.

Footsteps grew louder as the men got closer. She dodged a large wooden crate blocking her path and took three steps in before she looked down the alley.

"*Shit*," Hannah muttered saw the dead end coming up. The clamor of the men scrambling over the crate filled the alley, and she turned around and backed herself against the wall. Hannah lifted her hands in surrender.

She smiled, the humor never finding her eyes. "Fun game, guys. You caught me. I'm *it* now, right?"

"On your knees," the lead man growled as he approached her. He was the big brute and had a scar across his left eye.

"Seriously. I'm not what you think. Just a kid. My brother, he—"

"Don't look like just a kid to me," another said with a laugh. "You look like a woman. Ripe enough to eat." His eyes scanned her body, making Hannah want to retch.

The two smaller men started to chuckle but went dead quiet when the giant raised his hand.

"We've heard every excuse, Unlawful. None of them worked. No one's talked their way out before. You're certainly not going to be the first."

The leader drove a tall bronze staff into the ground. Its tip glowed blue.

Magitech, Hannah thought. She'd seen Hunters' weapons take men down before. It was not a pretty sight, but she never thought she'd experience its power first-hand.

Her eyes darted around the alley, both to the men and up to two visible windows; she doubted there was anyone listening who would intervene. She looked back at her attackers. "I don't know magic," she cried. Her heart pounded out of her chest as she pleaded, "I beg you, listen!"

But these were men of violence, who acted first and listened never.

The eyes of the two men behind the staff wielder were suddenly suffused by black, as if replaced by perfect midnight. It was the sign that they were about to do magic.

One of them swept his arms across his chest and followed the motion over his head, making two arcs. By the time they came to rest by his side, two perfectly round fireballs danced in his hands. The man laughed as he saw the look of fear and awe on Hannah's face.

He hurled a flaming orb just over her shoulder. It crashed behind her in a tiny explosion, and shards of brick bit at her neck. The other man extended an arm and flicked his wrist. She tried to move, but a barrel flew from the edge of the alley. Hannah ducked, narrowly dodging the missile.

"That is *real* magic, Unlawful," the man with the staff said. "It is for the few who are worthy, not for street scum like you. And we are the protectors of its use. We tag you as an Unlawful and enemy of Arcadia."

The man flicked something the size of a playing card towards her, which floated like a bird to find its home on her forehead. It burned as it made contact. She clawed at the mark, trying to peel it away, but she knew it was no use; only magic could take away the tag.

Restriction

Hannah eyed the alley behind them, looking for any way out. Nothing. She was caught, and a sense of doom washed over her. The feeling from the market square returned, and heat rose beneath her skin again. The young woman clenched her teeth and tried to get control of her body.

The monstrous man grabbed her shoulder and shoved her to the ground. As her knees smashed into the cobblestones, she screamed in pain.

"Now that I have you in the right position, time to take my prize," he said. He grabbed his staff, and with its glowing end tilted her head up to face him. "You wouldn't look half bad if someone washed the mud and muck off you. A shame to lose such a beauty from our fair city, but the law is the law. Since we're bringing you in DOA," he leaned down to whisper near her ear "we might as well play a little first."

A shit-eating grin covered his face. The sound of laughter and lewd comments surrounded her. Life for the bottom dwellers ranged from difficult to brutish, but she had never expected to meet her end in an alleyway, gang-raped by a group of the Governor's civil servants.

Her eyes narrowed in anger. "Go to hell!" she yelled at him.

She swung a clumsy punch to the man's groin, and he pivoted just in time to catch it in the ass.

He grinned down at her. "Ooh, feisty one. I don't mind some foreplay first."

The man dropped a right hook. The sound of her crunching nasal cartilage filled her ears as Hannah's world went blurry.

Reaching down, the Hunter grabbed a handful of her threadbare shirt and pulled. Her covering gave way with little resistance, and she instinctively wrapped her arms across

20

her bare chest. Sobs of fear and resignation leaked from the broken young woman. Her head dropped slowly toward the ground.

"Don't worry, little one." The large man gave her a feigned look of pity. "We won't kill you. Well, not before I have you first. And maybe the boys behind me, too."

Hoots and hollers followed. The man flipped Hannah over. One hand held her hair while the other grabbed the waist of her pants. The pressure cut a line into her stomach.

She closed her eyes and tried to hold back her emotions—the one thing she might be able to keep from them. But fear of ungodly violation gripped her soul. A tear escaped her eye, trailing a path through the dirt down her left cheek.

At least William was safe.

That was as much mercy she could hope for in a city like Arcadia.

"Hands off her!" The voice rang through the alley, clear despite the noise coming from the bazaar.

Hannah crumpled back to the ground when her attacker let go. Pulling the tattered shirt over her chest she looked up to see a figure covered in the folds of a brown cloak. He was hunched over, supporting himself with a twisted wooden staff. The hood of his cloak covered his head, face hidden in its dark cavern.

"Step away from the girl, you cur." He waved his staff back towards the only exit from the alley. "Take your henchmen and be on your way."

The three men looked at each other, then back at the new arrival. All three laughed at the stranger's demands, but it was the one with the scar who responded.

"Go back to wherever you came from, old man. This is official government business." He jerked a thumb at himself.

"We're Hunters, and we have a pocket full of tags to hand out. Careful," he pointed to the old guy "or we'll add you to our list."

They could see the stranger's eyes glowing in the darkness underneath his hood. They were bright red, like embers. Hannah gasped, and the men stepped back. The hooded man whispered words Hannah couldn't discern and tilted his head, letting the hood fall down his back.

She nearly screamed when the identity of her redeemer was exposed. Hannah had expected a wizened old face, but instead she saw the head of a monster; green, hairless, and shining in the midday sun. Two horns jutted from its head toward the heavens. Eyes big and round like an owl's darted around the alley.

The three Hunters screamed in fear.

——————— ◆ ———————

As the three thugs stumbled backward in terror of the demon standing before them, Ezekiel couldn't help but smile. The devil mask was an ancient spell not practiced in Arcadia, at least not as far as he knew. It was designed to scare the shit out of those who saw it.

He was glad it hadn't lost its effectiveness. He lifted his staff into the air, and before it hit its apex, dark clouds covered the quarter. Thunder rolled overhead and winds whipped through the tight passageway. He extended his left hand toward the men.

"Arcadians!" he spoke through the wind as the dirt and the trash whipped around them. "Magic is not meant to exploit the weak, but to rescue them. I would have thought they still taught that here."

A bolt of lightning screamed down from the heavens and connected with his staff. Channeling its power, he splayed his fingers and lightning flew from their tips. It was a secret art learned from the people of the Dark Forest.

The two smaller men were slammed against the alley walls, their bodies twitching from the current. The smell of burning hair and flesh filled the alley as the bolts danced over their unconscious bodies.

The large one, in an act of extreme stupidity, ran toward Ezekiel. He swung the weapon at the wizard, trying to cave his head in.

Ezekiel held out his palm; both man and staff stopped and rebounded slightly. The Hunter looked at his weapon, dumbfounded. His expression distorted into something sinister by the illusion on his face, Ezekiel smiled.

He closed his palm and twisted his wrist upward. The magitech staff began to steam. The Hunter screamed, but couldn't let go as his hand was fused to the shaft. It melted before his eyes, dripping liquified bronze across his skin. He fell to his knees and stared at his deformed arm.

Ezekiel stepped forward and glared down at the man. "Now it is I who mark you, as a fool and despised of Irth. You will never lay that hand on the innocent ever again."

With that, Ezekiel raised his wooden staff into the air and cracked the man across his skull, sending him crashing to the ground.

Sometimes it just felt good to deal out justice the old-fashioned way. He was told physical exertion was good for an old body like his.

The old man looked down at the Hunters crumpled in the alley's filth.

He spoke the word of release and the demonic face

disappeared to reveal his wrinkled skin and white beard underneath. The lines on his face relaxed. A sense of accomplishment like he hadn't felt in years washed over him.

Thoughts of the restoration of the old ways had consumed him since he returned home, and his quest had just started in this alley. This would be his first act of many.

If the Matriarch and the Patriarch were with him, he would find a way to cleanse this place. He looked up just in time to see the girl vault the wooden crate blocking the alley, the tatters of her shirt flying behind her.

Shaking his head, he realized that in the old days he would have tagged her with a tracking spell. He was rusty, and it seemed that the rust would need to be knocked loose. But he wasn't worried. His cunning and intuition would be enough to find her.

And find her he must. He pictured the green energy that had flowed from her and the strange lizard which had reacted to her power. Whether she knew it or not, she would have an important role to play in what was to come.

CHAPTER 2

Hannah swiped a shirt from a booth in the bazaar as she ran toward safety. It covered her physically but did little to ease the pain of what had just happened. Those men were going to hurt her, maybe kill her, for no reason other than they could.

They had the power.

Fear drove her legs as disgust churned in her gut. Remembering the tag, she pulled her hair over her forehead to try and hide the mark. The Hunters had branded her as an Unlawful—an illegal magic user and enemy of the city. Until she could find a way to remove the tag, the city would certainly be *her* enemy.

Which sucked in almost every way possible.

She finally made it to the small city park beyond the marketplace. It felt like a lifetime ago that she had been on her way here with her brother. She stopped and dropped to her knees behind a tree. The smell of the scar-faced man still haunted her.

She could still feel the tug of his hand on her hair; the rhythm of her heartbeat raced across her throbbing face to remind her of the blow he had delivered.

Doubling over, she spilled what little food was left over from breakfast onto the grass. Her body continued to retch, searching for something more to expel as if it might be able to rid itself of the memory of the assault. Finally, falling over on her side, she screamed into the dirt and pounded it with her fist.

"I only wanted to help William," she moaned through her tears in the empty park. "I only...*wanted to help.*"

She pictured the man grabbing her shirt as the words came, and a rush of anger came over her. It was the same energy she had felt as she held her brother in her arms and then again in the alley.

Powerlessness somehow turning to power. She pictured the strange lizard, the way it had stretched and grown in front of her. She saw her brother's sick form suddenly becoming well.

Then she imagined the demon-faced man drawing lightning from the heavens and hurling it at her attackers. Scared of the sensations, afraid that she was someone like that thing, she fought the surge in her body until it eventually subsided.

As she stared up at the sky, Hannah decided that she would do all she could to keep the power within her at bay. She also swore to herself that she'd die by her own hand before being treated like that ever again.

She vowed she would find the Hunters and make them pay, and that no other women would suffer at their filthy hands.

After what felt like hours, her thoughts turned from the violence in the alley to her brother. At least he was safe. Fear, anger, pain; none of that mattered as much as getting home to William.

She started the trip, hoping nothing had hurt him in her absence.

———— ◆ ————

Adrien stood in front of the window at the top of the Academy's single tower. As the Academy's Chancellor Adrien had certain advantages, such as the view from his office. From his vantage point, the highest spot in Arcadia, he could see each of the city's four quarters.

His assistant was standing behind him giving a report, but Adrien hardly listened.

Doyle had completed his studies ten years earlier. He was a half-grade magician who came from a noble family, so Adrien had little choice but to admit him. Even though Doyle couldn't cast a spell to scratch his own balls, he was hopelessly devoted to Adrien.

So instead of sending him out into the world, Adrien kept him by his side to serve as Special Assistant to the Chancellor. What Doyle lacked in magical acumen, he made up for in loyalty. Adrien knew the man would kill for him; that is, if he had possessed the ability to cause harm to anything at all.

It was time for the monthly update on financials. The numbers bored him. The Arcadian Academy was flourishing financially, not only from the astronomical tuition that the rich were willing to shell out to enroll their snot-nosed silver-spoon kids, but also, and maybe more to the point, because

Arcadia's Governor and the Leadership Council gave him whatever he demanded.

The Academy was the backbone of the community and the only thing keeping Arcadia on top in this world.

"I was thinking, Chancellor, that maybe it is time that we consider admitting more students. The demand is there, and we could—"

Adrien had continued staring out across the city. He lifted his hand and waved away the man's comments as if swatting a fly. "You haven't learned, have you, Doyle? Our job is not to fill beds but to control entry. You see, many in our place might keep the doors shut tightly because scarcity breeds demand. They're short-sighted fools."

He paused in his explanation to inspect his cuticles, then looked at his assistant. "But not us. Demand will always be high. Damned nobles would sacrifice their youngest to get their oldest in. And who can blame them? The chance to have a magician in the family is no small thing."

"What does scarcity breed, then?" the assistant asked.

Adrien lifted an eyebrow and waved his hand towards his window. "Scarcity breeds prestige. Prestige provides power. And power gives us whatever the hell we want. That's why we restrict access. Control the magic, control the world."

Doyle blushed and looked down at his papers. "Right then. Do you want to—"

"That's not all," Adrien continued, ignoring the man altogether. "How are we to keep track of all the authorized magicians?" Adrien turned back around to look out the window. "Can you even imagine the world that the Founder envisioned?"

The assistant twitched at *that* name.

"Let everyone study magic?" the Chancellor continued. "Ezekiel was a damned fool. If things had been done his way,

Arcadia would have been in ashes years ago. Hell, he thought that the old world was bad; went on and on about it. But that's nothing compared to what would happen if we let any damned fool practice magic. It would be bedlam. Chaos!"

Adrien slapped the frame of the window. "No! We'll keep the class sizes right where they are. Besides, what do we need more magicians for? We have the manpower necessary to complete my plan with the students that are here now. We have the pick of the litter. Our primary goals are research and design, not enrollment and financials. The Governor is pleased with the new prototype, and he wants to employ magitech as soon as possible."

"Right. Very good, sir. I'm sure he's pleased. Should I—"

Adrien observed a couple of carts stuck facing each other on a street three blocks over. "Damn right it's good, Doyle. And he'd better be pleased."

He turned and walked behind his desk, pulling out the chair and sitting down. "That asshat would still be pissing in a cracked pot in that little district of his if it weren't for the magitech weapons we've crafted for him. If it wasn't for me— me and the Academy—he'd have nothing."

The assistant looked down at his feet and pulled on the collar of his cloak. "There are, um, a few other things."

Adrien leaned forward, resting his arms on the mahogany desk and staring at him.

Voice quivering, Doyle continued, "It's the engineers, sir. Today's report was, well, troubling."

"Troubling?" Adrien asked, his voice soft.

Despite his love for the Chancellor, he was terrified at the moment. "Quite troubling, sir. Things are moving more slowly than expected. The lead engineer is saying that the first weapon won't be ready for another four months."

Adrien stood up and bent forward to tower over his assistant. "Four months is unacceptable!" His voice was much louder, his anger flavoring his reply. "Tell Elon that I can get them extra workers, but if he believes I'm going to wait another four months he's an idiot. Do I need to remind him what happened to the last head engineer who tried my patience?"

Doyle shook his head before stammering, "No, sir. I think that will be crystal clear."

"What else?" Adrien's voice boomed. Doyle's presence was becoming irksome.

He looked down at his notes and back to Adrien. "Oh, it's nothing. Just…there was an attack today. Three Hunters. Apparently they found a girl from Queen's Boulevard using magic in public. Unlawful, of course. They chased her down and attempted to make a passive capture."

"And?"

"Well, something went wrong. Only one of them is currently conscious."

Adrien knew the power his Hunters could assert. They weren't the brightest graduates of the Academy, but they were gifted in magic and were also given magitech weapons to assist in capturing or killing Unlawfuls. It was more power than necessary, but Adrien believed in being thorough.

Most Unlawfuls quietly developed their magic behind closed doors where they would never be found. As far as the Capitol knew, most of these folks could do little more than glorified card tricks. But allowing even the simplest magics to be practiced unchecked could lead to disaster.

There hadn't been a serious issue during a capture for over a decade.

Adrien's voice lowered. "Unconscious, you say? What happened?"

Doyle wiped his hands on his pants. "Apparently, sir, they were attacked by a demon that could control the weather."

Adrien dropped back into his chair and laughed. "A demon? Do they take me for an idiot? I'm guessing those three got drunk and were jumped by beggars or something. Once they're released from the hospital, make sure they're put to work in the factory. That will teach them to shirk their responsibilities."

Doyle continued his report, but Adrien had stopped paying attention. Something about the Hunters' story reminded him of a memory long since buried—a trick that his old teacher Ezekiel liked to use.

His mentor was powerful in ways that Adrien could never match, but Ezekiel was a fool. His notions of justice were always clouding better judgment—Adrien's better judgment. And it was that foolishness that had sent Ezekiel on his final quest.

The quest that would claim his life.

Despite what the halfwit priests on the street preached, Adrien knew that the Founder would never return.

And yet...

He put up his hand, stopping Doyle's recitation. "Actually, Doyle, I'll go talk to those Hunters myself. I might have some questions for them."

Doyle nodded. "Of course, sir. Anything else?"

Adrien waved him off. "That's enough for today. Thank you for your work."

The assistant nodded and turned for the door.

"And, Doyle?" Adrien called as the man grabbed the knob.

"If I ever hear of you speaking to anyone about this demon, you'll wish that it had been you in that alley today. You understand?" he asked.

"Yes, sir."

Adrien could hear his assistant swallow from across the room. He smiled, pleased by the extent of his power.

———— ◆ ————

Hannah paused on the step outside her house. She listened for any sign of her father. The day had already gone sideways, and the last thing she needed was a shit-show confrontation with the drunk head of the house. Hearing nothing, she turned the knob and stepped across the threshold.

The room was nearly bare, whether out of poverty or sheer laziness she wasn't sure. But since her mother had passed, their house was nothing like a home.

Tiptoeing across the living room, she turned for the bedroom she and William had shared since they were born. Although inconvenient at times, she didn't mind the arrangement, and knew that it was part of the reason she and her brother were so close.

They had spent hours lying in their beds deep in conversation about what life would be like if they ever broke out of Queen Bitch Boulevard—what the locals called Queen's Boulevard, the slums of Arcadia.

"What the hell happened to you?" the voice said from behind her.

Hannah spun on her heel and faced her second adversary of the day. Her fingers moved to her nose and felt the bump. She hadn't seen her face, but she could imagine it looked pretty bad.

The Hunter had tagged her in more ways than one. Of course, she wouldn't get sympathy from her father. Instead, she brushed more hair in front of her face and hung her head. "Nothing. Just… Nothing."

Her father's right hand formed into a fist, and she wondered if she would get a second beating. The man was aging, and his sedentary life, split between sleeping and getting drunk, did nothing for his physical abilities. But he had height and weight on her, and he could still do some damage.

Hannah expected the day would come when she finally fought back, but that would be a day of maximal commitment.

The day they would run from this town forever.

"Where's your take for today? With my…disability, you know I can't work. That's why you and your brother need to be out there hustling. And what the hell happened to your nose?"

As her father's rank whiskey breath spread over her, she considered lashing back. But she had learned her lesson before, and it was always better to just keep her head down.

"I'm sorry. I'll get twice as much tomorrow," she mumbled.

He growled, "Damn right you will." He pointed to the back. "And talk to your brother. He's been crying in his room since he got back. That damn boy is worthless."

She choked down a laugh at the irony of his words. The man in front of her was literally a waste of space. She couldn't hate him more if he were the Hunter that attacked her today.

Hannah sidestepped her father and headed toward the back of the house. It didn't take long; the place was small enough to fit on a merchant's cart. Cracking her bedroom door, she peeked inside. William levered up onto his elbows and smiled. The boy's color had waned again; black circles surrounded his eyes.

He spoke as she stepped in and closed the door. "Hey, glad you're back. I was nervous those men had gotten you."

"Yeah, you know me. I'm untouchable," Hannah smirked as she crossed the room and sat on his bed. "How you doing, anyway?"

The boy shrugged. "Not sure. I guess I feel almost normal. But something still isn't quite right. I know it's *not*, but I feel like my entire body is still shaking."

She knew nothing about medicine, but Hannah was sure that the onset of seizures was serious. Arcadia was known for some of the best medical services in all of Irth, which was great for those who could afford it. Instead, people in their quarter were forced to rely on home remedies and, at times, black-market potions, to try to cure the most serious ailments.

William had always been sickly, but today's seizure marked something worse and it terrified her.

She once overheard a trader say that people in other regions looked on Arcadia with covetous eyes. But they didn't know what life was like in the QBB. With her mother dead and her father a drunk, her little brother was nearly the only thing that made her believe life was worth a damn.

"Listen, when I hit the streets tomorrow, I'm gonna ask around. See if I can find out something about what happened to you. If I can, I'll get some medicine. But for now, get some rest."

He nodded to her. "OK. But what about what happened to you? That green light?"

Hannah subconsciously raised a hand to the tag under her hair. Whatever had happened back there in the streets was still freaking her out. "That's nothing for you to worry about." She ruffled his hair. "Go to sleep."

Moments later, Hannah laid in bed listening to the uneven breaths of her brother's labored slumber. Sleep never came easily for her, and after a day like this it might not come at all.

The Boulevard had come to life outside her window. Her quarter was safe for locals during the day; they were a group down on their luck with no hope on the horizon, and were all in it together.

But at night everything changed. The neighborhood was transformed into a den of prostitutes, drunks, and thieves. The only protection for someone like her or her brother was to stay in after sundown.

She thought about William and their miserable conditions. If she had a sure shot she'd take them both away from it all. Away from her father. Away from Queen Bitch Boulevard. Away from Arcadia. Hannah didn't know where they would go, but that didn't matter. Anywhere would be better than here.

As dreams of a better place danced in her head, sleep started to take over. Just as she was slipping away, a scratch on the shutters drew her back to consciousness.

She jumped, reaching for the dull knife on her bedside table. Really, it was less of a knife and more of a glorified toothpick, but it was better than nothing. Hannah held the point toward the window.

After a moment of quiet, her heart beating hard enough to split open her ribs, she figured it was just her mind playing tricks. She considered dropping back into bed when the scratching returned.

Keeping the knife extended before her, she slowly reached forward and pulled open the shutters.

Hannah fully expected to find a burglar lurking outside her window, or some drunk vomiting his mead into their rain barrel below. But what she saw shocked her. Two eyes stared at her from the window sill just inches away.

She stepped back in surprise. She half-expected the eyes vanish, but they didn't.

From her vantage point she could see the entire creature. It was that spiny green lizard she had seen transform in the market square. With all that had occurred, she had almost forgotten about that peculiar event. If she *had* remembered, she would have marked it up to optical illusion or maybe even delusion from the fear of losing her brother.

But there it was, sitting on her very own windowsill gazing back at her in the moonlight. It didn't look anything like the lizards that lurked around the cobblestoned streets of Arcadia. It was big; bigger than her old cat Thomas. Its skin wasn't pale like Arcadian newts; it was darker, the color of the waving boughs of the pine trees that grew outside the city gates.

If all of that wasn't strange enough, the creature had a dozen or so spines running down the narrow ridge of its back. Their points were silhouetted in the light of the full moon.

She stepped forward to get a closer look. When she did, the lizard leapt from its station on the sill directly at her. Hannah shrieked and swatted the thing away from her body. William wrestled around in his bed, obviously disturbed by the outburst but still asleep.

The lizard landed harmlessly on her pillow. It stared up at her without blinking, and she wondered if it was planning its next attack.

With its tongue shooting out and back in, it walked off her pillow and started walking in circles on her bed, wagging its long tail before finally curling up into a ball on her quilt— just like her old cat.

She lowered the knife and relaxed at the sight.

Seriously? How much worse could this day get?

"You're cute. But you got to go," she said, wondering how she would get the thing off her bed and out of the house. She approached it tentatively, having no idea what it was and if it were dangerous. She waved her hands at it. "Shoo! Get!"

It blinked and laid its head on the bed, keeping its reptilian eyes fastened on her. As Hannah drew close, she felt the hum of energy run through her body, just as she had in the market square. She reached out for the lizard and its tongue lashed out and licked her hand.

Hannah yanked her hand back, but it didn't hurt so she moved her hand forward again. Hannah laughed as the next lick tickled her wrist. It felt good, both to be tickled by the little creature and to laugh.

It had been far too long.

She smiled and whispered after a moment, "OK, friend. You can stay. But just for tonight."

Hannah closed the shutters and crawled back into her bed, shaping her body around the lump of creature that had become her second roommate in the tiny space she and William shared. As she drifted off to sleep, Hannah felt the lizard lay its head across her thigh.

CHAPTER 3

———— ♦ ————

Sunshine cut through the slats in the shutters, drawing Hannah out of her deep slumber. Years ago, beautiful tapestry blinds had kept the rays at bay. The window dressings were their only precious heirloom, a treasure passed down through generations.

Soon after the passing of her mother, they disappeared. Hannah never asked, but she assumed they were sold by her father or given to some Queen Bitch Boulevard whore for the sake of a few thrusts and grunts. The tapestries weren't the greatest loss, but their absence proved that nothing was sacred. And it showed what kind of an animal her father was.

The lizard curled between her legs and cracked an eye when she rolled over, then immediately went back to sleep.

"Lazy ass," she chuckled. It didn't seem to mind the insult.

She half assumed the thing would be gone when she woke up, just another wisp of a dream destroyed by the morning light. But whatever it was—and wherever it came from—the thing was flesh and blood, and it seemed to have made itself at home here.

"Well, if you're going to stay, I might as well give you a name. I've decided you're a boy." She tilted her head to the side and thought for a second. "How about Sal?"

As she said the name, the lizard curled itself tighter into a ball. With a little imagination, she pictured the thing smiling. It seemed that Sal would work just fine.

Getting out of bed was a chore. Her muscles and joints protested while her face throbbed. The Hunters had done more of a number on her than she thought, but not as much as they could have.

Hatred boiled in her blood, and she promised that they would get theirs someday.

She'd take extra time on Scarface.

Thinking of the Hunters reminded her of the demon from the alley. If she hadn't already been terrified, seeing it would have scared the hell out of her. But the more she thought about it, the less frightening its appearance seemed.

She had heard about magic users that had the ability to alter their appearance. In the light of a new day, with some time and sleep between her and the attack, she was convinced that the demon face was only some sort of scare tactic.

If so, it certainly worked. The last thing she saw before taking off down the alley was the demon with its staff raised high in one hand and the other pointed toward the Hunters in rebuke.

Perhaps they had already gotten what they deserved? She smiled at the thought, before frowning a moment later.

She swiped the back of her hand across her forehead; the Hunters' tag was still there. It was not only a reminder of the

Hunters' cruelty but worse, it would tell all of Arcadia that she was an Unlawful, or at least she stood accused as one.

But being accused and being guilty were basically one and the same. At least, that's how the other Hunters would see it.

Hannah dressed and pulled on a wool hat to cover the mark. By the time she got to the kitchen the wool already itched. She would have to find a way to remove the tag.

William was already gone, which was good. Two years ago they still worked the streets together, but since she had grown older, panhandling wasn't quite the return on investment that it once was.

In Arcadia, begging was children's work. And despite her thin frame, she was definitely no longer a child. She wondered about William's sickness and prayed that the seizures wouldn't return while he was out working on his own.

She didn't believe in the gods. If they ever existed, the Patriarch and the Matriarch had abandoned this world long ago.

But when it came to her brother? She was willing to give even faith a try.

———◆———

The woman's voice called out in the little rundown apartment. "Parker. Parker, wake up already! Your shift is starting soon."

"Coming, Mother." Parker stumbled out of bed as he rolled his eyes. His mother was sweet and conveniently naive. Many mothers along Queen's Boulevard became this way. He wasn't sure if she actually believed that a kid from the slums could land a job at the factory, or if she just fooled herself into believing he had the life she wanted for him.

Either way, Parker was glad she could brag to her friends over a game of Wicken, a popular card game in the city. He slid into his clothes and tightened the laces of his boots.

One snapped from too many days of wear.

"Shit," he hissed, tying another knot in the already tangled laces. He could scrape by working the streets of Arcadia. Although he couldn't get a more respectable job like his mother thought, conning shoppers provided a steady enough income.

And since the trading traffic had increased with the coming of summer, bringing more and more outsiders through the city gates, there was plenty of work. But money was still precious, and some would have to be put away for the off season.

Grabbing his bag of tools, he left his little room and headed for the kitchen.

"Here you are, lovely," his mother said, sliding a plate of eggs with a single strip of bacon across the table to the spot where his dad had always sat.

It took months before she accepted he wasn't coming home. The first day that Parker ate in his father's chair was when he knew for certain he had become the man of the house, and that was the day he stole his first loaf of bread.

Parker didn't necessarily like the life of a thief and conman, but it paid the bills and kept his mother from having to seek other questionable jobs. Too many women in the quarter did things no human should face, and he vowed that his mother wouldn't be one of them.

"Thanks, Mother. What's the plan today?" He asked the same question every day, and every day he got the same answer.

"Oh, I need to do some tidying up around the house and see if MacIntyre has work for me. If not, I'll swing by the park and sit with the girls." She smiled broadly at her son. "It's a good thing I have a working man in the house."

MacIntyre ran *The Arcadian*, the city's local paper. For a long time it had been esteemed as a reputable news source, but for the past few years it had published mainly political propaganda for the Governor and the Chancellor. The few remaining back pages were reserved for gossip and advertising. There had been little work for people like his mother since its transformation.

People said the business had been infused with special magitech—magic-powered machines that pretty much wrote, edited, and printed the paper all by themselves. Parker knew that was horseshit, but couldn't deny the fact that his mother's unemployment had *something* to do with the legal use of magic.

The magic was controlled by those in power, and it worked for them to make them more powerful. For as long as he could remember the Capitol had boasted of more and more progress while life in Queen Bitch Boulevard got worse and worse.

"Sounds like a good plan," Parker said, shoveling loads of eggs into his mouth. "I better get going. The foreman won't be happy if I'm late." He ate his last bite, kissed his mother on the cheek, and headed for the market square.

The morning fog was thick and the cobblestones were slick with dew. Few people were out that early in the quarter; not many had any reason to be. He exchanged greetings with those he knew better and nodded at some familiar faces.

Arcadia had grown exponentially over the past few years. People were flooding into the city from the corners of Irth, looking for a fresh life and a new hope.

Outside the walls, a skewed narrative about his home was spun for foreigners. People were told that Arcadia, as the heart of Irth, had good houses on every corner and that jobs were abundant for anyone willing to work.

Parker had no idea how this lie was spun or why. But he did know that when people came to the city they would eventually end up realizing the ugly truth of the place. Many of them landed on Queen's Boulevard doing the same work he did—hustling on the streets for whatever sustenance they could find.

This was why he had to go out earlier and earlier.

It was also why the con had to keep changing. Every few weeks he would devise a new plan. His work was always evolving. It had to be. And this morning, he was about to kick a new strategy into play.

"Morning, Mac," Parker said as he pushed through the growing crowd on the South end of the Market Square.

A burly man with a face only a mother could stand sat on an empty mead barrel chewing on the stump of a cigar that looked older than Parker himself.

"Hey, kid. What's happening?" the man asked as he sorted through a handful of coins, glancing up occasionally to watch the crowd gather for the first fight of the day.

Mac ran the Pit, a roped off little corner of the market that was reserved for daily boxing and mixed-methods fights. It provided entertainment for the lower classes, and a chance to cash in through the official bets that Mac facilitated.

He was a brilliant businessman. The odds were perfectly calculated and the earnings closely tracked. All bets were supposed to flow through him, and he collected a fee from each transaction. A portion of the fee went to the fighters.

Both the victor and the man who was left in a bloody pulp on the dusty ground would get their cut, which everyone knew was less than Mac's. Side bets weren't allowed, although everyone knew they happened.

"I want in today," Parker said.

"On the first fight? You know I'll take anyone's money, kid, but no one's stepped up to fight Hank. His reputation precedes him. After what he did to Grant last week, I can't find anyone to go toe-to-toe with him."

Parker looked around before answering him. "Not for a bet, Mac. I want in the ring. I want to fight Hank."

Mac stopped counting his coins and looked up as if confused for a moment, then laughed. Parker was tall for his age, his frame lean and muscular, but fully dressed he looked like a beanpole. "Be serious, kid. You can't go in there. You look like you couldn't give a stray dog a run for its money."

If you only knew, Parker thought.

Undeterred, Parker continued his pitch, "That's exactly why I'm the perfect man for the job. You'll be able to set the odds however you want, and you'll still draw plenty of action." He tried a different tack. "People would love to see Hank break me in half."

Mac shook his head and put up a hand, shaking it. "No way. If word spreads that I'm putting kids in the ring, the Capitol'll shut me down faster than you can say Queen Bitch."

Parker thought about saying 'Queen Bitch' but decided snark wasn't a good choice at the moment. "I turned eighteen last month, Mac. I'm legal now. There's no problem for you in this."

Mac chortled. "Just a number, kid. That argument won't

fly. Not with the Governor or the people." He pointed to himself. "I'm a businessman first and foremost, Parker. I can't have my customers turning away because I let you get mauled. It'd be bad for business."

Parker leaned forward on the table. "What's bad for business, Mac, is not having fights for people to bet on," he argued. "Come on. Give me a shot. If shit goes sideways, I'll call it."

Mac scratched his graying beard a few moments, considering before he nodded. "OK, kid. One shot. But don't get your ass handed to you. Your dear old dad would never forgive me."

The mention of his father only fueled Parker's appetite for the ring. His old man had gone off to strike it rich on a new mining operation deep in the Heights.

It was a fool's errand.

If his dad had told the truth about what he was doing, then odds were good he had been buried in a landslide or crushed to death by a mountain troll or whatever creatures lived beyond the walls of Arcadia.

But Parker suspected that his father was more coward than fool. He probably used the new mine as an excuse to get out of the city and away from his family. Either way, he was never coming back.

His mother, of course, believed that his father would return one day with a cart full of diamonds and enough money to take them out of the slums. But deep down, Parker assumed that the guy found his personal way out of Queen Bitch Boulevard, and the rest of them were left to fend for themselves.

"Thanks, Mac. I won't let you down."

——— ◆ ———

Ezekiel sat at the city gate, resting his legs. Traffic was picking up, and a long line of people waiting to make their way into Arcadia had formed. He watched in amazement as travelers took turns passing through the large gate.

A pair of Capitol guards lounged on either side of the roadway. Their inspections were done with a certain level of casualness, if at all. Most of those entering were farmers who made up the region immediately outside the city. The land surrounding Arcadia was lush, and agriculture thrived for miles beyond the walls. It was part of what made Arcadia great; why it was founded here to begin with.

The city had access to enough fresh produce and meat for its population to grow, and due to Capitol regulations, farmers had to sell within Arcadia's markets if their land was within ten thousand paces of the gate.

After a mile of farm carts had rolled through, a half-dozen mystics with their gentle faces and perfect robes ambled into the city.

The guards stood back, giving them more room than was necessary. The aura surrounding these monastic people preceded them, and most Arcadians offered a wide berth. Tales flowed like Mule Head Mead concerning the abilities of the mystics, though no one in town had ever seen their powers manifest.

Adrien had forbidden it within the city limits. Nevertheless, it seemed as if this small group of men and women still found it worthwhile to make the long trek from their mountain temple. They brewed a potent drink in the mountains, and were happy to sell it in Arcadia.

47

From what Ezekiel could tell, Arcadians were happy to buy it.

Ezekiel smiled as they passed; an aura of power flowed from their serene figures, one with which the old man was quite familiar. The demon mask he had used was a form of magic like their own. He considered reaching out to them, but held back.

Adrien had changed much in his absence. Maybe these people, whom he had once known so well, were his friends no longer.

Behind the mystics, a group of men several days' journey away from their homes trudged along. They pulled a cart along with them, filled to the brim with game and the pelts of smaller animals they had cleaned in the field.

When Ezekiel was forty years younger, before he had left on his half-century sabbatical, Ezekiel had hoped that Arcadia would become a place like this—a place for the nations, a place that would welcome all people.

And, at least in part, it had.

But in his absence, the city had become something more. More powerful than he could have imagined, more prosperous, and unfortunately, more cruel. He had seen that firsthand.

Stretching his legs, Ezekiel stood, then went back into town.

He had already seen the marketplace and all that it had to offer the city. Its bustling crowds and eager vendors were appropriate for a city the size Arcadia. And although it also attracted less seemly characters, it wasn't far from what he had imagined the marketplace would be.

Just south of the market, he had experienced Queen's Boulevard; what the locals called Queen Bitch Boulevard.

Named after the Matriarch, Irth's God-Queen of old, QBB had the lowest elevation of any of the quarters. The nobles liked to say, "Scum runs downhill in Arcadia." And in a way, they were right.

In contrast to Ezekiel's hopes, not everyone thrived in his city.

The slums were an irritating aberration whose cause Ezekiel had yet to learn. But the inhabitants persisted through their squalor, and, for the most part, were good folks. Nevertheless, some of the dwellers, down on their luck and desperate for survival, did things that would make a prostitute blush.

Queen's Boulevard was the most disconcerting of Ezekiel's experiences in the city he had once loved. The promise of magic and the hope of what it could offer shouldn't have resulted in a place like this.

The power of the art was meant to keep poverty and suffering at bay—to enhance prosperity and progress for all. It was clear that something had gone desperately wrong. The old man needed answers. And with the right information at hand, he could bring change.

He'd make a trip to the Academy later. Along with the Capitol, it made up its own quarter, and it was the most prestigious of all. But before making his way to the halls of higher learning, he had something else to do; someone to find. An old friend who lived in a humble home among the nobles.

CHAPTER 4

S he knew that the wool hat pulled down over her forehead looked ridiculous on the warm summer morning,
but Hannah had to hide the mark of the Hunters somehow. Walking around with the tag on her forehead was an
invitation she didn't need to make, and the ratty knit cap was
the best disguise she could find.

Hannah hoped that the men who nearly stole her final
shred of innocence might be in the hospital after what that
demon put them through. Despite the terror she had felt
when his hood fell off, today she thought of him not with
disgust but with appreciation. He'd saved her life.

Winding her way through the crowd, she found a spot
behind a group of rearick near the front of the Pit.

The rearick were short, stocky miners and craftsmen who
made their home in half-buried cities in the mountains south

of Arcadia called the Heights. Although these men were adults, Hannah stood a little taller than them.

Her dad always said that a life working in the caves made them short but ridiculously strong. The rearick unloading ore and crystals here in Arcadia had decided to take a break to watch the show.

There was no better entertainment in Arcadia than the fighting Pit. The audience for the first fight of the day was thicker than usual, and she wondered if her plan was going to work.

"Wildman" Hank paced the ring as the people cheered on their champion. "*Wildman. Wildman.*" His nickname was well deserved. He had been winning for nearly a year, ferociously tearing through anyone stupid enough to challenge him.

Hank had thrown the entire gambling system out of whack. The only way people bet on his opponent was if they were desperate enough to hope a long shot might pay off.

Shirtless and ripped, the Wildman slapped himself across the chest, muttering words to the sky. It was a tradition the crowd had become familiar with, but no matter how many times he stepped into the ring, he could still whip them into a frenzy.

Mac, the bookie in charge of the Pit, slid between the ring's ropes and waved his arms to quiet the crowd. Finally, the frenzy died to a murmur.

"Welcome to another day in the Pit!" Cheers rose and Mac's smile grew with their volume. "Now, I must be honest with you, good people of Arcadia. I was afraid that the Pit wouldn't get much action today." The crowd quieted, concerned that their beloved pastime was in trouble. "Because of the Wildman's violent performance these past months, I've been finding it harder and harder to recruit a suitable opponent, one brave enough to step into this ring."

"That's 'cause Ralph is still half-dead!" a voice shouted from the back of the crowd. The onlookers all laughed, but Hannah's stomach turned as she thought of her neighbor, who might not walk again without a limp.

There was no way Ralph, who used to be a baker before his shop went under, was ever going to make it against someone like Hank. But desperate times called for desperate measures, and the Boulevard was nothing if not desperate.

"We were even close to canceling today." Mac paused to let a round of booing pour out of the audience. "But thankfully, the Patriarch was with us! We have a newcomer who has, for good or ill, chosen to cut his teeth in the ring against the champ. Let me introduce to you, Parker the Pitiable of Queen Bitch Boulevard!"

A pathway cleared and Hannah watched a young man her own age cut through to the ring. As he made his way to the front, in his ordinary pants, shirt, and cloak covering what looked like a thin frame, the crowd hushed.

"Throw him back in the water, Mac. This one has some growing to do!" a voice shouted from the back.

Mac laughed for the crowd. "Who am I to deny such a brave lad his chance for glory? But if you all are so sure of his defeat, I will happily take your bets at my table."

Parker stepped through the ropes and extended a hand to the goliath standing across from him. Looking the kid up and down, Hank grimaced, as if offended by the amateur in the ring with him. The Wildman reached out and grabbed Parker's hand as if to shake, but then at the last second, he pulled Parker toward him and smashed his giant head into the young man's.

Parker stumbled backward, clearly dazed from the underhanded move. Even from where she stood, Hannah could see blood dripping down his forehead.

The crowd burst into laughter. The blood was what they came for, after all.

Mac quickly separated the two combatants. The fight hadn't even begun, but it already didn't look good for Parker.

The rearick in front of her talked amongst themselves.

"Wish I put all I had on me in dis fight. Kid's a goner," one said to the other.

The rearick dialect always tickled her ears. Hannah tapped him on the shoulder. "How much you have?"

"I've still got half my earnings from dis month's shipment, lass, but if I had bet dem all, I damn sure would be leaving Arcadia with a heavier sack."

The stocky men flanking him laughed. "Don't talk to da pretty girl about your sack, Kegan."

She watched the man blush, then put her hand on his shoulder. "Trust me, I'm old enough to know you hillmen aren't the only ones worried about the size of your sacks. I'll take your bet if you give me ten-to-one."

The rearick snorted and looked at his companions. "You should run along, missy. The Pit isn't a place for young women like ye."

"Hmm," Hannah sighed. "If you're not willing to risk a bet on such a sure thing, then I'd say the Pit isn't a place for girls like *you*." She shrugged, looking at his friends before she turned back to finish her comment. "I guess you have no sack at all."

The men surrounding him and some other onlookers laughed at her insult. She lifted and then rattled the small bag of coins she had saved up and hidden precisely for a shot like

54

this. It represented all of her savings, and she had taken every ounce of precaution to hide them from her drunken father. It was a risk, but with the right idiot and the right odds, she might just get lucky.

"With a mouth like yours, maybe you *do* belong at da Pit," the rearick said with a grin of admiration breaking through his beard. "I'll take your bet for eight-to-one."

Hannah nodded, keeping her eyes on the kid in the ring as he removed his cloak.

———— ◆ ————

Parker and Hank circled each other as the crowd swelled around the ring. People were hungry for a good fight, and although they didn't expect one, they'd gladly pay to see a nobody like him get pummeled.

Watching the Wildman for any tells, Parker kept his eyes trained on his opponent. He had spent enough time hanging around the fights to know Hank had seen everything. Well, nearly everything. Parker hadn't been in a fight for years, and that childhood nonsense had meant nothing compared to Hank's experience. But sometimes, if your opponent was cocky enough, inexperience might be used to your advantage. It was just about the only advantage Parker had.

"Let's get this over with," Hank sneered through gritted teeth.

"What?" Parker asked with a smile. "No foreplay? Fine, we'll do it quickly, since that's what you're used to."

Hank's sneer turned to rage, and he came in telegraphing the right hook from a mile away. Parker easily ducked the fist and spun behind Hank, landing a playful kick on the man's broad ass. The kick, plus Hank's own momentum, carried the big man forward until he nearly stumbled into the crowd.

They responded with loud cheering. Parker turned to them and gave a deep bow.

Hank's face was wine red as he turned back. "All right, you little shit. Was going to take it easy on you, but no one makes an ass of me."

Parker smiled. "Of you or your ass?" The crowd laughed again and began hollering when Parker mimed a little kick.

The man charged again, head aiming for Parker's torso. With the agility of a dancer Parker avoided him, then used Hank's head to vault. The big man hit the ground, kicking up dust into the air. Parker danced around the edge of the ring, waving and blowing kisses.

The onlookers whooped and hollered in return. They were starting to enjoy Parker the Pitiable, and Parker was certainly taking the moment to enjoy the crowd. But his bragging stopped as he turned just in time to take a left jab on the chin followed by a heavy right. Hank's fists were like bricks, and Parker's head spun as he dropped to one knee.

Hank gloated over his victim. He raised his arms overhead, roaring like a pagan warrior. It was his signature move, and the crowd had been waiting for it.

But so had Parker.

As the Wildman stood over him playing to the crowd, Parker put all his weight behind a kick at the man's groin. Hank's roar of delight turned into a high-pitched squeak as he doubled over. Parker wasted no time pushing his advantage. He slammed a fist into Hank's throat, then placed his foot against the larger man's knee and pushed with all the strength he had.

The winded man fell like an oak, dropping hard to the

packed dirt. Before he could catch his breath, Parker was on him. The kid delivered a flurry of blows, aiming as best he could for the soft spots beneath the man's ribs before rolling away to safety.

Parker leaned over Hank as he rolled on his knees. "Need a hand, Henry?" Parker asked in his best impression of a concerned friend. Mockery would get him everywhere, or at least that was what Parker was hoping for.

Hank finally pushed himself off the ground, but it was clear that the fight had gone of him. His eyes were bloodshot and his breathing was ragged. All that was left was for Parker to stay out of range of Hank's fists until he could land the final blow.

Parker had never been strong, but growing up on the Boulevard taught him to be smart and fast. The strong preyed on the weak, but not if they couldn't be caught. Hank was used to fighting men who either matched his own brute-force tactics or cowered in fear.

The insults, the acrobatics, and the speed of this kid left him disoriented. But Hank was a seasoned professional, able to change his strategy on the fly. He hadn't given up yet. This time he came in cautiously, working his feet like the experienced fighter he was. All Hank needed was one shot to pin Parker down, and this kid would be toast.

Parker offered him that chance. He stepped up to him and dipped his shoulder as if going into another roll. Hank took the bait and bent to catch the shifty fighter. Slamming on the brakes, Parker transitioned his move into an uppercut, clenching both hands together and putting all his strength and momentum into the blow.

—————◆—————

"*Scheisse*! Da damned fool," the rearick yelled as the kid swung his double fists into the man's chin. The crowd went silent in awe and admiration. They had loved every minute of Parker's dancing, even his cheap shot to Hank's balls. But they never thought the kid would actually come out on top.

Not until that uppercut.

This time Parker didn't stop for celebration or to work the crowd. Hannah knew her bet was going to finish things right then and there. She held her breath as she watched him stomp-kick Hank's knee, chopping him down to size. The big man buckled as his leg twisted out from under him. Stunned, the champion looked up at his adversary like prey who knew the hunter had won.

Parker dropped and swung his elbow into the man's temple to finish him. The crowd went silent and then roared with glee as the Wildman went out like a light.

Hannah placed her own elbow on the rearick's shoulder and leaned on him like she would lean against the side of her house. "Sorry friend, better luck next time." She held out her hand, asking for the payment he had promised.

The man's face turned from white to red underneath of his bushy beard. "You...you swindled me? You knew he was going tah win? You knew it all along?"

She grabbed the coin purse out of his hand and shrugged.

"Now, how could I have planned something like that? I'm just a little girl, after all." Her look of innocence turned into a wry smile as the man from the Heights blustered in rage. She quickly melted into the crowd before he could try and take his money back.

As she moved away from the Pit, she counted her winnings. She had risked everything she had on that bet and it had paid off. Glancing over her shoulder, her eyes locked with the rookie fighter's. Blood trickled from Parker's nostrils, but his wounds didn't dampen his smile.

She nodded, then turned and headed back down the alley away from the market. Hannah would let the crowd and the victor have their moment. She had a pocket full of coin and plenty of work to do.

———— ◆ ————

"Stay seated," Adrien told the receptionist with a wave of his hand as he crossed into the Capitol's infirmary.

The receptionist, mouth wide, stood anyway, which was precisely what Adrien had expected. The Chancellor was a damned celebrity in Arcadia, and the fact that he seldom left the Academy grounds made an encounter something common people would talk about for days.

He'd learned to hold back years ago, but a small smile still pulled at the edges of his mouth. "I'm here to see them."

"Sorry, sir, who?" Her mousey voice was hardly audible above the hum of the magitech equipment. The infirmary was one of the most technologically advanced buildings in the city.

He raised an eyebrow. "The Hunters," he responded, his answer causing a blush.

"Oh, right, of course." She looked down at a clipboard and back up at Adrien. "They're just down the hall. But, sir, the doctor is about to discharge them. Wouldn't you rather I just sent them directly to your office?"

He pursed his lips and shook his head. "Oh, no…"

"Helen, sir."

Adrien flashed his perfectly white smile. "No, Helen. I wanted to see the men before they were released. Raise their morale a bit. Thank them for their service. Means a bit more if I do it here."

"Oh." The woman sounded pleased with his answer. "Would you like me to show you to their room?"

"I'm sure I can manage," Adrien said as he left the front desk. As soon as he was out of her view, his smile dropped like rotten fruit off a tree.

Adrien found the small room, entered without knocking, and shut the door. When he turned back around, he was greeted by three surprised men, each one built like a prize fighter. He looked them over to see an assortment of bandages and slings; bruises covered their bodies. When they recognized him all three men got to their feet, though it took one of them great effort.

The arm of the biggest man was completely wrapped all the way down to the elbow. It hung heavy at his side. "Chancellor, what a surprise, I mean, honor!" the man said, his voice trembling a little with fear.

Adrien knew the man wasn't excited to see him. "Well, Jasper, I do care about the men protecting this city. The Governor and I work very closely on the issue of patrolling for Unlawfuls. And I heard the three of you had quite the run-in, so I wanted to look into the matter."

Adrien smoothed out his cloak and leaned back against the wall by the door. "Please, gentlemen, sit down and tell me what happened." He crossed his arms.

The two smaller men looked at Jasper, waiting for him to respond.

Finally he sat down. "Hard to say, really. I mean, at the beginning everything seemed pretty cut and dried, Chancellor. We were on the street and some kid, a girl, was sitting on the cobblestones with a younger boy in her arms. As far as we could tell, something was wrong with the kid. Really wrong. It was evident that the girl had used magic. We could feel it, and the effects were immediate. The boy just healed in front of our eyes. We announced ourselves as required, and she ran. So we set off after her and finally cornered her in an alley. It was all aboveboard."

One of the other men chimed in. "Cut and dried. It was by the book."

Adrien knew they were lying. And they were fools for doing so. "By the book, was it?"

"That's right," Jasper said. "Squeaky clean. Just doing our duty."

The brazen deception angered Adrien, but it wasn't at the top of his list of concerns. He didn't really care that his men took certain liberties, as long as they got results.

Order required a strong hand and strong men had needs, after all. But these men had failed in their task and he wanted to know why. Doyle's description still rang in his ears.

A demon that cast lightning bolts.

Adrien looked at each man before returning his focus to Jasper. "If everything was aboveboard, then why are you three here and not patrolling my streets? Tell me about the other one. The one that did this to you."

Just the mention of the magician rattled the three Hunters. They exchanged glances, each man hoping another would respond.

Adrien waved his hand in a circle. "Come on, dammit. I don't have all day."

The third man, the one who had been silent since Adrien entered the room, finally spoke. He was smaller than the other two and smelled of smoke. Adrien guessed he was a fire user. "Never seen anything like it before. It came out of nowhere, had green skin and large red eyes. Horns on his head and powerful, like the devil himself—"

"You fool." Adrien cut him off, his anger escaping through gritted teeth. "That was no demon creature. It was only a mind trick. It's obvious this magic user is one of the mystics." Adrien rolled his eyes. It was apparently true about quantity of muscle being inversely proportional to intelligence.

At least sometimes.

He shook his head and continued, "If you three little boys weren't such cowards, you'd have seen that."

The fire user swallowed hard and glanced at the others for help, but they kept their faces down. He looked back at their boss and continued, "Begging your pardon, sir, but I thought those mystics were all peaceful. I thought they couldn't do physical magic. That thing, I mean, that magic user, it did physical magic like I've never seen before."

Adrien sneered. "Explain." The man looked like he had just been stabbed.

"Well, he had this wooden staff, and he used it to throw lightning bolts at us. Never seen a magic user do that before. And Jasper's magitech staff, the guy melted it like it was nothing…"

The brute kept talking, but Adrien heard nothing more. He retreated into his own mind. The description of the wizard reminded him of his mentor, who had left the city in his hands decades ago. He remembered their parting well, and thought about the level of trust that it had taken for the old man to pass the mantle of magical stewardship to his protégé.

He had given Adrien the keys to the kingdom and then wandered off into the mountains, never to be heard from again.

The Chancellor shook his head and convinced himself it couldn't be the same person. That man was dead. And if it were him, by some miracle, then what was the connection with this young Unlawful woman?

Merely circumstantial?

Jasper, the large one in the full arm bandage, had taken over the talking. "I'll get him back for what he did to us. And that little boulevard bitch too, sir."

"No, not the magician," Adrien snapped. "Leave him for me. But let this be a lesson to all of you to be on your guard. Remember, I don't stand for this kind of anarchy. Unlawfuls like this need to be kept in line."

Jasper nodded. Sweat beaded up on his forehead. He knew the Chancellor was short on patience and shorter on mercy. "I won't forget, sir."

Adrien's sickly smile didn't relieve their concern. "I know. Not after I give you a little reminder," Adrien told the three.

The Chancellor turned to the sidekick on Jasper's left.

The man was either a coward or an idiot. Neither was acceptable, and he didn't have enough resources to kill all three men at the moment.

Adrien raised his hand in the shape of a "C" and slowly squeezed. The Hunter tried to gurgle out a scream, but nothing emerged as Adrien crushed his throat. His eyes rolled back in his head and his body slowly started to slide before ending in a rush, his head sounding like a melon as it cracked on the floor.

Once the Hunter's body motionless was on the ground, Adrien turned to the man on Jasper's right.

"Please, no…" the fire user said. He raised both hands before his face as if that could do anything to stop the Chancellor's wrath.

"It's not your day to die, fool. At least by my hands. Find the girl. Both of you. Bring her to me alive. If you must get rough, so be it, just so long as she can still answer my questions. Destroy anything that stands in your way."

Jasper looked down at his deformed arm and smiled. "Gladly. But what if we see the other magician?"

Adrien raised an eyebrow, thinking back to the power his old mentor had wielded. The power to change lives or destroy them.

"If you're smart you'll run for your useless *bloody* lives."

CHAPTER 5

———◆———

Few Arcadians he had approached had ever heard of Eve. And it wasn't a surprise. She was as meek as she was beautiful. The ironic thing was that she, like Adrien and Ezekiel, had been there at the beginning with its opportunities to seize wealth, power, or celebrity status along with all the privileges that accompanied them. But these were not important to Eve.

From the founding, her pursuits had been different, purer. All that she had wanted behind the giant walls of Arcadia was a small plot of land to garden and a house in which to raise a family. The old man had loved her for her unpretentiousness, among other reasons.

Eve had gotten one of her two desires.

Ezekiel found her home, a small, single-level house with pristine sandstone walls, bright blue shutters, and a welcoming oak door. Settled among houses that were nearly palatial compared to the rest of Arcadia, the tidy little place was austere without a trace of presumption. A tiny garden was nestled in the back.

It had taken a long time, but Ezekiel finally found an old man who knew exactly who he was looking for. Leaning his staff against the wall, he pushed back his wild, white hair and smoothed his beard.

He'd fought men and monsters of all kinds in his younger days, but standing in the doorway of the only woman he had ever loved terrified him more than any wild beast. Finally mustering his nerve, he rapped on the door.

Within seconds it was flung open, and a beautiful young girl with blond curls halfway down her back stood in the entryway. Her eyes glimmered like sapphires. "May I help you, sir?"

He stepped back as she watched him. He checked that he had the right house before stepping back up to the doorway. "I'm sorry, I'm looking for a woman named Eve. I heard she lived here once?"

The girl laughed, and the old man felt his ears burn. "Yes, Auntie Eve lived here once and still does. Well, we live here…I mean, we both do."

"Auntie Eve?" the man repeated. "Well, you must be Jessica's daughter, then." His face brightened as he took in the girl. It had been forty years since he'd seen Eve or her sister, but the similarities between the girl and her mother were striking. The blue eyes made it all come together. "Is your mother here?"

The girl looked down at the cobblestone path and back again. "She's been gone since I was young. Don't even remember her." Her eyes grew moist.

"Oh. Terrible. I am so—" he started to mumble. He had spent too many years away from people to remember how to be polite.

She raised a hand. "No, forgive me. This is not our kind of hospitality. It's good you're here. She's been waiting."

"For me?"

The girl nodded. "Come along."

———— ◆ ————

Fingers as frail as fallen twigs reached up and brushed Ezekiel's cheek. Her touch felt the same as it had decades ago, only now it was at once gentler and somehow stronger. But the strength was deceptive. Eve lay still, her face as pale as the winter moon. Surrounded by pillows, the bed had been her permanent residence for the past eight months. Death was calling, but she had held him off to wait for this day.

The old man sat next to her. "I'm sorry, Eve, I—"

She pressed her fingers against his lips and slowly shook her head. "No. Not like this. I knew you had to go. Don't you remember? I gave my blessing." A faint smile spread on her lips. "The only thing you ever let me give you."

He nodded, knowing she was right. This was not a time for sadness. Gritting his teeth, he forced a smile. "It is good to see you, Eve. My heart has longed for this day. I imagined you'd have married, been surrounded by grandchildren."

His words drew a laugh—not the kind of laugh meant to tear down but rather to build up. "Well, now *you* make a presumption, my old friend. I did in fact marry. Not long after you left. He knew our love was a balm for my broken heart, but he didn't mind. Peter was a good man, strong. The Matriarch gave us two good years together, and then I lost him in an accident at the factory. I'm told he died quickly."

She nodded as she lost herself in thought. Finally, she continued, "No children, though, but Madelyn is as good as mine. We've done well together."

The old man smiled, this one took no work on his part at all. "Good. I'm glad for the two of you."

"We have so much to speak of, but I am afraid we have little time. Let us not share our lost loves."

"Arcadia," he said. The word was like honey on his lips.

Her face lightened. "Yes. Our home and great experiment."

"But what has it become?"

Madelyn cleared her throat at the bedroom door and walked in with a tray of tea and cookies.

"Thank you." The old man reached for the tray. Handing it to him, she smiled and backed out of the room to leave the two alone.

Eve continued her story. "It worked, dear. The city. The place we built together with the others blossomed like a flower bed touched with the magic of the Druids."

He bit into a cookie. "But how could it come to this then?" He pointed at the walls. "The things I've seen since I returned. So much pain, Eve."

Her lips pressed together. "Ezekiel, this is a hard story. One that none of us ever thought would come to pass, but one you must know. When you left, everything was in place. And the steward you left in charge was filled with energy and vigor. For years, Adrien kept building and creating things of beauty.

"Farms developed outside the walls and the peace we enjoyed drew people from the ends of Irth. Arcadia was becoming the society that we all thought might not be possible after the Age of Madness.

68

"Adrien and his friend Saul worked day and night. They were tireless and single-minded in making the dream, our dream, a reality. As more and more came, the city filled with life. It was truly beautiful. But the more people who flooded the gates, the more problems arose.

"Those boys were whip-sharp, though. Adrien and Saul gathered us all and shared the plan. Our magic had almost completed the place, but one-quarter of Arcadia was left wild. Trees grew tall and animals roamed free.

"Of course, that's where I spent most of my time. But then the city needed my wild place, and I knew it was for the best. The quarter would be cleared and reserved for two structures. The Capitol from which Saul would govern the city, and the Academy where Adrien would train magicians based on your principles."

Memories of his final conversation with his student ran through Ezekiel's mind. A smile crossed his face, then faded because he knew the story had a sorrowful end.

"It was like that for years," she continued. "The city grew and grew. Saul appointed people to oversee the quarters, and created a government that would help us flourish.

"And Adrien," she said, "was certainly in his element. The Academy was free and open. He had magicians running classes in all the rooms and sometimes out into the corridors. For the first time, we no longer felt like little children playing house, but like founders. We were rebuilding paradise in a world that had been torn and twisted…."

She stopped and looked down at her hands, her voice soft. "But it wasn't long until paradise was lost. Nothing happened overnight. Rather, it crept in gradually, like evil tends to do. There came a time when everyone you met was some kind of magician. I mean, most of them were harmless. Many were using their powers for great acts of good. But shadows of vice hid in the corners of many hearts.

"Before long, some people started to use their powers for ill. And one day, a group of magicians from Queen's Boulevard tried to take the Capitol with their magic. Power begets a lust for power, and these men wanted more. They were thirsty for it."

He pulled his drink away from his lips. "And what did they accomplish?"

She shook her head. "Nothing. How could they? They were amateurs at best. Saul had a military guard and Adrien oversaw the most powerful magicians for miles around. They put down the uprising in hours, but its effects lingered. Adrien barred any new students from the Academy until the first-years were on the verge of graduation.

"By the time he permitted new students, he had instituted an admissions policy that only allowed the best and brightest from what had become the noble class. The damnedest thing is that we all voted for it. Even *I* voted for it, Ezekiel! And why not?"

Her voice firmed as she relieved her memory. "We were all scared to lose this place, scared of what magic could do if it were left uncontrolled. And we trusted Adrien with our lives. I trusted him."

The woman's eyes teared over, and she turned out of pride toward the window looking out on the garden; her remaining wild patch of Arcadia. The old man gently squeezed her arm and allowed her the space she needed. She finally turned back to her friend.

"He changed everything. Adrien didn't just regulate which magic could be taught, he also changed the narrative about its purpose. I know now this is why the other students needed to go before his new classes could be initiated. No longer was magic for the commonwealth, but rather for the good of the state, which amounted to nothing more than the good of Adrien."

"But Saul wouldn't have let him do this."

"At first Saul had no idea. Adrien was curing a disease that had needed to be addressed. Over time the uprising fizzled out, so we all thought Adrien had made the right decision. But a year into Adrien's solution, it started to become clear. The two would fight into the early hours of the morning over the fate of Arcadia. And then—" A coughing fit came over the woman, and her pale face turned pink, then red.

The old man leaned over and held her in his arms. Compared to watching her suffer, the story of Arcadia held little weight. Ezekiel reached out in thought as subtle as prayer. His eyes turned, and the tiniest waves of power left his body.

Her coughing stopped. She leaned back and raised her eyes to his. "You *have* learned things."

He smiled. "You thought I was only taking it easy these last forty-odd years? I have learned much. I could help you, heal your body."

She patted his hand. "Magic can only sustain us so far, my friend."

He shrugged. "As far as we know, all magic is limited. But I have seen things. There are powers from the Matriarch and Patriarch that have yet to be understood or revealed."

She nodded. "In them is our hope. But it is a hope in a future that I will not see, and that, honestly, I don't want to see it. I am happy we have met again. I must rest now, Ezekiel, but the story isn't over. There is one more thing you must know."

"Yes?"

"There was never any proof, and even if there had been it wouldn't have amounted to anything. But your student Adrien? He murdered Saul."

Ezekiel closed his eyes and absorbed the shock. If that were true, then his protégé was truly gone. He hung his head. "How could he have done such a thing? They were closer than any friends I have ever known," he asked, his pain lacing every syllable of his words

Her voice was firm, but little above a whisper. "All things can break, Ezekiel, but all can be rebuilt, too. You are here now, to make things right. Here to put an end to Adrien's rule."

———— ◆ ————

Parker sat on a flour sack at the opposite edge of the market from the Pit. His canvas bag, a relic older than him, was wedged between his legs. The satchel was now stuffed full of his tools and the winnings from his first—and last—fight in the Pit.

Taking a beating wasn't his idea of a viable livelihood, but he was behind for the month and desperate times called for idiotic measures. Between his earnings and his partner's winnings, it had been well worth taking a few lumps. Not to mention that it was likely the word of his exploits would spread throughout Queen's Boulevard. And being the badass from Queen's Boulevard for a few weeks would have its perks.

Eyes open for his friend and partner, he scanned the crowd as he gnawed on a slice of stale bread. His jaw hurt with every bite, and he knew he would dream of Wildman

Hank's fists tonight. He held a handkerchief some admirer from the crowd had handed him on his exit from the Pit to his bloodied nose.

Theatrics may have worked to win the fight, but it also cost him some blood and a blow to the face. Part of him was glad he wouldn't be able to play that con again. His ears were still buzzing as he watched the crowds shift around the vendors' stalls in the square.

Morning was his favorite time of the day. Arcadia was fresh and buzzing with new life. It made him feel like things could actually be different. Most of the citizens were rushing to get a jump on their day's work.

"What the hell happened to you?" he asked Hannah as she wove out of the crowd. Her beautiful nose was swollen to the size of an apple, and raccoon eyes spread out from its mass. Parker couldn't help but think she was still a knockout, even with the adjustments to her face. He chuckled at his friend. "Looks like you were the one in the ring."

"No biggie," Hannah said, adjusting her wool hat. "You doing OK?"

She sat next to him and pulled out her own chunk of bread. They went through this every day. The habits they formed gave a sense of normalcy to their thoroughly abnormal life. Hannah winced as she looked her old friend over.

"Not so bad in there, huh?" She nodded in the direction of the ring. "It would have taken you weeks to pay back my losses if you didn't win. And what the hell was up with the blowing kisses? Nearly got you creamed."

Parker smiled, then winced as pain shot through his face. He waited for a second to let the throbbing pass. "That's what won it for me. Had to get under Hank's skin. But screw the fight. What the hell happened to your face?"

She ran a fingertip across her nose. "Hard to explain, really. I'm still making sense of the whole thing. Will and I were on our way to the park, and something, don't know what, came over him. He started shaking and convulsing—white-faced and drooling."

"Holy shit," Parker whispered.

"Right? I didn't know what to do. He was in my arms, and I started to scream and then something felt different, like I was about to explode from the inside out. And then, he was just better. Almost like it had never happened."

She considered telling him about the lizard, but thought that would be too much for one conversation.

Not to be deterred, he kept up his questions. "So where did the black eyes come in? And what's with the hat?"

Hannah bit her lip and looked down. He'd known her for years—since they were children—and he hadn't seen her like this before. Something bad had happened. Really bad.

"Hunters," she finally admitted.

"No shit?" he asked.

"Chased me into an alley…" She trailed off, and Parker gave her time. Finally, she looked up and locked eyes with him. Even through the pain, her eyes held something different. Something special. Parker knew that if it weren't for their circumstances, she could have been something great. "They were going to kill me, with other things beforehand, I think."

"Wait. Why the hell would Hunters give a shit about you? I mean, no offense, but you don't know a lick of magic."

"That's the crazy part. I don't have the faintest idea, but they were convinced I had practiced magic in the market square. Right over there." Hannah pointed to their left. "Must've been what was happening with William, I don't know. They chased me and cornered me in an alley."

"You were caught by Hunters and lived to tell the tale? You have some special skills you haven't told me about. Because if so," he lifted his sack to gently jingle the money, "I say we put you in the Pit tomorrow."

Hannah smiled. "Guess I have a guardian angel. Some, well…*guy* showed up. A magician. At least, that's what I think he was. He looked like a character from a cautionary tale for children. Long robe, staff, and his eyes glowed brighter than I've ever seen."

"And?" Parker pushed her forward.

"Didn't see too much. The guy dropped his hood and his face was all demonic; horns and everything. But now I kind of wonder if it was only part of the magic. Either way, the guy totally kicked ass. Magic was flowing, but also his staff had power. I didn't stick around to ask questions. Ran as fast as I could."

Hannah was holding part of the story back, and Parker let her. There was more hurt below the surface and he felt it himself.

After enough time, he asked, "So what did you do?"

"I just told you," Hannah replied. She wanted to punch him in the shoulder, but even as annoyed as she was, she wasn't mean enough to hit him after his pummeling by Hank this morning.

"No, I mean to your brother. How did you heal him?" he clarified.

She shrugged, looking around the market. "I didn't do anything. He just…just got better. It was a misunderstanding. They were going to brain me in some back alley over their… misperception, I guess. And what's worse," she lifted the hat quickly to show off the tag still burning on her forehead "they stuck me with this. I don't know how the hell I'm gonna get it off, Parker. But other than that, I'm fine. Really. Let's just get to work."

Hannah looked tough, but Parker didn't buy it. Something else was going on, but he would let it be for the time.

The morning didn't stop for stories, and they needed to strike while the iron was hot.

He placed his hands over his heart and batted his eyelashes. "Well, I'm glad you're OK. I'd be lost without you."

"Screw you." Hannah laughed. "What's the play today?"

"Well," he said as he patted the leather bag at his side, his eyebrows dancing up and down before he winced, "I thought I'd play with my balls."

CHAPTER 6

H annah pulled her legs up underneath her on the sack of flour as she watched Parker move toward the crowd. He carried a crate discarded from a produce vendor in his arms and his leather bag was strapped tightly to his back. As he wove through the crowded marketplace, he bumped into shoppers along his way. His feigned clumsiness was drawing quite a bit of attention.

"Excuse me," he repeated as he made his way forward.

Shoppers and vendors kept looking over their shoulders at him as he spun through the crowd. Finally, he bumped hard into a cart filled with fresh bread. It pitched over onto its side, and the loaves spilled out onto the ground, tumbling in every direction. Parker fell in a heap among the mess. The shopkeeper who was pushing the cart loomed over her friend.

"What the hell is wrong with you? Look at this..."

Parker stood, hands raised in defense like a kid caught trying to steal candy. "Sorry. I can—"

"Damn right you can. Clean this shit up. And you're going to buy the bread I can't sell."

Almost nothing draws a crowd better than a public confrontation. A semicircle formed around the disruption as the bald baker continued his tirade against Hannah's friend. A few shouts came from the crowd. Many of them wanted to see another fight.

"Now!" the shopkeeper snarled.

"OK. I'll do whatever you want, right after I do this," Parker said.

He bent at the waist, placed the crate on the ground, and in one swift move, arched up into a perfect handstand, toes pointed to the sky. Gasps came from the onlookers, and even the shopkeeper stared in disbelief.

Hannah smiled as her friend performed ten perfect push-ups from his handstand, counting each one off. Although she knew he could easily do a hundred, the crowd was awed by his perfect combination of strength and balance. Some were muttering about his performance earlier that day in the Pit.

On the last pushup, a single red ball dropped out of his leather bag. Holding himself on the box in a one-armed handstand, he caught the red ball with his other hand as it fell toward the dusty ground.

The crowd gasped, then cheered, the shopkeeper with them.

Parker vaulted off the box onto the ground, and gave a bow for the crowd. Reaching into the bag, he drew out two more balls and started a simple juggling routine as he stepped back onto the crate.

Hannah took a moment to enjoy his routine, even though she knew it by heart. As the crowd watched and laughed, she could picture each of his moves in her mind's eye. She knew that her friend's role in their partnership was harder, but hers was by far the more dangerous.

Convinced that the marketgoers were thoroughly entranced, Hannah got to work. She wove through the intoxicated crowd, bumping into bodies as she went.

Most ignored her tiny frame. She was just another body pressing against them, trying to get a better view of the show. They were also unaware of her hands reaching into their coat pockets and handbags.

Parker's clowning grabbed their attention as Hannah grabbed their purse strings. She worked quickly, and by the time she got to the opposite side of the bazaar, she'd filled the pockets of her cloak with whatever items of value she could lift.

———◆———

Ezekiel leaned against a pillar at the back of the market. If his face hadn't been veiled by the low-hanging hood, one might have seen the smile spreading across his face as his eyebrows raised in anticipation.

The young man was causing a ruckus in the small square, everyone turning in his direction to watch the market's jester. But the old man wasn't watching him.

Ezekiel's eyes were locked on the girl.

Smart, he thought. *Both of them.*

She wore a thick wool cap on her head, but Ezekiel could see the bruising around her eyes and cheeks. The previous day hadn't broken her; she was obviously stronger than that. She sat on the edge of a flower sack, watching her partner's perfect setup.

The sound of the crowd rose and fell with anticipation as the young man did amazing feats with a set of red juggling balls. He'd pass a can when he was finished, the old man had seen it many times before. Street performers like this would make more than a simple panhandler, but not enough to live on. But the old man knew that the performance was not their primary game.

He watched as the girl cut through the crowd. Her hands moved deftly; the old man observed her draw secretly from each of her marks. No one so much as stirred as she picked their pockets. She was heading in his direction and had nearly broken through the crowd when something went wrong.

"Pardon me," he heard her say as she knocked into one last mark on the edge of the circle—an overweight shopkeeper of some sort wearing brightly colored clothing, obviously not a resident of the Boulevard.

The young lady slipped her hand into the pocket of the man's coat. In a flash, he reached out and snatched her forearm.

Ezekiel watched the young thief's cheeks turn white.

The shopkeeper opened his mouth, but before he could say a word, Ezekiel had waved his hand in their direction. He spoke a word of power and his eyes glowed red in the shadow of his cloak. The man froze, mouth still ajar. His eyes were blank, like he was sleepwalking.

Ezekiel spoke another word, and the well-dressed man released the girl and turned his attention back toward the juggler on the wooden crate.

The girl slipped away but made sure to grab a ring from the man's hand first. Why waste a good opportunity? She disappeared into the crowd without a backward glance.

She's determined, the old man thought. *A little rough around the edges maybe, but you needed some grit if you were going to succeed.*

———— ♦ ————

Parker leaned his back against a large oak tree at the edge of Capitol Park and stretched out his long legs.

An expanse of green grass spread before him, terminating at the steps of the Capitol building. The sandstone building itself was a large stately-looking structure sitting on a rise, its pinnacle just a little lower than the Academy tower.

He had heard that it took a hundred magicians a month to build the place, and two had died in the process. But then, lies and exaggerations flowed through Arcadia like water in the River Wren.

Capitol Park was a gem in their city. Precious resources, both magical and mundane, had gone into its creation. It was the most beautiful area inside the walls.

Public works like this were built every few years. Nothing like a show of magnanimity to keep the common folk satisfied. It allowed the Governor and Chancellor to focus the rest of their time on projects that advanced their own purposes.

The lawn had become a primary gathering point for people of all classes and from all neighborhoods. It was patrolled by the Capitol Guard, a group of soldiers in pristine uniforms who were more of an accessory to the Governor than anything.

Parker watched a group of mothers from the noble class sit and talk as their kids played in the grass. Several students from the Academy, with their fancy clothes and stacks of books, took up a stone table not far away.

He noticed a crowd beginning to gather around Old Jedidiah, the town's adopted "Prophet," as they titled him.

Jedidiah had become a popular figure in Arcadia a few years previously. He came into town from outside. The man wore rags and lived on a diet even the poorest would turn up their noses at. It was said that he spent decades wandering in the wilderness.

Some claimed he was raised by animals.

The Prophet had no home, as far as anyone knew. Rather, he dwelt with his followers, moving from place to place. He spent his days in Capitol Park. The inner circle, standing closest to Jedidiah, was made up of his followers.

A multitude always gathered on the outside. Many just wanted to hear the Prophet's words of the day, and others came to heckle, tossing insults at him and his disciples. But ridicule only fueled the flame of his preaching.

Hannah limped toward Parker from the opposite end of the lawn. He had known she was hurt, but seeing her walk from a distance made him realize just how badly the Hunters had abused her.

His lips pressed together as he cursed them, the Governor, and this city. Parker wanted the Prophet's words to be true, to be *real*. The hope that someday there could be a different way of living in Arcadia, ushered in by the one that the people referred to as The Founder. The dream inspired many.

The man who had laid the foundation for the city would come again and bring justice on his shoulders. But it was hard for Parker to keep the dream alive when the world around him was shit. Well, mostly shit. He got to spend his days with Hannah, after all.

But seeing her in pain made believing in a better world even harder.

"How'd it go?" Parker asked, being sure not to show his concern. Hannah was strong. She wanted none of his pity or anyone else's.

She dropped onto the grass, then spread her cloak out between them and emptied the contents of her pockets onto it.

There were a pile of coins and a few bills, a small magitech lantern that had a little juice left, and a bunch of other trinkets that might be of some value. Maybe they could hawk it on the Boulevard. The thing about being a pickpocket is that you never really knew what you were going to find, you just took whatever you could grab and tried not to get caught.

That was rule number one. And probably rules two, three and five if he were being honest.

"Went all right," Hannah said. "Your little trick with the bread cart worked well. The crowd ate it up. Something strange happened, though. Just as I was breaking out of the crowd, I was going for a bulge in some guy's pocket."

"Whoa, we're there to steal stuff. Reach for bulges on your own time," Parker said with a wink.

"Screw you." Hannah returned the smile.

She never minded his jokes, so he was dished them out.

Hannah continued with her story. "I reached into his pocket and he grabbed me. Based on how he was dressed, I bet he'd been picked clean before. Should have just skipped him. Anyway, I freaked. I mean, I thought he was gonna call for the guards. And with this still stuck on tight..."

She pointed to her forehead. Even though Parker couldn't see the Hunter's tag, he knew it was there. He shuddered to think of what would happen if the guards saw it.

Parker furrowed his brow. "What'd you do?"

"*I* didn't do anything. This guy was big. My hand was in his pocket, he had me by the forearm, and then, out of the blue, he let me go and turned back to your show."

Parker smiled. "I *am* a pretty good juggler." Parker pulled a stick out of the grass and rolled it between his fingers. "Or he must've seen how much of a badass you are."

Hannah laid back on the grass and stretched her arms out to the sides. "Yeah. I'm pretty much a badass." She looked over at his left eye, which was still swollen from his fifteen minutes of fame in the Pit. "How's your face?"

"Beautiful. Yours?"

"The same," she said.

"Who knows, maybe the Matriarch and the Patriarch were smiling down on you," he said, hoping to get a rise.

It worked.

She punched him hard in the shoulder. "If the Bitch and the Bastard exist, they don't give a shit about folks like us. I gave up on fairy tales after my mom died."

Parker rubbed his arm and looked over at Old Jed. "Yeah, you're probably right. We don't need them. And besides, given my stunning good looks and charm and your spindly little pickpocket fingers, we will make our own magic."

She leaned back over and smacked his arm again. He made an effort to exaggerate how much it hurt.

"They aren't spindly, they're dainty. And I wouldn't bet on your looks. Maybe the crowds come to see the douche nugget from the Bitch's Boulevard make a fool of himself."

He smiled. "You know me. I'll gladly play the fool if it means we can eat."

The two lounged in the sun, their heads nearly touching. It was one of their rituals, to divide the wealth and then spend some time just watching the world go by. Other than his mother, she was all Parker had. When they were together on the lawn, it was a little taste of what the Founder, if he were real, would bring back to Arcadia.

———— ♦ ————

Ezekiel sat on the steps of the Capitol, a sandwich from Morrissey's wrapped in brown paper clenched in his fist. Much had changed since he left Arcadia. Many things that once were part of his native city were now gone, and strange things had taken their place. But Morrissey's, the first restaurant established in the newborn city, still remained. It was almost exactly like it was four decades earlier. A mix of nostalgia and longing washed over the old man as he ate but he pushed it down. Now was not the time for sadness.

He was back in Arcadia, and on a mission.

A smile spread across his face as he watched the groups on the Capitol's lawn. There were certainly differences. This monstrosity, for example, sat in a place that had once been dense woods; the little piece of the wild he and his friends had chosen to maintain inside the walls of Arcadia as a reminder of the wilderness they had emerged from. But the wild spaces within the city walls had all been tamed now.

Ezekiel watched as the man in the tattered robe rose before his congregation, his arms lifted high to grab their attention.

"Good people," the Prophet started. "I greet you in the name of the Matriarch and the Patriarch." He paused dramatically, waving an outstretched arm over the crowd in welcoming benediction.

"You mean the Bitch and the Bastard," a mocker shouted from the crowd. "They've left us, old man, in case you didn't get the message!"

Ignoring him, the Prophet bent slightly at the waist toward the people sitting close. "Ah, beloved. Your presence brings me peace in a tumultuous time, and a glimmer of a future which will appear with his most certain coming."

Ezekiel sat up, wondering where in fact the Prophet's speech was headed. It was always interesting to hear people talk about you.

A bit like being at your own funeral, without the messy dying part.

"Yes, faithful ones, a day is coming when the Founder, the one who gave us magic and taught us to use it, will return. It is the Founder, the one who brought us out of greatest darkness, the Age of Madness, who will come back to the city. He will revive it, restore it again with the Matriarch and the Patriarch's blessing. Do you look forward to this, beloved?"

Murmurs came from the crowd at his feet, but those on the outside continued to mock and hurl insults.

"Keep waiting, ya old sonofabitch," his heckler called back.

The Prophet lifted his chin and smiled. "I will wait for as long as I must. The Founder will return in due time. It is said that he anticipates the day when magic is once again used properly."

"When the Unlawfuls have been wiped out and the purity of magic returns to Arcadia. Never forget my children, unlawful magic is a scourge upon our city. These criminals and heathens do dark deeds by night. Only the pure will know the Patriarch and the Matriarch's blessing."

Ezekiel shook his head, angry at the preacher's words. To hear his life's work become so distorted was a shock he had not expected.

There's something wrong with this world, he thought, but it's not the Unlawfuls' fault. And if the Matriarch were here, it wouldn't be the poor from Queen's Boulevard begging for mercy. She would have her fair share of dark deeds to do by night; hell, probably during the day, too.

If this fool only knew.

———— ◆ ————

"I've gotta get back to QBB," Hannah said, finally sitting up. She nodded toward the small crowd. "Not to mention, I can't listen to this idiot anymore."

"The Prophet? We always get a kick out of him." Parker looked from the crowd to Hannah and back.

"Until yesterday," Hannah agreed, thinking of the Hunters who had assaulted her in the alley. She pulled on the edge of the knit hat to make sure the tag was still covered. She was now exactly the kind of person Old Jed was preaching against.

"Right. I forgot you're a heathen devil worshiper now," Parker said with a smile, but part of her thought he was right.

The Prophet and his ministry only served to distract people from their real problems; to have them blame the Unlawfuls rather than the nobles. The Governor's decrees and the Academy's restrictions—the things that really hurt people—were only supported by the Prophet's perverted message.

The Chancellor, the Governor, and Old Jed preached the same ideas. They divided and conquered, each of them finding a place in the hearts of a different part of Arcadia. The Prophet drew the lower-class people, and the institutions held sway over the upper class.

Hannah expected Old Jed's disciples to take justice into their own hands and become vigilantes with pitchforks and torches instead of magic and magitech. The Prophet was mobilizing the people against Unlawfuls.

Soon, if the witch hunts began, no one would be safe.

"It's all horseshit anyway," Hannah said, getting to her feet and knocking off some grass. "Gods? The Founder? Purity of magic? All horseshit. Magic just is. Don't need to create a freaking religion around it. Some people are born with it, just like some people are born rich, and others are born ugly like you. Just luck, not the blessings of the gods."

"Sure," Parker said. He could have been blind and still see her anger.

Hannah stuffed her share of the spoils into her pockets. "Nice job today. I gotta run. Need to see if I can score something for William in case he gets sick again."

"Be safe," Parker said. She knew exactly what he meant. As far as she knew, the Hunters were still on the prowl, and she didn't want to see what a dose of her angry energy added to their violence.

CHAPTER 7

"Half your take in the box, Hannah." Jack was as big as a cart and as fit as a milk cow. He wasn't half-bad, except for his breath and the fact that he worked for Horace, the manager of Queen's Boulevard.

Horace extorted the people under his care as much as he was able, and the Governor didn't give a shit about the evil he worked on the streets of the slums. The people who lived there had neither voice nor power, so it really didn't matter what they thought of Arcadia's governing authorities.

Most of Horace's men were terrible. It was common knowledge they did their own skimming out of the toll box—the place that every street kid had to drop half their earnings to make it back into the quarter. At least Jack wasn't a big douche over the whole thing. He did his job, sometimes with a smile, and never gave her much trouble.

Hannah dug into her pockets and dropped almost half of the cash in. She figured Jack wouldn't check, so keeping some out was worth the risk. "A small price to pay for a safe neighborhood, right?"

Her sarcasm was lost on Jack, whose straight face looked as dumb as it did ugly. Everyone knew that Queen's Boulevard was the most dangerous quarter within the walls. Most Arcadians wouldn't dare come into her part of town for fear of muggings, murders, rapes, or all three at once. But it was different when you lived there. Residents were safe, at least during daylight.

"Good girl," Jack said. "And tell your old man that it's time for his drunk ass to get back to work. Time to contribute, that's what Horace says."

Hannah nodded and passed by. Fat chance that would happen. As far as Hannah could see, her dad's working days were over. If Horace expected more money from her family it would have to come from her.

The tension in her neck eased a little as she crossed onto her home turf. All day she had been nervous about the Hunters, waiting for them to jump her around every corner. But back on the Boulevard she knew she was safe.

She couldn't help but feel at home in the Boulevard. She'd never lived anywhere else and probably never would. Many in the ward felt a sense of hopelessness with their lot in life, but Hannah was resigned. She'd been dealt a shit hand, with a shit dad, and, for the most part, a shit life.

She smiled. With *shit* to look forward to, up was probably her only direction.

Or death…

Hannah's mind shifted to William, and she realized that between him and Parker, all wasn't lost. At least they would always have her back, and she would have theirs. As she walked down the dirty cobblestones, she saw neighbors she considered fine people.

Taking a right into a back alley, she stepped down two stairs and knocked on a battered steel door. A tiny window opened near the top; a single crazy eye stared out at her.

"Ah, Hannah," a voice said through the opening.

The peephole slid closed with a bang. A series of locks, magical or mundane—Hannah was never sure—snapped open. The steel door creaked on its tired hinges.

In the doorway stood Miranda, all four-foot-eight of her. A set of bifocals sat on her crooked nose, which terminated in a wart on its sharp point. A shawl hung from her shoulders and dragged on the ground. If there were ever a quintessential witch, it was she. But Hannah was careful never to call her that.

Miranda insisted she was only a chemist, and only for friends. Mention the word alchemy and one might never be served again. Which was awful, since Miranda was really the only source of good, affordable medicine on the Boulevard.

Miranda's work would fall under the Chancellor's prohibitions. The Academy regulated all kinds of magic, not just the physical stuff. But Hannah wasn't certain if the woman was an Unlawful practicing magic in secret, or just good at healing people.

Nevertheless, Miranda's brews packed a punch and had were extraordinarily effective, which is why Hannah always came to her. That and the fact that Miranda had known Hannah since birth. The woman had always taken pity on her mother and once she was gone, that pity was transferred down the familial line.

"Come in, come in, dear," she called over her shoulder as she walked back into her hovel. Hannah stepped in, closing and locking up the door behind her. Miranda trusted Hannah to lock up, which made her feel good.

One more item in the good column. Screw you again, Death.

She followed behind the tiny woman and joined her at a squat table near the wood stove that burned year-round, regardless of the weather. Hannah peeled off her outer cloak, hoping it might not offend the lady of the house, and settled into a stiff chair. She sat quietly and let Miranda inspect her face.

"You've seen trouble, girl?"

"Not so bad. A misunderstanding, really," Hannah said.

"If I had a dollar for every time a woman came in here because of a misunderstanding I could retire and move into the Capitol building." Miranda stopped and considered her words. "Your mother, she had her share of *misunderstandings* as well. Is this of the same sort?"

Hannah raised a hand to her swollen nose and thought of the men in the alley. Her father wasn't a man who would shy away from the rod for the sake of punishment. But neither Hannah nor William had ever been brutally beaten by him, not to this extent anyway—at least not yet. Not to mention that her father preferred to keep his children's' scars away from the prying eyes of neighbors.

Looking Miranda directly in the eyes, she told the truth. "Not him, other trouble found me. I'm OK."

"Well, lovely," the old woman said, rising from her chair, "you've come to the right place. I have something that will take away your black eyes and make that nose pretty again."

"There's one more thing," Hannah said, peeling the wool hat off her head to expose the Hunters' tag adhered to her forehead. She held her breath, praying that she could trust the old chemist.

"Ah, that kind of trouble." A nervous smile appeared. "Dear, I didn't know you were a—"

"I'm not," Hannah interrupted. "No idea what happened out there. It was a misunderstanding and they saw what they wanted to see. But it didn't stop them from beating me up, or...or anyway, it almost cost me my life."

Miranda nodded her head knowingly. "Those bastards. Can't do their job or keep their nasty cocks in their pants, hmm? When will the Founder return to clean up this mess?"

Hannah blushed, embarrassed that her mother's old friend would believe in superstition and children's stories.

While Old Jed preached that the Founder would return to cleanse Unlawful magic from the land in the name of the Matriarch and the Patriarch, some of the *really* old timers told it differently.

Folks like Miranda thought that when the Founder returned, it would be the nobles and their minions who had it coming. Hannah thought it was hogwash either way. There was no magic in the world strong enough to clean up Arcadia's problems.

Miranda's voice faded as she left the room to rummage in another area of her little home.

Sitting in the warmth of the fire, for the first time in a long time, Hannah felt completely safe. Miranda, with her tiny body and warted nose, had scared Hannah and the other kids as they were growing up.

A lot of mothers in the quarter would tell stories about how "Miranda the Witch" would take bad children from their beds at night and use them to make her potions.

Hannah was only ninety percent sure they were just old wives' tales to this day. But growing up in the Boulevard, you didn't have the luxury of choosing your friends, and Miranda had always been good to her—witch or not.

The little steps came back into the room as the old woman hummed something under her breath.

"Here we are," Miranda said, sliding a tube across the table. "Rub that on tonight, and in the morning, you should be as good as new. Now, as for that tag. I've removed a few in my life. Damn Chancellor with his damn academy and damn Hunters, grabbing more and more good people each year. But usually, if they tag 'em, they bag 'em. Not sure how you got away."

She turned away from the table to her stove, where she dropped a few dried leaves from her left hand into a boiling kettle. It produced an awful cat piss kind of smell.

Miranda lifted the kettle off the stove and set it on the table. "Lean in, dear."

Hannah leaned across the table, and Miranda let the steam hit the girl's forehead.

"*Shit*," she screeched as the scalding mist hit her forehead. But as quickly as the words left her lips, the Hunters' tag lifted from her head and fell to the table. Hannah stared at it until the harsh symbol burst into flame, then disintegrated.

Hannah forced a smile as she rubbed her still-burning forehead. A sense of relief washed over her; her dark future had now had a lone sunbeam come crashing through the clouds in her mind. "Thank you, Miranda, this means a lot!"

"Wasn't so bad, was it?" Miranda chuckled.

Hannah looked down at the table, back to Miranda and then at the table again as she rubbed her forehead one more time for good measure and wrinkled her nose. "Better than drinking it."

"I'd guess so," Miranda said with a laugh.

Miranda turned to put her small box of herbs away, and Hannah reached out and grabbed her hand.

"Actually, I didn't come here just for me. It's Will."

"William? I haven't seen that boy for ages. He OK?"

"Well, we're not sure."

Careful not to expose too much, Hannah told the story of what had happened to her brother on the streets of the market. She left out the detail that she might have stopped the seizure with magic.

It's not that she didn't trust the old woman, but if Hannah were an Unlawful, the quarter would be searched. People would be questioned. The Hunters who had defiled her would be back, and nothing would stand in their way. And no one, including Miranda, would be out of the line of fire.

Better for her to have a good excuse. Plus, the fewer people who knew, the easier it was for Hannah to deny it to herself.

Miranda left again and returned with a bottle of pills. "Now, I can't be certain, but sounds like the tremors have taken his body. If that's the case, two of these in the morning and evening will stave off the convulsions. Bring William to me in a few days. Let's have a look together."

For all the terrible things people said about QBB, Hannah had people who truly loved her here, including Miranda. She felt her throat constrict, and her eyes grew glassy. Hannah had to get out of the room before she lost it. She hated showing her emotions.

"Thank you." She slid nearly half of her earnings from the day across the table.

Miranda covered Hannah's hand with her own. "Your money's no good here, girl."

"You are kind, but I'm not a child anymore. It is time for me to pay what is due."

Hannah turned for the door and left before the alchemist could resist.

She made a quick stop at the only grocery in their ward. It was small and cramped, and the food was overpriced and often spoiled, but Hannah knew if she went home with money her father would take it for booze.

Within minutes she was standing on the doorstep of her home. More anxious than she'd been all day, the young woman listened for her drunk father.

———— ♦ ————

If one believed that the Capitol was magnificent, the Academy was downright heavenly. Ezekiel marveled at its stone architecture, each block laid perfectly atop the others. He ran a finger along a seam. When they had started construction of the city, the magicians had taken particular care to build it strongly. Their hope was to make it a place where all could dwell in harmony.

Beauty was important, but they believed that virtue came with a modicum of humility, so they constructed the walls, houses, and shops with such a philosophy in mind. It was obvious that the original viewpoint had been jettisoned after Ezekiel had left decades ago.

Two wings stretched out in either direction, each identical to the other. They met in a massive hall with an entryway held up by arches reminiscent of the great buildings which had existed before the Age of Madness.

In the center of the building a tower reached toward the sky, marking the highest point in all of Arcadia—an metaphor for the ascendancy of magic.

Students littered the lawn in front of the Academy, all of them sons and daughters of nobles. Some leaned over books and scribbled in leather-bound folders. Others stood in small circles practicing the spells assigned to them in the classroom.

Ezekiel could feel power coming from the students, which paled in comparison to the sheer force that lay within the walls of the building. He couldn't help but smile.

Part of his dream was to build this place. A school for all to study; somewhere young adults could take time to learn the arts with no other cares. It would cost a lot, and they had discussed that. But they all knew that supporting a university of magic would be worth any amount, making Arcadia into the paradise he had dreamed of.

He stepped up the wide block staircase, which lead to a set of oversized doors. Before he could reach for the handle, they hummed and swung open to welcome him.

Clever, the old man thought.

One of the advances that Adrien had made was his application of the magical arts to tools, both common and spectacular.

Magitech doors undoubtedly impressed the nobles; just a little incentive to help loosen their grip on the piles of coins that would procure a spot for their children.

Thinking of the market and Queen's Boulevard, Ezekiel knew the magic in the doors could have been put to use elsewhere to ease the life of the broken and the poor. Injustice ruled in Arcadia, and sometimes it came in packages as innocuous as a set of doors.

"May I help you, sir?" a young man asked. He was most certainly a student as he was dressed in official academy formal wear.

Ezekiel nodded. "Yes, I was hoping to get a tour," he answered and then stood quietly waiting for an answer.

The young man looked Ezekiel up and down, taking in his mundane cloak. It wasn't customary to give commoners tours of the Academy.

People in the lower classes generally never bothered asking. He looked over his shoulder at the crowd of nobles gathered at a reception desk in the magnificent rotunda.

"OK, well, tours are by appointment only. If you would like to schedule a time—"

The old man tapped his staff on the marble floor. Its tone echoed through the cavernous space. "Looks like there's a group ready for you now." He grinned at the young man. "I'll stay in the back."

The guy flushed and looked back again at his group. In Chancellor Adrien's Academy, rules were made to be followed. "I'm very sorry sir, but—"

Ezekiel stopped listening to the man. He closed his eyes and found his center. When he opened them, his eyes were fire red, but hidden from others. "It would mean very much to me to see your school. I expect you will oblige me."

The guide paused as if lost in thought. Then, he said, "Of course, sir. Luckily, there is a tour only now about to begin."

Ezekiel's eyes faded back to their normal steely gray as his face broke into a smile. "Fabulous! I'm glad that reason still has a place in Arcadia."

As promised, Ezekiel stayed in the back, shuffling along behind the group of noble parents and their snotty children. Although the prospective students were on the cusp of adulthood—all of them eighteen to twenty years old—they nevertheless looked like children to the old man. He had not been much older when he had set off to build Arcadia, actually. The difference was that these kids had grown up in privilege.

Ezekiel and his companions had aged quickly from the trials and toils of a world groaning for redemption in the years after the Age of Madness.

Mothers doted over the kids and fathers joked with one another about how good the kids had it there. Ezekiel thought it might do the noblemen good to spend a day in QBB to see just how good *they* had it, with government jobs and businesses running on the backs of the poor.

Things certainly *had* changed in Arcadia, and this ship needed to be righted. Up to this moment he had been annoyed. Now he was royally pissed off.

The guide stopped in the middle of a long hall. Artwork from the days before the Age of Madness was displayed on either side of him. Everything glistened as though it were just made.

"The Academy was founded only a few years after the last block was laid on the southern wall. Construction began before the Capitol. I'm always impressed by the fact that higher learning was in the mind of our founders from the very beginning of our city—a true testament to the fact that magic *is* the bedrock for a flourishing Arcadia."

He took careful steps backward, recounting the history— at least the *official* history—of the Academy with each stride.

"Several magicians were involved in the construction of Arcadia. They were all powerful for their time, but magic in those days was certainly different than it is now. It was learned in the woods and throughout the wreckage of the old world. As you can imagine, it wasn't as elegant as the magic taught here in the Academy. Nevertheless, it was obviously quite effective."

Ezekiel followed and smiled as he remembered those early days in Arcadia. The guide didn't quite have everything right, but it was close enough. Certainly, he and the others had been scrappy magicians in those days.

They had learned on the run and under pressure. Their magic came from discipline and training, and with a cost.

The young man continued. "But even in those days, there was one magician who stood out from them all during the founding of Arcadia. He was more skilled and powerful than the others. But thankfully, that man didn't regard his power as something to hold over the rest. Instead, he understood that his gift was one which held great responsibility. Our Chancellor Adrien was that man. And this hall in which you stand now is Adrien's dream."

A chill spread over Ezekiel's spine as he listened to the revisionist history.

Eve had warned him; the new narrative should have been no surprise.

Rewriting history allowed those in power to keep their influence and increase it. Adrien had always been smart, but Ezekiel had believed that he was also virtuous.

It had been the main reason why he was confident leaving Arcadia in his hands. He thought that he had trained Adrien in both magic and morality, but he was clearly mistaken.

As the guide continued to back down the hallway reciting more history of the Academy, he stopped before a massive marble statue. Ezekiel recognized it immediately: It portrayed Adrien in his youth. The figure looked almost as Ezekiel remembered, except it was a little more beautiful. The features were more angular, and his body was shaped in a gymnasium.

The guy looked up at the statue in awe. "And here he is. The Founder of the Academy."

Mothers gawked at the striking image of the Chancellor as their kids shifted in boredom. They already knew that the path to prestige flowed through the Academy. A tour with all the boring history wasn't necessary to convince them to apply.

"He really was quite striking," the guide added with a smile. "And most would say he has matured just as well. Let me assure you, as a student who is just about to finish his final term, he is as kind and benevolent as you have heard. All our instructors are fabulous, but the one course the students really look forward to is Chancellor Adrien's <u>Magic in the World</u> class. It's the capstone, a way for us to receive our final instruction magic's real purpose. I'm in it right now."

"What are you learning?" the bravest and most interested kid asked.

A smile cracked across the guide's face. "The question is, what *aren't* we learning? We began the term with the Chancellor explaining what had happened in the days before the Academy. Of course, we had covered this in our History of Magic course with Professor Burns, but it was good to focus on it again. Before the founding of the Academy, people ran around doing anything they wanted with magic. As you can imagine, there were times when pure chaos would break out in the streets of Arcadia. Particularly on Queen Bitch…um…Queen's Boulevard.

"Adrien realized that magic in the hands of undisciplined people was the worst thing for the future of the city. So, he did something about it. Today the magical arts can only be learned here, as you know. The academy trains magicians and licenses magic's use in the world. But what people don't talk about is the proper application of power. We're taught that magic used at street-level is *wasted*."

Ezekiel could hold back no longer. "Wasted?"

The guide, for the first time, turned his attention to the old man. "Yes, sir. Wasted. It's like this: there are only so many magicians admitted to the school. One's magic is limited because it wears the caster out. So it only makes sense that there is a limited amount of magic to be applied in the world at any given time.

"The available magic could be used to do silly little things like mending a neighbor's fence, or it could be used for the sake of the city at large. That's what magic is for, to fortify the city and to help it prosper. Because—"

"Pardon me, son," Ezekiel interrupted. It took effort to keep his anger out of his voice. "But did you say mending a neighbor's fence is silly?"

"Yes, you see there is only so much magic—"

"How about using your magic to save a family, or, say, a child from evil men?" Ezekiel pressed.

The guide laughed uncomfortably. "Yes, sir. Because there is only so much magic in the—"

"If you were being eaten alive by some unknown disease that was treating your body like a rancid piece of meat, and I or someone used their magic to save your life, would that be silly?"

The guide, not used to people asking questions, let alone challenging the status quo he was taught to spew upon the noble visitors, was clearly flustered. Ezekiel, though cool on the outside, was reaching his own limit.

"Adrien…the Chancellor says that magic used on the weak is worthless. Magic's place is for the city and for the strong. When we flourish, the city flourishes."

"Well, the Chancellor is a damned *fool*!" Ezekiel ground out, his eyes turning pure crimson as he released the frustration and anger he held within.

Ezekiel cupped his hands in front of his chest, palm in. The eyes of the visitors went wide as a pebble appeared, floating in front of him. It quickly grew into a boulder.

The onlookers took a few steps away from him. Turning his palms out, Ezekiel pushed the object, sending the giant rock careening toward the statue. It hit with a loud crash and marble shattered in every direction.

The guide and his guests all hit the ground, covering their heads as shards of rock bounced off the walls.

When the dust cleared, the old man had gone.

CHAPTER 8

L iving with a drunk all your life teaches you to walk silently and always keep your guard up. Hannah had mastered navigating the house during her father's perpetual binges. The worn boards didn't make a peep as she snuck past her father, who was passed out in the dining room, and into the room she shared with her brother.

Hearing the door, William rolled onto his side. He was small for his age, with a boyish face. But today, the fifteen-year-old looked like a child.

"Happened again?" Hannah asked, sitting on the edge of the bed. The old mattress was barely better than a board.

He looked up and replied, "I'm fine."

She didn't push him. Didn't have to.

Most days, Hannah was sure she knew her brother better than she knew herself. He wouldn't give her any extra opportunities to feel badly for him. And he knew that he was the reason she still lived in the house in Queen's Boulevard. If it weren't for William, Hannah would have been miles away—maybe even in another city, if that were a possibility.

"I visited Miranda today. She gave me something for my face," she told him as she reached up and touched her cheek.

"Finally. I was wondering if we could do something about your ugly mug." William laughed.

Hannah landed a soft, playful punch of her brother's arm before reaching into her pocket. "Gave me these too." She rattled the bottle of pills. "Says they could help with the seizures."

Her brother looked down. "Hannah, you shouldn't have—"

"Of course I should have," Hannah argued.

"No," a heavy, slurred voice said behind her. "You should listen to your brother. You shouldn't have."

Hannah's father Arnold loomed in the doorway, looking like he hadn't shaved or bathed in months. They used to talk about their dad going on a bender, but that term implied there were also sober days.

"Where's the rest?" her father asked.

"Rest of what?" she asked.

"The rest of the damned money. You go out there every day, the two of you, and you're supposed to come home with something to show for it. So where is it?"

Hannah's throat tightened and her body tingled with electricity as it had in the market square. "I have food and medicine to show for it. That's why I work—to take care of this family. Not to buy your damned firewater!"

She froze. Placating her father was always the wiser decision, but now Hannah had kicked the beehive *hard*.

Arnold's face turned a brighter red, adding contour to his puffy, drunken eyes. "Well, I guess you're like your mother after all—an ungrateful little bitch."

Her dad strode into the room to add to Hannah's already battered face. She flinched as the roundhouse came in her direction, but her father's massive fist froze inches from her. Not just his hand; his entire body was as still as a statue.

Hannah stiffened, expecting to get hit, but then relaxed when the blow failed to land.

The hell?

"What's your name, sir?" a clear voice called from the hall behind her father.

A robed man with white hair and a beard to match stepped into the small room. A staff was steady in his hand, and his eyes glowed fire red.

"Arnold," her father answered. Hannah, mouth open, looked between this newcomer and her father.

"Arnold, I want you to listen very carefully. You will never lay a hand on your son or daughter again. From this moment on, you will cease to bother your children. Leave this house immediately, and don't return until you have found work. Because you're a drunken louse, and because it's nighttime in the Boulevard, I don't imagine you'll have luck anytime soon. Nevertheless, this is now your number one priority. Nod if you understand me."

Arnold nodded. Hannah couldn't believe her eyes.

"Good. Now get out, you poor excuse for a seed donor." The old man waved his hand negligently. "I need to speak with your daughter. And one more thing," the man said. "From this day forward, any booze that passes your lips will taste like donkey piss. Do you understand?"

Her father nodded and slowly left the room, stepping carefully around the old man. The visitor's face softened as he turned toward Hannah and William.

"Now that that is taken care of, let's get down to the important stuff, shall we?"

Hannah's jaw dropped in disbelief. "Who are you?" She heard the front door slam behind her father.

"And what the hell just happened?"

———— ♦ ————

For most, eating alone night after night would be lonely, even at the majestic table in the Chancellor's Mansion, but Adrien didn't want it any other way. His days were spent running the Academy and, for all intents and purposes, the city of Arcadia.

The Governor would be lost without him, which made sense since Adrien had basically made the toothless bureaucrat his puppet. The Governor didn't do shit in his position, and that was precisely what the Chancellor wanted from him.

Dinner was prepared by an executive chef who was available around the clock, but that night Adrien hardly took notice of the quality of his viands.

His mind couldn't shake the report that Jasper and the other Hunters gave about the demon-magician in the market. Ezekiel had mentioned such magic before he left Arcadia for the last time, but it was impossible that his mentor could be back. Everyone knew he was gone for *good*.

Magic was powerful, but the dead didn't return. Perspiration beaded his forehead and he dabbed at it with the cloth napkin.

If the Master *had* returned, Adrien would have to be ready for him. The man would certainly not agree with the direction in which the Chancellor had steered the city. But what did he know? Adrien's teacher lived in a world of imaginary ideals. He knew nothing of real politics, let alone real education.

"Cynthia!" Adrien yelled, his fear making his yell sound like frustration.

Footsteps clattered down the hall toward the dining room. A beautiful woman in maid's garb quickly entered from the hall and halted across the table from Adrien. "Yes, Chancellor, what can I do for you?"

"Horace is the manager of Queen's Boulevard, isn't he?"

"Yes, sir. He is."

"Send one of the boys to tell him I need to see him one hour from now in my private office."

The woman offered something between a bow and a curtsy before shuffling out of the room, relieved to be leaving.

———————— ◆ ————————

Shock had washed over Hannah when her father left the room on command. No one told him what to do, not in his own house. She spun back to the old man, who was standing in the middle of their bedroom.

"Let me see that, son," he said to William.

The boy held out the bottle of pills with a quivering hand. After giving it a little shake, the man opened the bottle and sniffed its contents. Pulling a pill out, he held it up and inspected it.

"Interesting," he said, more to himself than to the room's residents.

Hannah watched him break the pill open and pour the contents into his left hand as he stirred the contents around with his right index finger. He raised his right eyebrow and looked over to the young man. "Where did you get this?" he asked.

Without a word, William's eyes cut to his sister, then back to the man.

Ezekiel turned. "Young lady?"

If a kid learned anything growing up in Queen's Boulevard, it was not to be a snitch. Sure, the guy saved her from certain death, but she still didn't trust him.

Her lips remained tightly pursed.

"Ah, a woman of principle, I see." The man smiled and his eyes glimmered. They were a steely gray when they weren't glowing red. "Let's play it this way: whatever you do, don't think of the alchemist's name right now."

Naturally, the first thing to flash through her head was Miranda's name and an image of her sitting across the table from her in the little basement room. As she thought it, the magician's eyes flashed red and then back to gray.

"Miranda?" he murmured.

Hannah narrowed her eyes, annoyed. "How did you..."

He cocked his head to the side. "Really? Are you so surprised? Well, I expect I don't know her, but this Miranda has made a very good mix for the boy. I'm sure it would have worked after some time. A few days, a little more, a little less. Alchemy is such an imprecise science."

"I recognize you," Hannah pointed at him, "even without the green skin and horns." Her anger could take her only so far before her question came out, but it was now only a question, no frustration left in her voice. "But who the hell *are* you?"

The man laughed again. Each time he laughed it was more comforting for Hannah than the last. "That is the burning question, isn't it, young one?"

Untying the cord around his neck, the man pushed his arms back in one swift move, allowing the brown cloak to drop to the floor. Underneath were stunning white robes.

His transformation occurred before her eyes.

While his hair and beard were still white, he looked decades younger and stronger. He seemed to have grown six inches as he straightened. The entire thing made Hannah step back and sit on the bed with William. She grabbed for her brother's leg.

"Whoa," William said in almost a whisper.

"No shit," Hannah replied.

"Ah," the transformed man said. "This looks a bit more like me. But I couldn't be out there without something of a disguise." He rolled his neck as if working out some kinks. "I am the one that people here call the Founder. My given name is Ezekiel."

"Whoa," William said again.

"Horseshit," Hannah said, rising from the bed and pointing at the man. "There is no such person as the Founder. It's like wood nymphs or…or…" she threw her hands up in the air, "I don't know, something else that isn't real."

She continued her argument. "The Founder is a story told by some to manipulate and others to comfort. Like the Prophet." She stabbed a finger at Ezekiel. "That guy is a cultist! Drawing everybody in with stories and then feeding off their admiration and attention. And his disciples?"

Her voice rose an octave.

"They're even worse! The way the Prophet talks about the Founder, it gives them a false sense of hope about the future. But that ain't the way of the world. Not here in Arcadia. And it sure ain't *my* life." Hannah realized she was sweating, and for some reason, close to tears.

Her emotions were taking over, and she wasn't certain why. "You're not the Founder, and we're not going to be your disciples." She breathed deeply, willing the tears to stay away as she speared Ezekiel with both eyes. "Go mindscrew somebody else, you sicko! Just because you saved me back there in the alley...and...and now with my own father...."

Hannah felt nauseous, as she had much of the previous day. She curled her hands into balls and considered attacking, but something deep inside told her to stop.

Just Wait.

Listen.

And watch.

The magician finally took his eyes off Hannah and turned towards William. "Young man, do you believe as your sister does?" he asked, an eyebrow raised in question.

William's eyes were wide and his mouth dropped slightly open as he looked to Hannah and then back at Ezekiel. "Um, yeah. I think so."

Ezekiel pursed his lips for a moment. "How are you feeling? The seizures."

"Fine."

"No." Ezekiel shook his head. "Tell me the truth."

William glanced back at Hannah, and she gave him the slightest nod. She wanted to believe, but at the same time she just couldn't.

Her life didn't lend itself to fairy tales.

"OK," he shrugged. "I feel terrible. Like the world is spinning. Only slowly now, but then it speeds up and the shaking comes. I can't stop it."

"I can," Ezekiel said with a wink. "Do you want me to?"

Another glance in Hannah's direction, and she knew she had to make a call. A lifetime of suspicion meant she couldn't trust this man, but when it came to her brother, no wager was too high.

"Do it," she finally answered, her voice a whisper.

Without a word, the man stepped forward and leaned over Hannah's brother. His eyes turned red again. She could feel the power coming off him, like in the marketplace.

Placing his hands on the boy, the man stood motionless for a moment. It was as if his body was there, but nothing else. After what felt like an eternity, William's face came to life. His color returned and he looked better than he ever had. The man took a couple of steps back and then slumped in the chair in the corner.

"Whoa!" William cried, looking at his hands. "That was amazing."

Hannah came back to the bed. "What? What is it?" she asked, looking him up and down.

"I've never felt like this before." He looked up at his sister, his eyes glistening. "I feel...I feel...great!"

For as long as Hannah had known her brother, the boy had had moments when his health was bad and other times when it was worse. He'd never felt great before.

Hannah's heart burst with joy. Looking back at Ezekiel in the chair, she questioned, "You fixed him?"

The old man gazed at her for a moment, then nodded. "Now that I am back," he told her as he looked towards

William and then out the window, "I have a mind to fix a lot of things." He turned back to the two of them. "William here is only the beginning." He waved towards the outside. "It is time to make Arcadia what she was meant to be. Time to create a kingdom where magic is used for the good of all."

Having regained his strength after the casting, the man stood. He didn't look like the old man who had entered their house minutes ago.

Although still gray, he seemed strong and filled with life. "The one problem is that I'm going to need help. I can't change the world on my own. And there are going to be those who want anything *but* change. We're not talking about just the little things, though those matter. What I'm talking about is a whole new order," he told the two of them.

Hannah stood up, arms crossed in front of her. "Even if I bought all of this, what can I do?" Her voice dropped, as close to admitting defeat as she had ever been. "I'm nobody."

"Hannah…" His eyes seemed to disappear for a moment before she could focus on them. "You are a *magician*, with the potential to unlock power you can hardly dream of. The question is not what you can do, but rather, what you have the *will* to do."

The old man held a hand out in her direction. "So, you answer me this, Hannah," he asked her, his eyes seeming to dance between colors.

"Do you want to help save the people here?" He waved to those in Queen's Boulevard. "Are you willing to help save Arcadia?"

CHAPTER 9

A caged bird forgets how to sing, Hannah thought as she walked through the front gates of Arcadia and into the unknown. It was a line her mother had said to her over and over when she was young. It was a tale, which, as far as she knew, was older than Irth.

As a child she had never really known what it meant, but as she got older, Hannah found that her life was the cage, and the bars had gotten thicker and thicker as she grew older. She had never realized until now that her mother was a caged bird herself and she didn't want Hannah to follow in her path.

Stepping through the broad gate and out of Arcadia for the first time, all terror was washed away, and she felt a sense of liberation she didn't know was possible.

The taste was sweet, and she wanted more.

Glancing over her shoulder, she took one last look at Arcadia's walls as she walked beside the magician who had offered her freedom.

The choice hadn't been made lightly.

For years, she *could* have run, but responsibility to her brother kept her within the walls. She had traded love for freedom, and had resigned herself to that decision. His declining health had held her. That, and her abusive father.

There was no way in hell she would leave Arcadia with her sick brother in that drunk's hands. So, she had stayed, and had no regrets or resentment toward her brother because of it.

But Ezekiel had changed everything.

He had placed his hands on William, and all signs of weakness disappeared. William had gone from looking like a shriveled child to the strong young man Hannah had always known he was on the inside. With William's health back, Hannah's impetus to stay was weakened. If Ezekiel's magical spell on her father was real as well, the decision to became even easier to make.

Ezekiel had spoken to her father, and he had listened. He was now crawling the streets of Arcadia looking for work, something he had stopped doing well before her mother died.

But even with the apparent reversal in circumstances, Hannah's skepticism had not been easily overcome. Her life had taught her that bad tended turn worse. That lesson had made it hard to accept that some all-powerful godlike figure would just show up at her door with free handouts.

It took hours, but Will had finally convinced her that going with Ezekiel, at least on a trial basis, was worth a shot.

Even if the whole thing was some elaborate scam, the rewards outweighed the risks. And the guy *had* healed him. Hannah was willing to break a lot of rules where William's health and happiness were concerned.

Will was a smart kid, and Parker would help him when necessary. So she had finally consented to listen to the magician's plan to save Arcadia and her role in the whole endeavor. Even as they walked their first paces beyond the walls, she wondered, why her? What did she have to offer the mighty Founder whom people had talked about for decades?

Apparently this old man was convinced she could use magic. She didn't doubt the fact that something weird had happened to her—the strange lizard tucked away in her bag was proof of that—but it was hard for her to grasp that she might ever be able to do the things she had seen the Founder do.

There were many questions to be answered, but she turned her mind from her queries to take in the new world around her instead.

"So, um, Founder—"

"Ezekiel."

"Yeah, OK, Zeke." She looked around at the trees and the path before gazing back to look at him. "Where the hell are we going?"

He lifted his staff and pointed toward the horizon. Peeking up over the dark green boughs of the pines was a tower. Even from her vantage point, it looked like a relic from the old world. She could see places where the structure had crumbled. It looked like the hand of a god had reached down and torn off the top.

Having grown up in her cage of a city, Hannah was clueless when it came to judging distances that encompassed more than a walk across the four quarters, but she made a guess. "Going to take us hours to walk there."

"Yes it would, if we were to walk."

Ezekiel's eyes flashed bright red and a flood of power washed over her. The hair on her skin stood up, and a mighty wind rushed through her hair. She blinked and realized she was no longer outside the city gate, but instead stood in the middle of a great hall with high arched ceilings. The place was filled with crumbled rock and rails of steel—a metal from the old days before the Age of Madness. She cleared her throat, and the sound echoed through the cavernous interior.

Well, it was cavernous compared to her little hovel in QBB.

"What the hell?" she got out as she rotated in place to look around.

"Not hell. This will be our little heaven," Ezekiel said, just as a piece of the ceiling crashed to the floor some thirty feet away. "Or at least purgatory. It is where we will train and ready ourselves for the first steps of taking back Arcadia." He reached up and scratched his beard as he looked around. "It needs a little cleaning first, but nothing we can't handle."

The man's face was drawn and sickly. He slumped more than when he had first entered her father's house, leaning his weight on his staff. "But for now, I must rest."

Hannah hesitated before reaching out. "Are…are you OK?"

The man laughed. "Of course, but magic comes with a price. Teleportation is one of the most exhausting arts I know. Takes even more to move both of us." He pointed with his staff. "I made you a place at the end of that hall." He gestured with the staff to the left. "Mine is over there. I need to restore some of my strength. You should get settled in. This place will be your home for some time. But for now, stay inside the tower. The surrounding forest is not as tame as Arcadia."

He was as good as his word; he headed for his room. Hannah watched him go in silence, then turned to explore her new residence.

A thin mattress was pushed into a corner. Other than a side table and a tiny desk with a chair, the room was bare. Settling in wouldn't take long, but it was more than she had ever had so Hannah was grateful. And although she loved William with all her heart, sharing a room with a boy allowed for little privacy. She tugged open the leather bag and pulled out her spare shirt and cloak, the only clothing she had.

Two beady eyes stared up at her. "Here we are, Sal. I'm not sure what's ahead of us, but I'm glad I'm not alone."

She turned and placed the creature on the bed, where he rolled into a ball; he was a lazy beast. She thought he had grown since the night he made himself a part of the family. She considered about rolling him around the bed for a second, a mischievous smile on her face.

She could hardly remember the way he looked when she first saw him, nothing more than a common newt. If Ezekiel was right, then maybe magic was the reason this thing changed into his new form. Either way, Sal didn't seem too upset with his new lot in life.

She folded her clothes and slid them into a drawer, then paced the room, wondering what the strange building would have been in the days before the Age of Madness. While walls in Arcadia were constructed with the precision of magic, the walls of her room were different.

Somehow even more precise.

She had heard of machines in the old days that had run on something like magitech but required no magician. There were so many stories floating around Irth about the past, one never knew which were true and which were bullshit.

People generally chose the ones that benefited them and discarded the rest.

After three complete laps around the little room, boredom took its toll. At that time of day, she and Parker would normally be working together running some con.

She wasn't used to taking days off.

Hannah turned for the door. She walked toward the great hall where she had first landed and marveled at the way the ceiling soared upward. The pitter-patter of Sal's footsteps followed behind her and she turned to look at the little guy. "You bored too?"

His tongue flicked in and out of his mouth. She smiled at the memory of Sal tickling her wrist.

Curiosity pushed her, so she tried all the doors to the rooms that adjoined the hall but none of them budged.

She was unsure if they were shuttered before the last humans fled, or if Ezekiel had done the job himself when he came back. One of the doors must have led into a stairwell because she was stuck on the ground level.

Stay in the tower. The magician's words echoed through her mind.

Naturally she knew that the world outside Arcadia was different, but certainly, it wouldn't harm anything to stretch her legs a few steps, right?

Finding a door to the outside, she pushed and was surprised to find it unlocked. Hannah's inquisitive nature trumped caution, and she took the first steps into the new world.

Hannah hadn't realized just how musty the tower was until the cool afternoon air struck her face. It was altogether different from what she had breathed in the city her entire life.

As she inhaled deeply, a smile lit her face. The air smelled of pine, earth, and freedom. Hannah stretched her arms toward the sky and let the breeze from the forest blow through her hair. It was only a few hours since she had left her brother on Queen's Boulevard but she already wanted to talk to him, if only to describe what she was seeing right now.

During their conversation, before he had given his blessing, she had been inclined to try to bring him along, but William had insisted on her going alone with the Founder if only to see what he had planned.

As her mind had contemplated all that had happened and the hope she had allowed to bloom since the magician had healed her brother, she headed toward the shadows of the trees.

No more than twenty feet into the forest, Ezekiel's admonition returned.

Stay in the tower.

"As long as I don't go too far, I'll be fine." She looked around, trying to see between some of the branches in the trees.

Hannah was a kid from the Boulevard. She had spent her life around danger.

What harm could a few trees do?

Glancing over her shoulder, she spotted the door leading into the decrepit tower and convinced herself that she was close enough to the magician's fortress to return if something bad happened.

The crunching of little feet on the forest floor was easily heard as Sal came scampering across from the building and jumped into her arms. She absentmindedly rubbed his scaly body as her eyes scanned the woods.

He wriggled as she ran a fingernail down his back, outlining the base of each of the peculiar spikes. When she finished, he crawled up onto her shoulder. "Ouch!" She flinched as his sharp claws bit into her shoulder. "I'm not your pincushion." He settled down, his tail draped down her back.

Hannah let the pain recede into the background as she considered just how much her life had changed in a few short hours. If it weren't for the Hunters in the square, or even for William's seizures, none of this might have happened.

Life had dealt her a shit hand, but it seemed she had finally drawn a lucky card.

Now the question lingered in her thoughts, *Would the luck remain?*

The answer to her question came sooner than she expected. As she stepped farther into the trees, a series of grunts echoed around the woods, and she heard what sounded like city goats pawing around in the dusty square of the market.

Looking up from the pine needle-covered earth, her eyes fastened on a creature that looked like one of the pigs the farmers brought to Arcadia for slaughter. Only this pig was twice as big and had tusks jutting from its jaw. Thick black hair ran down its back.

"Oh, this is bad," she whispered, eyes flitting left and right before locking on the pig.

The animal continued to paw the ground and snort and roll its massive head as it stared at her, saliva dripped from its tusks.

Hannah backed up slowly while she gawked at the creature, until she stood with her back planted against a tree. Sal moved his tail so it didn't get squished.

"It's OK, boy, girl, whatever you are," she said in the most soothing voice she could muster, but her words did nothing to calm the beast. Hannah's eyes cut to the tower's door, and she wondered how fast the animal could move.

From the looks of the tusks, she assumed the thing could deliver significant damage. She took a test step in the direction of safety, and its grunting increased to a frenzy. And then, without warning, the oversized war pig jumped towards her and ran head-down in her direction.

A lifetime of instincts honed by the dangers of the Boulevard pushed Hannah to action. She turned and sprinted back toward safety.

Sal's claws tightened on her shoulder.

Branches whipped across her face and arms, but she ignored the pain. She could hear the pig closing in on her. The tower was just ahead, but she was afraid she wouldn't make it. She glanced over her shoulder to see how much time she had but as she did, a root caught her foot and sent her sprawling on the ground.

She landed hard but quickly rolled so she could see behind her. The large beast was nearly on top of her, its tusks like spears. Hannah raised her arms in defense, a pitiful attempt to block the creature's charge.

She refused to give up, but she knew in her heart that death was upon her.

Her eyes caught movement from her left; an object streaked through the air and struck the beast in the head. The animal dropped, rolling to a stop just a few feet in front of her with its skull crushed beyond recognition.

The projectile, a giant metal hammer with a spike on the handle's end, lay bloodied on the ground to her right.

As Hannah stared wide-eyed at the weapon, she heard a branch snap behind her shoulder.

"What da hell is a little lass a doing out in da forest by her lonesome?" a gruff voice asked in the rearick dialect.

A man with a thick beard and long hair falling over his leather armor approached and bypassed the pig to pick up his hammer. He grunted as he took in the animal before he turned to Hannah.

He was half as wide as he was tall, and his face held no hint of what might be considered kindness as he eyed her up and down.

He didn't seem impressed.

Hannah stammered at her savior. "I…"

"It ain't safe out here, as ya now know. And who da hell are ya? And what's dat?" he asked, pointing to Sal with the head of his hammer.

The strange feeling of power under her skin enveloped her, and Hannah breathed deeply to stifle it. "*That* is my pet. And I'm not sure if anyone of your stature should be calling anyone else little, sir." She cracked a half-smile and raised an eyebrow at the rearick.

Without warning, the man pulled a knife from his belt. Hannah jumped back, thinking the man was a monster, saving her from the war pig only for his own vicious pleasure.

But before she could react, the rearick flipped the knife over and extended it toward her. The blade was made of silver, its hilt ornately crafted.

She stood up, knocking the worst of the dirt and needles off her. She was right; he stood inches shorter than her.

He offered, "Ye might not be very smart, but ye sure got some balls, and I like dat. And sassy, too. This is for the next time ya decide to do something as stupid as ye did this day." He jerked the blade a couple of times in the direction of the pig.

Hannah accepted the knife and turned it over and over in her hand, eyeing the craftsmanship. To her trained eyes, it had some value.

Holding out a beefy hand, the man said, "Da name's Karl."

Hannah took his hand. Suspicious or not, he had just saved her from a proper goring. "Hannah," she replied with a smile. Looking down at the beast and back at the knife, she said, "I really don't know what to do with this."

Karl shrugged and pointed to the pig's head. "With an animal like that, always aim for da throat. Works with a man, too, but it's a wee bit harder to land it." He winked in fun.

She looked back toward the path he had approached from before asking, "Do you live around here?"

"Around here? Bah. No." He jerked his chin toward the horizon. "I'm from the Heights. But I can make a lot of scratch escorting farmers and traders through these woods to Arcadia. Just dropped a group off, and I'm picking dem up again tomorrow."

"Oh. Then what are you doing around here?"

"Have you ever been to Arcadia, lassie?" he asked.

Hannah laughed. "This is my first time *out* of Arcadia. Been there all of my life."

"Figures. That explains your performance with this boar here. But if you're from the city, then ya know that Arcadia is no damn place for a man who loves the shade of trees and the feel of wind in his beard. Gets so damned claustrophobic in there, I can hardly make it through the gate before I need to get my ass back out of there."

"I didn't know that rearick could get claustrophobic."

The man tilted his head. "Under the ground's different, eh? I trust the earth. People, not so much. Now, let me escort ye back to yer palace, my lady."

Hannah flushed a little and tucked the knife into the leather belt that held her cloak in place. "What about that?" she asked, nodding at the boar.

"Dat's dinner, if you care to join me."

She wrinkled her nose. "Gross."

He laughed. "Nope, not gross, *good*. Damn good meat and she's a fat one. A little heat and a lot of salt, and I'll sleep with a full belly."

They walked to the tower. She would have been caught by the big pig, boar, whatever, for sure. She had gone farther than she thought.

The man stopped at the base. "Want to come in?" Hannah asked. "I could introduce you to my friend if he's up."

Karl's eyes scanned the tower from top to bottom. "Not in there."

"More claustrophobia?" she asked with a grin.

"Sure, kid. Something like dat." Karl nodded then took a couple steps backward. "Pleasure to meet ya, lass." He pointed at belt. "Now do me a favor and keep the knife close and stop being so damned stupid in these woods." His words were gruff, but Hannah could sense warmth beneath his granite exterior.

She watched the man sling the giant hammer over his shoulder and disappear into the woods before she retreated into the safety of the tower with Sal on her heels.

CHAPTER 10

C ome on, just one more time, sir? Give a boy from
Queen Bitch Boulevard a chance to win his money
back."

"Sure. Once more," the middle-aged man said as he
counted the coins in his palm. His fine clothes and trimmed
hair indicated that he was a noble who had wandered out
of his quarter. "But, I'll tell you, son, if I win, I'm keeping
the coins. Only way you boys will learn."

Parker placed his hands in front of his chest, palms
together, and bowed. "I am always willing to take a lesson from an elder. Especially one who is both wise and
refined." He turned to the crowd that had gathered at the
corner of the market square. "What do you think, folks?
Should I try it again? He's good, but I only have a handful
of coins left."

The onlookers hooted and hollered, urging Parker on.

"OK, I don't want to let the good people down. But I can only do ten this time. My dear Ma still needs her medicine." Parker lifted an imaginary glass and pretended to drink. The crowd roared.

"Here we go, then. Three shells, one ball. As everyone can see, the ball is here, under this one." Parker tilted back the middle shell, showing a tiny green pea. "Now, sir. Last chance and I need the money, so I'm going to make this one a little tougher. Ready?"

The man kept his eyes on the shells and nodded.

Parkers hands moved fast, his mouth even faster. "Keep your eyes on the shell as they go around. Where's the pea? That's the plea. Where's the pea? Can you tell me?"

He went on for another thirty seconds before pulling his hands back from the shells. "How do you feel?"

Sweat glistened on the man's forehead. "Good. I got this." His finger hovered over the shells as it finally settled on the one furthest to his right. "This one."

"You sure about that?" Parker asked. "Really sure?"

"Yes. This one. I'm positive."

"Last chance."

The electricity in the crowd was thick. Everyone leaned in waiting for the reveal. Parker closed his eyes and let his head dip. Flipping the shell, he said, "Well, they say the nobles are smart, kind, and good looking. At least you're one out of three."

The green pea sat under the shell.

Scooping up his winnings, the nobleman said, "Get an honest job, kid. Sweeping the gutters is a sure thing, and you're not very good with those shells."

As the man moved out of sight, Parker looked back at the gathering. "Well, I guess my ma will go to bed sober tonight.

Might as well give it another shot. Who's feeling smart or at least lucky?"

The crowd shifted as a man stepped forward, landing twenty coins on Parker's crate. "I'm in for twenty."

"Sorry, sir. After the noble, I need to be cautious. Are you a farmer or something with all of that coin?"

The man shook his head. "Trapper, and I just dropped off a cartload of furs."

"Ah, and you want to go home with even more. All right, let's give it a go."

Parker shifted the coins to the side of the crate and started the routine again. His hands flew, as did his mouth. Finally, he came to rest. The man inspected each of the shells. After a moment, he pointed. "This one."

"Ah, close." Parker flipped over a different shell showing the tiny pea. He swiped the man's coins and stuffed them into his bag. He asked, "Try again?"

"Nah. That's all. The wife said no gambling."

"Perfect," Parker cried. "This is a game of skill." Sliding the pea under the middle shell, he flipped the empty ones over. "You saw it, right? Here, look again." He tilted the shell back up. "Three moves on this one. No need to put money on it if you're not sure."

Parker slowly slid the shells around, shifting each of them one space. "Last chance for a bet. I'll let you win it back."

The man rubbed the back of his neck with his hand. "How about I win it back and more?"

Parker shrugged. "Guess I'll give it a chance. Forty coins?"

The man laughed and pointed. "Stupid kid. It's here."

Parker grinned and flipped the shell. It was empty. "Sorry, mate. Thanks for playing, though."

The crowd cheered as he grabbed the coins.

"You little cheat," the trapper yelled.

"Sir, I resent your comment. I am an honest—" Without finishing, Parker kicked the crate into the man's legs and shot through the thick crowd. He had to circle the whole quarter before he knew he was safe.

Collapsing on a bench at the edge of Queen Bitch Boulevard, Parker counted his coins and caught his breath. The shell game was always a risky con. It could only last so long before it was broken up by an angry tourist or the Governor's Guard, but he had made enough for the day.

"You want to try again?"

The nobleman stood over him.

"Pretty far away from your quarter now, aren't you sir?"

Glancing down Queen's Boulevard, the man smiled. "Dunno, looks quainter here than I imagined. Maybe I'll move in."

Parker laughed and the man dropped onto the bench next to him. "Can't wait to get out of this stiff cloak. Makes me feel stuffy, like those noble bastards. How'd we do today?"

"Not bad, Sam. About two-fifty. You did pretty good—almost believable as a man from the Capitol quarter." Parker dropped half the earnings into the man's hand. While Parker knew he deserved more of the take, he split it evenly with the man because that's what he always did with Hannah. And most hustles needed a partner. "It was a good day."

The man nodded, grabbed his share, and headed toward Queen's Boulevard. He stopped and turned. "I know it's usually you and Hannah running the cons, but if you need me, I'm happy for the work."

"Sure thing, Sam. We'll have to change it up tomorrow, but I might need you again."

Parker hid half the coins in his shoes and made his way into the Boulevard. Stopping at the toll, he paid the cut to Jack, who would hand it over to Horace, the scumbag manager of their quarter. Life was hard enough in Queen's Boulevard; it felt harder every time he handed over hard earned cash to the "civil servant."

He was halfway down the Boulevard when he heard a hushed voice call his name. His face lightened when he saw it was William.

"Come with me," he said.

"William?" Parker looked around quickly and hissed back, "Where the hell is Hannah?"

"Just come with me. I'll tell you everything."

Parker followed William as he wound his way through an alley and climbed over a broken-down fence. After crossing an empty lot littered with trash, the boy looked over his shoulder at Parker and around the edge of the lot before ducking through a hedge.

William stepped through a broken window into a building that appeared suited for demolition. While the outside was falling apart, the inside was neat and tidy. Pieces of discarded furniture lined the walls, and it looked as though someone had recently swept the worn-out floors. Condemned buildings were a dime a dozen in Queen's Boulevard, but he'd never seen one cared for like this.

"What is this place?" Parker asked looking around.

"A clubhouse, I guess you could say. Hannah and I found it years ago. We'd come here whenever we got the chance. You know, kids' stuff? We'd play house, or school, or magic. Called it our own. Two years ago when Hannah started running the streets with you we stopped coming, but I decided to keep it up. Only felt right. I come when I can."

Parker walked the perimeter of the room and tried the knob on the only door. "The rest of the house like this?" he asked.

"Nah. Just this. I don't know why, but we usually stayed in this one room. Only ventured into the rest of the house a few times. Smells like cat piss and death. Everything's a mess. But, you know, when you carve out a little corner of the world, you find you can actually care for something. We started small. Thought that someday the place would be ours and we could do the rest. But you have to start however you can."

William sat down on a chair in a corner arranged as a sitting area. He rubbed his hand on the arm of the chair and tilted his head back.

Parker dropped into a chair across from William. He noticed the color in the boy's face and the steadiness of his hands. Hannah's sick little brother looked like a different person.

He started to ask about it, but reconsidered. "Where is she, William? It's been days. I don't want to be the overbearing street partner, but I'm starting to worry. You know, with the thing in the alley."

"Yeah, that's why I found you. I think she would want you to know she's gone."

"Gone?" Parker asked. "When? *Where*?"

His mind raced, but once it started to settle down, Parker realized he shouldn't be all that surprised.

They all had it bad in the quarter, but some kids, like Hannah and William, had it worse. At least Parker had a mother he loved and who cared for him. He also had his health. But not them. They had a mother who was dead and buried, and a father they wished was.

Some people got the short end of the stick. Hannah and William got the short end up their asses. But he never thought she would leave William behind. He was all she ever talked about.

"I don't know for how long, but she's gone to study magic."

Parker laughed. People from their quarter didn't study magic. It was impossible. "Come on, where is she?" he pressed, his anxiousness diverted by the outlandishness of the answer.

William looked at Hannah's partner. "Really. A powerful magician saw her potential. He was watching in the market square when I had my seizures. I have no idea what he saw, but he saw something."

Parker thought about Hannah's description of the attack. If the Hunters were after her, then maybe she *could* do magic.

"So she's at the Academy?" Parker asked.

William fidgeted. Parker could tell that he wasn't sure how much to share.

Finally, the boy looked up and spilled the beans. "The Founder, Parker, he came and healed me. And then he asked my sister to go with him, to train or something. He just kept talking about saving Arcadia like he saved her life. Like he saved me."

The boy filled in the gaps of the story. Parker smiled along, nodding at all the right times, but deep down he didn't believe there was a Founder and neither did Hannah. He wondered how much trouble his friend was really in.

"Where did they go?" he finally asked.

William shrugged. "To a tower outside the city. At least, that was where the Founder told her they were going."

———— ◆ ————

Hannah sat in the great hall thinking about the incident with the wild boar and Karl. She cursed herself for needing his help. She needed to get stronger. Guts came naturally, and toughness had been honed over time, hustling in the streets of Arcadia. But she needed skill, so training would be necessary.

Zeke had brought her to the tower to teach her magic. Despite her reservations, she was willing to learn.

"Are we ready to begin?" The magician's voice echoed through the hall.

"I've been ready since you zapped us over here. You're the one napping." She gave him a slight smile and wondered if the old man had a sense of humor.

"When you're my age, little girl, simple things like kicking ass and teleportation take a bit out of you." He nodded to her. "You will see soon enough."

"All right, old man. Teach me some magic."

"Call me Ezekiel. And the magic will come, but you need to learn some history for context. Walk with me." He turned and headed towards the now-familiar door.

At the door he waited for her to catch up, then pointed ahead of him down the length of the building.

The teacher and his new student started the first lap around the tower. Hannah chose not to mention that she had already taken a self-guided tour outside. The man's strides were long and she had to move fast to keep up with him.

She was clueless as to his actual physical stature since much of what she had seen had either been a disguise that made him look weaker or an enhancement that made him appear to be physically powerful. The walk was the first clear indication that the man was strong, which made sense if he'd spent a major portion of his life walking Irth.

"What do you know about the history of Arcadia?" he asked.

She thought about that. What *did* she know? The temptation was to either say too much or admit too little. If she was going to be trained, Ezekiel needed to know what he was working with.

A lot of good that was going to do him.

"Not much, I guess. As much as any other kid from QBB might know. I mean, I never really went to school or anything. More of an education on the streets. My mom told me some things before she…" Hannah paused.

"Died?"

Hannah's throat got tight and a quick nod of agreement got her over the hump.

"Yes. Died. My mother's parents had come to the city soon after the Age of Madness ended. Arcadia was new then, and opportunity was everywhere. My grandfather got a job working on the final stages of the walls. There were plenty of magic users at work, but he provided muscle. Magic doesn't run in my family."

The man nodded along with her story. It was a travesty that hunger and desperation drove a smart kid like her to the streets instead of a life of learning and exploration.

Ezekiel was fortunate to have found her.

When she concluded her story, he added, "Well, you know part of the tale, but you have made an assumption about magic that is only partially correct, like most truths. The old world— the world before the Age of Madness, and the Second Dark Ages before that—didn't have magic as we know it today.

"But, in most senses, their society would have seemed incredibly advanced in comparison to ours, at least in the technologies they had available. For the people of the Early Age, science and technology *were* their magic, and many worshiped it like a god."

Ezekiel pointed at the buildings they were passing. "They built huge edifices that reached to the heavens, and developed all kinds of machinery and technologies such as flying ships. Just before the coming of the Madness, the people had all but mastered communication technology. Just through their technologies, they could talk with anyone around the world." The old man waved his hand toward the sky. "And even in the heavens."

"Wait." Hannah stopped walking and motioned toward the clouds. "People lived in the freaking *sky*?"

The old man turned, seeing her incredulous expression and laughed. "Eventually, yes. We had just started traveling there, but as the time went on it became home to some."

"But what the hell powered it? Magitech?" she asked as she started walking again.

The old man shook his head and turned to continue his circuit. "Magitech is something Adrien has introduced into the world. In the old days, the humans would harness the energy from the sun and dig fuel out of the ground. It was really quite something. Just before the end of the Early Age, they had learned how to split an atom to make power beyond our imagination. Beyond what *any* magician can do."

"Split a what?" she asked as she stepped over the same broken ground she had dealt with for the past seven laps.

"Mm, yes. An atom." For some reason he didn't seem bothered by the rough terrain. She tried to catch him cheating, but it didn't seem like he was using any magic to float across.

He was just more agile than her, apparently.

"The technicalities aren't that important. But you should know that this source of energy is what got us into a lot of trouble. Seemed the smarter people got, the more foolish they became. Eventually, the power in those atoms was used to destroy the world and most everything in it.

"Almost no one lived through the release of that energy, but those who did worked to rebuild Irth. They began making the place we now call home. But during the process, something even more terrible than their science emerged. Something even more deadly."

Hannah answered as he paused in his story, "The Madness. It was the judgment of the gods upon the wicked."

This made the man laugh. Apparently, children of Arcadia—at least those who had grown up in Queen's Boulevard—had cobbled together pieces of the stories of their past, but they had filled in the cracks over the years with their own imaginations.

"Again, you understand only part of the truth. The Madness was also the result of technology gone awry, although this technology was quite different from the bombs and the planes. It attacked us from within."

Hannah quietly took in the old man's words. While some of it made no sense to her whatsoever, the idea of being attacked from within was perfectly clear.

Her words came out slowly. "You mean like a sickness…"

She could hear Ezekiel's feet hit the ground, so he wasn't floating. She would have to find out how he walked so easily on some of this terrain.

"Mmm, yes, exactly! It was a disease; one that could attack anyone at any time. But instead of giving people fevers or making them shake like your brother, this disease attacked the mind. It turned people, good and bad people, into monsters. One day someone living in your small village would be normal, the next they ate their own children alive."

Her face, if Ezekiel could have seen it, would have made him chuckle. "Ugh. Now I know why it's called the Age of Madness."

"Yeah. It's had several names throughout the decades, but that seems to be the one that has stuck. Probably because it was so fitting. At the beginning of the outbreak, people were spread out all over the world. Little communities fended for themselves and tried to protect their own from other groups. They were rather uncivilized societies. But when the outbreak happened, people realized that there was safety in numbers. The disease pushed the people to gather in concentrated areas, to work together. That is how the early cities were developed."

"Are there, um, other inhabited places like home?"

"Oh yes. It is hard to fathom just how large the world is. There are places just like Arcadia, filled with cities and people. But there are huge swaths of Irth that are now left uninhabited—places the infection wiped completely clean of humans."

They walked in silence for a lap. She had heard stories from the old days, but they had always seemed like children's tales. Much like the gods and the Founder. But now, as Hannah walked side by side with a man powerful enough to heal her brother, she found it easier to accept that maybe some of the old stories were true.

She allowed just the smallest amount of hope to grow in the secret place we all protect.

Her innermost place where she had stopped allowing hope to enter so many, many years ago.

———•———

Ezekiel looked down at his new student, trying to assess how well she was taking all of this.

The girl was shocked, and rightfully so.

He had just dropped a serious bomb on her; the world she lived in was nothing like she had imagined. Her silence betrayed her skepticism, but that was fine.

Belief must be *owned*.

He had seen too many people swayed and manipulated by clever rhetoric before. The truth had to become *hers*. He considered letting their history lesson stand, but she pushed for more.

"And that's when the Founder, I mean...you...stepped in. If you are the Founder, then you brought us magic. They say you were the one who ended it all and drove away the Madness. The Prophet even calls you a god, like the Matriarch and Patriarch. Should I bow down, Almighty Zeke?" she asked, looking at him with a smirk on her face.

Well, if she was starting to believe, it hadn't made her any more reverent.

The man laughed. "It's Ezekiel, and I'm no god. And from what I can tell, the Matriarch and the Patriarch weren't gods either. But that's a story for another time. What I *can* say is that I didn't overcome the Age of Madness on my own. I had help. Some really powerful help," he admitted.

She stopped walking again, her hands on her waist, lost in thought. He paused and gazed around as he waited for it to come, wondering how long the questions would bubble in her brain before she asked.

"But how did you do it? And if magic didn't exist before, then where did it come from?"

Ezekiel nodded to himself. Her questions were getting to the heart of it. She was even more clever than he had realized.

"The answer to both of those questions is the same. But let me ask you, when you helped your brother that day on the street, how did you feel?"

Hannah cocked her head as she thought through her answer. Ezekiel waited patiently.

"I guess I felt like there was something inside of me trying to get out. All my fear and frustration, plus my concern for my brother; it was like they were feeding something. Something that was hungry for more."

"Exactly! That force that's inside of you is what lets you to do magic. It allows you to tap into a world of pure energy called the Etheric. That's where our magic comes from. But that power needs to be controlled. At first, only a select few had it—those you refer to as the Matriarch and the Patriarch. Then it spread to the whole world, but most didn't have the will to control it.

"They couldn't tap into the Etheric like you can. So that desire turned into hunger, and flesh and blood were the only ways to satisfy their absolute need to get at the energy."

The two of them started walking again. "The Madness spread this potential throughout the world, destroying people in its wake. But from the ashes, something wonderful arose. A switch was flipped that turned that hunger from something monstrous to something wonderful. From madness to magic."

Ezekiel had gotten lost in his words. When he finished his speech, Hannah watched him with a look of awe on her face.

"That's what you figured out," she asked, completely into his story as well.

"Me?" He waved his hand in negation. "No. I got my switch flipped, but it was the Oracle who figured out how to do it. How to save the human race."

Hannah's look of awe quickly disappeared as she rolled her eyes in annoyance. "Shit. You're telling me that the Oracle is real, too?"

He regarded the young woman, a frown on his face. "Of course she's real. Why wouldn't she be?"

The girl shook her head. "Zeke, you've missed a lot while you've been out walking Irth. Arcadia, it's a different place. Most of us don't go to school to learn things. We educate ourselves on the streets. The Capitol, they like it that way. Our ignorance, our powerlessness gives them control. But you hear a lot of stories, and it's hard to figure out what's real and what's a steaming pile of pig shit."

She breathed deeply and then continued, "My mom used to tell me about the Oracle. But I thought those stories were just like the Queen Bitch and the Bastard. Cute stories to keep us all out of trouble, or try to give us some sort of hope and meaning."

Ezekiel felt his face tighten with the girl's words. He had to remind himself that there was no reason why she couldn't understand the world as it really was.

He spoke firmly, his conviction balanced with compassion. "Hannah! First, never speak of the Matriarch and Patriarch that way. They are as real as you and me, and they deserve—no, they *command*—our respect."

"But—" she started, an arm already flinging out.

This time he put up his own hand. "No buts. Just hear me out. You can wrestle with what you believe later. For now, you need new information. Second, the Oracle is real and has a name, which is Lilith. And she is a *very* powerful creature who holds knowledge about truths so complex that even hearing them would likely scramble your brain."

He could see her brain firing fast as she analyzed how he described the Oracle. "Wait, creature? She's not human?"

The man realized there was so much the girl would have to learn. "Lilith can't be categorized in simple ways we might understand. Someday I will show you, but now is not that time."

"OK, I guess, Dr. Mystery. So, back to the zombies."

Ezekiel nodded. "My colleagues and I followed Lilith's instructions and were able to stop, and in some cases even reverse, the effects of the outbreak. It was an amazing and dangerous time. We lost several of the best and the bravest. But what we found is that once people stopped manifesting the disease, something else was appeared in its place.

"The power that was within every person—the power that indiscriminately poisoned its host—was the source of magic in our world. We started to realize that it was in all of us, but the power was still dangerous. Only those who were strong enough to control the power could use it as magic. Some died trying. Others, scared of its effects, bottled the power up inside of them."

"Are you saying that everyone can do magic?"

"Not quite. Everyone does have the power within them. It's not unique to the nobles. Even back then, we didn't make this publicly known. To try and draw on the power is *very* dangerous. Many people harm themselves in the process. One should only practice if they are led by a mentor—someone to teach and contain them.

"My friends and I focused on the magic and how to use it. It was by magic that we started to heal the world. And we wanted to spread this knowledge, so, using magic, we built Arcadia."

"And you're afraid that Adrien is going to tear it all down using magic?"

Ezekiel looked at his new student. He wondered how much to tell her. How much of this world should he keep from her, to protect her? But the look on her face told him everything.

She had been through hell already. It's what made her strong enough to fight the devil.

He breathed out, resigned to telling all of the truth, as much as it hurt him. "That's precisely what is going to happen. Unless we stop him."

CHAPTER 11

A drien shuffled through paperwork as the sun outside the giant bay window overlooking Arcadia drifted closer to the horizon. A document updating him on the progress with the machine indicated that things were better, but still not up to speed. The Chief Engineer had increased their pace, but it came at a cost. Several of the men assigned to the project had burned out.

That could easily happen when the young and inexperienced pushed their power too far. Now they were being carted to the infirmary two by two. No matter. It was a cost this city could bear. He shook his head and turned to the list of prospective students the Dean had sent him.

He had an academy to run, after all.

A number sat in the side margin next to the names; the goal of how many students to accept. In reality, the more important number was the remainder; those denied access.

That was the key. Deny access. Create scarcity. Elevate prestige. It made the few who were accepted eternally grateful to their Chancellor.

Picking up his pencil, he drew a line through the number and increased it by twenty percent. What are a few more, especially when the ones you have are dropping like flies? He would need additional fodder for what was to come.

A knock on the door interrupted his calculations. "Enter!" he called out, still considering the increase in the number of students.

Doyle stepped in, closed the door, and walked up to the desk, waiting silently.

Adrien looked up from his planning. "Speak, damn it. What is it?"

Doyle glanced down, taking in the altered numbers. He cursed his bad timing. When Adrien got mad, everyone around him suffered.

"Sir, you asked for the Hunters and Guard to be on the lookout for anyone matching the description of the magician who attacked our men. Well, I think we've had a hit."

A sinister smile spread across the Chancellor's face. "Is that right?"

"Yes, sir. I mean, he didn't look like a devil-monster or whatever, but everything else seems to check out. Do you want me to send in a team of Hunters to secure the Unlawful?"

Adrien stood up from his desk and reached back behind him. "No. I will take care of this one myself." Before Doyle had a chance to respond, Adrien threw on his blood-red cloak and made for the door.

———— ◆ ————

The Chancellor hardly ever left the Academy, let alone traveled into the other quarters. As he made his way through the crowds, people gawked at his presence. He was a celebrity, and it was the closest that many of the commoners would get to greatness. Following the path described to him by Doyle, he wove through the dirty streets toward the heart of the market quarter.

The smells of rotting food and other filth wafted up from the gutters. It reminded him exactly why he stayed within the walls of the Academy, and why magic would be wasted on people who lacked any sense of dignity. Turning a corner, he ran into a beggar with hands outstretched.

"Alms, sir?"

"Out of my way," he said, as he drove his elbow into the old woman, knocking her over.

He stood dead center in the square and rotated, looking for the man who had taught him magic. Ezekiel had given him the keys to the kingdom, and Adrien had made that kingdom great. But something told the Chancellor that his old teacher hadn't come back from the dead to congratulate him on his progress. Arcadians prayed for the day when their Founder would return. Adrien intended to see to it that their prayers were in vain.

Adrien caught a glimpse of an old man in a long brown cloak out of the corner of his eye. Just as he turned the corner to leave the square, the man glanced over his shoulder and cast a smile in Adrien's direction.

Ezekiel. I've got you, old friend.

Adrien moved towards the man. Ten yards down the road, the man turned left and Adrien followed, walking as briskly as possible without drawing too much attention.

Although Adrien was hurrying and the old man seemed to take his time, he somehow maintained his distance.

The Chancellor could feel his pulse rising and sweat gathering in the small of his back. Casting aside all semblance of self-control, he started to jog. At the seam where the market transitioned into Queen's Boulevard, he turned a corner and stood face-to-face with his old mentor.

"Hello, Adrien," Ezekiel said. "I wondered when we would meet again. It's been a long time. You look good. Better than you should."

Adrien's stomach tied in knots. He worked to compose his breathing as he stared. "I must say the same. All this time we thought you were dead."

"Sorry to disappoint you. But imagine my disappointment at returning home to learn that my trust was misplaced all along."

Adrien tried to turn on his charm. "Come now, Ezekiel, you have to understand. After a year we sent out parties looking for you at Eve's urging. They scoured the corners of Irth, but here you are. Finally returning to our dear Arcadia." He forced a smile onto his face.

"Yes, Adrien. Wait, should I call you *Chancellor*?" A sneer spread under the magician's beard.

"Adrien is fine," he said, wanting to wrap his fingers around the old man's wrinkled neck.

"Ah, then Adrien. Good to know that you were so concerned. I saw Eve. She isn't good. And strange that she urged you as she did. She knew why I left and, in the end, never expected me to return. And you mentioned our great city, but is it really so great?"

Ezekiel waved his arm in the direction of the squalor of Queen's Boulevard that spread out behind him. "Look at what you have done. You've turned our dream into a damned nightmare. They're people, Adrien, and they *suffer under your hand*."

Adrien sneered, keeping himself in check. "You are quite a fool, aren't you, Ezekiel? I thought that maybe some time wandering Irth might change you, but it's apparent that you are as stubborn as ever. You always were the consummate idealist, and at this point I believe you will never change. Ideals are for children and idiots. We were both children once. Our dreams grew together, but one of us has evolved into a man, the other," he looked Adrien up and down, "into a fool. Yes, you can patronize me with your high-mindedness."

Adrien pointed around them both. "You can point to the lazy scum that huddle in masses in *Queen Bitch Boulevard*, you can groan about your *precious* kingdom perverted," he slammed his fist to his chest, "by my shrewd machinations. But you know nothing of what I have built and the greatness that is Arcadia. And when everything is in place, we will be the greatest city in all of Irth and beyond its boundaries. We're creating a legacy here that will rival the old days. And you and your dreams will be *nothing*."

Adrien spat the last words at the old magician.

Ezekiel narrowed his eyes and pointed at his prodigal student. "Enough. You make excuses and rationalize your works, but truly you bring only ruin. And one day the ruin," he looked around before finishing, "will catch up with you. What plans of yours could be worth that risk?"

Adrien shrugged. "It doesn't matter. You will never live to see it."

This time it was Ezekiel's turn to laugh. "Adrien, Adrien, Adrien. How cute! You could never beat me back then. What makes you think you can beat me now?" He raised his bushy brows, a twinkle in his eye, and waited for a response.

Anger and rage grew inside of the Chancellor. His blood boiled and his power swelled. The new Master of Arcadia would end it right there, in an alley that probably had no name.

"I am no longer that boy you left behind."

Adrien laughed more ominously than before. He drew on the passion inside of him and his hatred for the man standing before him. Adrien's eyes turned coal black.

Cupping his hands in front of his chest, he brought all that was within him into focus. As he spread his hands apart, a sphere of radiant blue light grew larger and larger until it blocked his view of the wizard.

He drove every ounce of energy and intention into the ball of power, and just as he felt the last ounce of energy leave his body, he drove his arms outward and toward his old mentor.

Adrien watched as the most magnificent magic he'd ever created passed right through Ezekiel and collided with a brick wall forty feet away. The wall exploded, sending bits of shrapnel in every direction. Some bounced back to hit him.

Adrien shielded his eyes, and when he looked up, the wizard was exactly where he had been a moment ago, a serene smile on his face.

Ezekiel shook his head. "I'm sad to see I was able to teach you so little, Adrien, but there's still time." His smile turned to ice. "Soon I will teach you one more lesson that you won't live long enough to forget."

With that, the image of Ezekiel flickered and disappeared, leaving Adrien panting and alone in the forgotten alley.

———◆———

Hannah stumbled out of her room, still rubbing the sleep from her eyes. Sal had finally woken her up and now skittered along next to her. He looked like he had gained more weight.

"What the hell are you eating?" she asked the no-longer-small lizard.

Entering the great hall, she found Ezekiel sitting on a mat on the floor, back straight as a board, legs crossed. His eyes were open, but they glowed a brilliant red and stared off into the distance. She was used to the black eyes of the magicians in Arcadia, but she had never seen this before.

She waved her hand in front of his face, but there was no response. Next to him was an empty mat with a mug holding a mysterious steaming liquid. She took the cue and sat down, pulling her legs up under her.

Picking up the mug, she sniffed it and scrunched her nose. It smelled like dirt, if dirt could die and rot. She sipped it, and the elixir tasted almost good.

Nothing like its odor.

"Root tea. I learned to brew it in the Heights," Ezekiel explained, looking at her after he took in the larger green lizard perched to the side.

Hannah jumped at the man's voice. His eyes were back to their normal steely gray.

She looked at him over the mug as she sipped more, before replying, "Not bad, even if it smells like the ass of an orc."

The man laughed as he sat up. "You make it sound so appealing. The power is not in its taste, but its effects. Just keep sipping it. The tea will give you extra focus, and you're going to need focus."

"More of your history lessons?" Hannah closed her eyes and faked a yawn as she stretched. "You're killing me, Zeke."

"It's Ezekiel, and somebody *will* be killing you if you don't know your history. The paths of our future have been trodden by someone else in the past. Always. However, we don't have time to retrace all those paths. Today we start your training in physical magic." He slowly stood up. "Sit up straight."

Hannah cranked her shoulders back and pretended a magician's staff ran the length of her spine. "This is comfy."

"It will be."

"Sure, whatever you say, Zeke. What were you doing when I came in here anyways?" She pointed to his mat. "That didn't look like physical magic."

The old man stared down at her. She read a sadness in his eyes. "I was...visiting an old friend. It went poorly. But enough of that. Today we focus on you."

"So are you going to teach me to call down magic or something?" She peeked at him from the corner of her eye, but the man stared at the wall across the room, unmoving.

After a beat, he said, "You don't call anything *down*. Weren't you listening yesterday?"

"Mostly," she admitted. She practiced holding her breath and took a sip.

His voice seemed to echo in her ears, and inside her mind.

What the hell was in this tea?

"Magic is inside of you, me, everyone. The work of the magician is not to conjure anything from outside, but to draw the power from within and direct it with intention. But it is a practice that needs complete focus. Not something for a smart ass like you."

She looked over and saw Ezekiel smiling.

"OK. Focusing." She nodded.

"Good," he said. "Now, magic is most easily directed when the user has a desire to change the world in some way. The deeper and stronger the desire, the more potent the magic. Remember your brother on the street? That was your magic, without you even knowing how to use it, streaming out of you to heal based on your subconscious desire. That sort of thing would have likely destroyed someone less strong than you. Most don't have the will you possess."

He looked around the room and continued, "At this stage, you need training and guidance. Also, we will talk about what magic is and *isn't* for." He sat back down in front of her, his back straight.

Her eyes were closed. "You mean, so I don't become a douche nugget like your first student?"

"I don't have the faintest idea what that means," he replied.

"Yeah, never mind. OK, focusing again." She made sure her back was as straight as his.

They sat like that for what felt like an hour. Hannah was starting to wish they were doing a history lesson.

After some time, her mouth disobeyed. "Hey, Zeke?"

"Mm hmm?"

"Pretty sure I'm focused enough to blow fireballs out of my ass."

"That would be a very unorthodox style," Ezekiel snapped. "Now be quiet."

After what felt like an eternity of waiting, the man finally stirred.

"All right. Come with me," he said as he stood up.

She wasn't going to admit that her back seemed to have a little kink in it. If someone as old as Zeke wasn't complaining, she wouldn't either.

At least, not yet. She would reserve her final decision until later.

Hannah followed the magician to a room that had been locked since her arrival. She expected to find something marvelous waiting behind the door—glowing goblets, strange creatures, mystical tablets—but there was nothing. Well, almost nothing. In the middle of the room was a rock the size of a large potato.

"Thrilling," she told him, staring at the rock.

"Physical magic is first. It is the easiest of the arts. Well, at least *I* found it to be. It is the one that humans are most naturally connected to. And, after the Age of Madness, it was the one we discovered first."

Hannah thought of the men in the alley and their fireballs. She felt sweat gather across her body, and the now-familiar feel of the magic danced inside of her. This was why she was here. It was her reason for being.

She would be a magician. She *was* a magician. Damn, what she knew was true in Arcadia was playing hell with the facts she was learning. Old beliefs were warring with new information not fully owned, yet.

Ezekiel continued explaining. He was either ignorant of her concerns or unbothered by them. "Physical magic gives you the ability to control and even change non-living matter. The better you get at it, the more complex your magic can be."

He looked at her, making sure he had her attention, and said, "I've seen physical magicians do powerful things. Raise towers and initiate rockslides. The confluence of physical magic and a healthy imagination could allow you to cast workings that would blow your children's stories away."

She looked from him to the potato rock. "Got it. So what do I do?" she asked, thinking how she might blow it to bits.

He laughed at her assumption while enjoying her gumption. "Not that simple, Hannah. Magic doesn't work because of an action taken or a spell spoken by you. The only thing you need to do to cast magic is to focus your energy out and direct it to do the work. But we found early on this was more easily said than done. So, as we developed the art of physical magic," he moved his arms around, his hands held certain ways, "we created routines and practices, each one connected to a different kind of spell."

He stopped and looked at her, a mischievous gleam under his bushy eyebrows. "There is no power in the ritual. It's all within you."

She pressed her lips together, head cocked to the side. "The man in the alley and the fireballs. He swung his arms across his chest," she exclaimed as she mimicked his action.

"Impressive, right?" Ezekiel asked, beaming.

"Um, not exactly. I was about to get gang-raped and killed, which kind of dampened the mood," she answered.

He ignored her. "I invented that one." His smile remained. "Magicians don't require the same motions to focus the magic, but the rituals are passed down through generations from teacher to student. I taught Adrien that move over forty years ago. He taught one of his students, who became a faculty member."

"And she taught the monsters with an appetite for barely legal girls."

He nodded. "Which is why you must learn it, too. Those barely legal girls will need someone like you to protect them as we take back Arcadia."

The notion of reclaiming Arcadia was appealing.

But the idea of wiping the streets with the asses of the men who assaulted her was downright captivating. "OK, let's get started."

Ezekiel nodded toward the stone in the middle of the room. "Move it."

Hannah took a step toward the rock, and the magician grabbed her arm. "With magic." His steel-gray eyes sparkled.

"OK. I've got this." Hannah stared at the rock, thinking about it moving. Nothing. She pictured it hovering over the ground. Nothing. Raising her right arm out before her, she flicked her fingers. Nothing. Finally, she gave up. "How the hell?"

"It's much harder when you are trying." He answered, cryptically.

Sal, who had followed them into the room, stood up and turned in a complete circle, then laid down again, ignoring the two of them.

She blew out a breath. "Zeke, you are one confusing whitehaired son of a bitch."

He nodded in agreement; he'd heard it before.

"Think about sitting on the mat in the great hall. Empty your mind first. When all is gone, don't focus on the rock. It's not about the rock. It's about what's in here." He leaned forward and tapped her chest, and Hannah could swear she felt the tingle of magic come through his fingertips.

She nodded and tried to clear her mind.

The thought of failure rushed over her. Hannah pushed the fear away as if her life depended on it.

Images of the men in the alley appeared. She struck them away.

William. Parker. Her father. The tower. The lizard. As each thought came, she pushed it away, and soon there was nothing.

Breathing slowly, she turned her mind inward, toward the power that had become a part of her existence and awareness. Once in tune with the energy within, she felt like she could slow her heart to a stop if she wanted to. Then she tried to direct the internal flow outward toward the rock, an excited smile on her face.

Nothing happened. Her anger rose in her frustration.

"Shit bucket!" she shouted.

Ezekiel stepped up next to her and spoke quickly. "You're frustrated. Good. Channel that frustration *now*. Let it build, Hannah, without holding onto it. We're going to use it. Now, do what I do. Copy me."

Ezekiel spread his feet shoulder-width apart and slid his right foot out a few inches further than the other. Raising his right hand, he kept a flat palm up, and his elbow bent at ninety degrees.

Hannah mirrored his every move.

"Good. Just like that."

Extending his arm, he turned his palm down toward the floor. He pulled his fingers back, and then quickly extended two, like he was trying to flick away an invisible object. The rock in the middle of the room shot toward the opposite wall. He turned his hand over and pulled his fingers back toward him, slowly this time.

The rock slid back into the middle of the room.

"Do *that*," he told her.

Hannah laughed. "Really simple."

The old man stepped away, giving Hannah her shot. She went through the process of clearing her mind again, focused inward, and made the motion exactly as he had shown her. Power surged through her body and then burst free. The rock didn't fly across the room, but it did roll over once and come to rest five whole inches further away.

"Did you see that?" she called out, excited. "I'm a bloody *magician!*" She exhaled. "Whoa!" She wavered, then dropped to her knees, a little lightheaded.

Ezekiel chuckled. "That's right. Foul mouth and all. You'll fit right in with the physical magicians. Now practice. I'll be back soon, and I want to see progress. And be sure to rest between attempts. Energy is energy, and when you shoot some of yours out into the world, you need to recuperate."

"Like the teleportation?" She looked over her shoulder at him.

Ezekiel nodded. "Just like that."

She heard him leave, and Sal chose to move around in a circle again and plop his lizard ass right back down in the same spot. Maybe he had warmed it up and he liked it?

She eyed the rock and enjoyed the feeling of triumph after throwing her first spell, well, *on purpose.* Hannah realized that taking down the Hunters would be a hell of a lot harder than nudging a rock, and take a thousand times more energy.

Her eyes narrowed. "Let's do this," she said as she stood back up and got into position.

CHAPTER 12

———— ◆ ————

E zekiel puttered around in the area he was using for a kitchen.

The smartass girl was special, there was no doubt in that, but seeing the amount of energy that it took her to move the tiny rock, he started to wonder just how long the training would take.

She was old—to start in the arts, that is. Hannah had learned how to be normal. Her body, for the sake of self-preservation, had taught itself to withhold her magic since she was born.

A body would go to extraordinary lengths keep itself from implosion. It always amazed him.

Students in the Academy didn't start fresh. That's why Adrien had created a prep school in Arcadia. While the younger children weren't taught magic proper, they were trained in the arts of meditation and mindfulness. By the time they got to the Academy, they were ready for what it had to teach them.

Hannah had none of that.

Her body had learned to defend against itself. Now Ezekiel had to breach the self-control the girl never knew she had. Aware that she would need some food to replenish the energy her body was using, he grabbed a tray with his right hand.

This might not work, he thought as he turned the knob of the door to the training room.

But as Ezekiel stepped through the doorway, the rock launched toward his face at lightspeed. Hannah screamed a warning at him. Raising a finger, he stopped the rock a foot from his face and let it float in the air. When he snapped his fingers, the rock burst into a thousand pieces inside the three-foot sphere he created.

Hannah gawked at the little tiny pieces enveloped within the perfect globe before he waved his hand again and it all dropped to the floor.

He managed to do all of this without dropping the food tray in his hand. There was a small smile on his face.

My doubts were ill-founded. She's ready for the fire.

"Making some progress, I see," the old man said, raising his brows.

"Shit," Hannah sighed. "I didn't—" she started.

Ezekiel put a finger in the air. "No apologizing for your magic. Now let's go. It's time for fire."

He led her to another locked door. Behind it was a room identical to the last, only this one had a pile of wood and a bucket in the middle. A leather couch was shoved against the far wall. "Let's sit. Why don't you eat some of this food while I tell you what's next?"

Hannah sat back on the couch and dove into the lunch he had prepared—a meaty soup with a thick piece of bread. Crumbs rained from her mouth as she tore into the bread. Ezekiel sat on the edge and told her about fire magic.

While it was part of the physical arts, it had been years before Ezekiel had discovered fire magic, and even longer until he mastered it. His first use was completely by accident. His ability to manipulate matter had grown, and he had begun to teach Adrien all that he knew. The boy, not much younger at the time than Hannah was now, had shown marvelous potential.

Ezekiel had welcomed him, an orphan, into their community early on. He demonstrated great skill, particularly in the way he could easily channel his power with simple mechanics. Adrien was so good that Ezekiel realized he had met his protégé.

One night he took the boy beyond the little village that would one day be Arcadia. They walked for miles, telling stories and talking magic. The boy never knew the trip was an exercise, something Ezekiel had planned for days.

Once deep into the forest, the magician feigned confusion, claiming they were lost. The warmth from the sun passed as the night grew dark. They huddled at the base of a giant oak.

"Looks like we'll have to spend the night out here. It's been awhile since I've slept outside a proper house," Ezekiel had said. "Though, years ago, the forest was the only home I knew."

Ezekiel had laughed, but the boy was not happy about the situation. Adrien kept complaining about the cold and how his cloak was just too thin.

Finally, the wizard said, "So do something about it. You're a magician now."

The boy's eyes turned black, and he rubbed his hands together as if he were warming them. A moment later, the twigs at their feet burst into flames.

"By the Matriarch," Ezekiel had shouted. "How the hell did you do that, Adrien?" It was the first time that the student had become the teacher.

As Ezekiel watched Hannah eat her lunch, he expected that the young girl would have much to teach him—like that trick with the lizard.

That was something he had never seen before.

"It didn't take me long to understand and even master fire magic once I had seen it. However, until someone pointed out the path, I was ignorant," he admitted.

"They all love fire magic," Hannah told him. "All the bastard students running around Arcadia. It's the most impressive."

Ezekiel laughed. "Yes, well, it's useful as well. But certainly not the most useful."

"How does it work?" she asked around a spoonful of meat.

"All magic comes from within you, including the fire magic. The more passion, the hotter the flame. Remember the man from the alley?"

"How could I forget that asshat?" she grumped.

"He was actually quite good with it. The way he taunted you. Throwing the balls in the air and then over your head. Now, *that* was some magic."

"No, *that* was a jackass."

Ezekiel smiled as he watched the girl's face tighten with anger. He just needed to push a little harder.

"Yes, but his form was really quite beautiful," he mused.

"Nothing beautiful happened in the alley that night," she told him, fairly stabbing the bowl.

"Oh, don't be a closed-minded little—" he started, his eyes half closed, watching her.

Hannah shot to her feet and the bowl went flying, but Ezekiel caught it off to the side. She never noticed as she spun her hands across her chest, just as the man in the alley had done. When she completed the rotation, the logs burst into flames.

"Yes!" Ezekiel screamed, watching her eyes fade from red. "That is it. PASSION! *Directed* anger and rage. Extraordinary."

Hannah extended her hand, as she had with the rock, and lifted the bucket into the air. She twisted her wrist, and water drenched the wood, smothering the fire to nothing. Steam and the smell of burned wood permeated everywhere.

She collapsed back on the couch and looked at the smiling geezer. "That was a shit trick."

Ezekiel winked. "I am full of them. And the trick worked. The magic is there and it's ready. We just have to get you to direct it. Soon, fire will be yours. Second nature. But you need to be careful, control both your desires and passions. Like your friend back in the Boulevard."

Hannah bristled as Ezekiel mentioned Parker and passion in the same breath. "What do you mean?" she snapped.

"It is a balancing act. Like your friend's trick with the pushups. You need to be able to balance your emotions with your desire for control."

"Or what?"

"Or the world will go up in flames, and you will be the fire-starter. Patriarch knows the last thing I need on Irth is another Adrien to deal with. If you unleash passion without control, you could blow up this whole damn tower if you feel too much in your core." Ezekiel tilted his head. "That said, the negative consequences aren't always so drastic."

"Oh?" She looked over at him. In the corner, Sal's little tongue went in and out, tasting the air. The lizard got up to study the logs.

Ezekiel shrugged his shoulders. "No, sometimes the effects are a bit more local. I've seen magicians burst into flames or sever bones—one just disintegrated into oblivion—doing no harm to anyone or anything around them."

Hannah swallowed hard. "Well, uh, that's comforting."

———— ♦ ————

The hair on the back of Hannah's neck stood up as she entered the shade of the thick trees overhead. It was shocking just how much the temperature dropped when they got into the woods.

They had passed the place where Karl saved her from the boar only days earlier. Drag marks remained on the ground. The girl Silently hoped she would meet the rearick again someday.

She kept her eyes open in case that war pig had tusky family around. Just for a moment she considered sharing the experience with Ezekiel, but held her tongue instead.

The magician had told her to stay in the tower, and it was likely he'd not be happy if he knew that she had willfully disobeyed on her very first day. But now, fully aware of his powers, she thought it was a good bet he already knew about her field trip.

"Your physical magic is coming right along," Ezekiel said, striding just ahead of Hannah. "It's the most basic, so if it didn't come quickly, we'd be in trouble. Now it's time to try something a bit more complex. Physical magic is about manipulating objects in the world. It's easier to control, and you've seen it a lot in Arcadia. But have you ever heard of Nature Magic?" he asked her.

Hannah considered trying to sound more impressive, but answered, "Nope. Never heard of it."

"Well, that's no surprise. When I was here last, few in Arcadia were aware of it. I imagine Adrien might know some things about Nature Magic, but it might be beyond even him."

"What makes it so much more difficult?" Hannah asked.

"Well, once you understand how it works, it's not that much more difficult. There is a fundamental difference, though. If you don't understand the distinction and you're trained in a particular way, it can be tough to cross over. Those who use nature magic were raised in it. They've seen it everywhere, every day of their lives. So they struggle to use physical magic.

"You, on the other hand, are starting pretty much from scratch. That's why we're doing a little bit each day. Learn them all together, and hopefully they'll grow together as well."

She thought about how it worked in her city. "Starting a little late, though, aren't we?"

"Oh, I've taught older dogs new tricks," he answered.

Her eyes shot lightning bolts at the back of his head. "Hey, Zeke? I know you've been in the woods for a while, but *never* call a lady a dog. Not cool."

Ezekiel laughed and continued. "My apologies, fair maiden. As I said, physical magic is the direction of our inward power out into the world. We can influence and modify things that already exist. And some things, like fireballs, can even be created. Everything except gravity is energy. It is certainly powerful, but has its limits like all the arts. Each has its own strengths and limitations."

The two walked down what could, if one were generous, be called a path. Not far from the tower, the sound of running water filled the air. Dropping down at a slight rise, the two sat on the edge of the River Wren under a short, stout willow.

Ezekiel continued without missing a beat. "Unlike physical magic, nature magic requires a willingness to call out," he pointed around them, "to the power hiding in the natural world, not to the power within you. Whereas physical magic is a form of domination," he opened his hand, palm up and a small flame flickered into life, "of a strong will imposing itself on the inanimate, nature magic is more like supplication. With physical magic, we tell the object to act."

He pushed away and the small flame leapt out from his hand, flaming out a few feet away. He clapped his hands together. "With nature, we ask and it responds. It takes a lot of time to form this bond with the natural world around us; it cannot happen overnight."

Sal popped out of Hannah's bag on cue and curled up at his mistress's feet. She reached over to run a hand over his head. "Tell this guy that."

Ezekiel watched the two of them for a moment, scratching his beard. "Yes, the lizard."

"Sal."

"You've named the creature Sal?"

"You know, like—"

"Oh, I get it. Like salamander. I just thought you might have been a bit more creative." The magician stole another glance at the. "Yes, you and the lizard are indeed a peculiar case. It was what first caught my attention. When I saw the reptile change, I knew something was afoot in Arcadia. As far as I know, no one practices nature magic there, not even the Unlawfuls.

"And yet he," he pointed to Sal, "well, he is something different. I don't think that the masters of nature magic could do what you've done with your little friend. At least, *I've* never seen it. When I found you, you weren't a magician, or at least you said you weren't. But I knew that there was something special about you."

Hannah kept her eyes directed downward as he spoke. She wasn't used to being praised, not like this. "I get it. I am the special bloody snowflake. Now back to the magic; I don't have all day. Why would someone want to chat with a grouse when they could torch some baddies with a big-ass fireball? What else can you do with it?"

Ezekiel's face spread into a smile. He held out a finger and clicked his tongue. His eyes flashed red, and a brown and white robin with an orange breast flew down and perched on his finger, tweeting and flicking its head. He clicked again, and the bird took flight.

"Nice. Birdy control. I'll put that one in my back pocket for the next time a Hunter is trying to rip off my shirt," she muttered, unimpressed.

"Don't be so shortsighted. Not everything needs to be viewed through the lens of that one bad experience. However, if that is the approach you need to take for any of this to pierce that skull of yours, think on this. What if it wasn't a bird, but a giant black bear, ready to do your bidding? Or what if it was something even more powerful? Something mythical." The old man glanced back down at the spiked-backed lizard.

"You get the picture. But it doesn't end there. The supplication of nature is as vast as one's imagination. I can control the weather, call down lightning, animate plants, and even ask the River Wren here to stop its flow to allow me to pass. It took a long time to master, but I now use nature magic more than the physical arts, at least for the past few years. There is something fulfilling about working *with* things, not just *on* them," he finished.

"OK," Hannah had to admit, "that sounds cool. I hadn't considered all of that. It will take some time to digest it, though. Anything else?"

"Yes—the most important bit, really. The secret hidden power of nature magic is the power to heal. The world will grant us some of its own life energy if we ask it, and we can channel that energy into another being."

Her eyes got a faraway look. "Like my brother Will." Hannah's eyes sparkled as the memory of his healing flitted through her mind.

"Exactly like Will. Theoretically speaking, I might have been able to heal him by passing on my own power, I suppose."

Ezekiel rearranged his robes and bent a leg before continuing. "But the combination of the fatigue of the casting on the body and the imparting of energy could have had disastrous effects. The natural world gives with pleasure, if we borrow with a deep sense of responsibility and stewardship. The relationship is quite symbiotic. The interaction of the power within us and the world's energy is like a dance. We just have to lead without stepping on too many toes.

"Sadly, I've never been very good with animals. It takes a special kind of bond. I can call birds and a few other things." He pointed down at her feet once more. "But I don't have anything close to what you and that lizard do."

Hannah tossed a small rock into the Wren. She watched the ripples get washed downstream by the current. "You mean Sal."

"Dreadful name, but yes. The two of you are connected now, and that bond would be hard to sunder. From now on, part of you is in that little creature and part of him is in you.

She leaned forward to pick the lizard up and held him in her lap, trying to understand the connection between them. She could feel something, but couldn't put words to the feelings. "Maybe I should have picked a bear."

The old man smiled. "Seems like he picked you as much as you picked him. And don't worry, I have a feeling this little one is full of potential."

"Yeah. It's a shame no one practices nature magic."

The man clapped his hands and laughed. "Now, why in Hades would you assume that no one practices it? My girl, your world is as small as Arcadia itself. The druids practice nature magic all of the time."

She stopped petting Sal for a moment, turning to face Ezekiel. "Druids? They're real? I thought that was just more horseshit."

This young woman had made him want to roll his eyes more times in the last week than his whole last decade.

"They're very real, although they might think that one who lived her whole life trapped in a city was *horseshit*."

"Have you seen them?" she pressed.

"Not only have I seen them, I've spent years with them. Delightful folk. Far too secretive; you won't see the druids often, if ever at all. Unlike their physical and psychic magic brethren, they have found life in the natural world more compelling. They have left the society of other men and gone to live deep in the Dark Forest where they can better commune with nature. And, like Arcadia, they are building a civilization that lives up to their ideals. At least they were when I last saw them. And by the time I got out of the dreaded Dark Forest, I was glad to see the sun again."

This time, her mouth stayed open in amazement. "Wait. You, like, lived with freaking druids? That's crazy. Did they teach you the nature magic?"

The man blushed. "Actually, it was *I* who taught *them*. Not the other way around. Though they have far surpassed the master."

Hannah looked at him with disbelief.

He kept his eyes trained in the distance as he continued, "The Arcadian legends about the Founder didn't only begin because of physical magic and the beginning of our city. It goes deeper than that. I, of course, despise the name, as it takes what is due from the Matriarch and Patriarch."

Her voice, this time, wasn't so pushy. "Where'd you learn it all?"

"That is a long story for another time. The short version is this: the Oracle Lilith herself trained me in the arts. I simply passed them down to others. Just like Adrien was my disciple in Arcadia, I tutored others in the other arts, trusting each of them with the stewardship of their own disciplines. But enough talking."

He stood up slowly, and continued, "Time for magic, Hannah." Ezekiel pointed at a tiny wildflower growing at their feet, several buds waiting to blossom. "Make that little one bloom and then come find me at the tower." He turned to walk back toward the building.

"Wait. Do I use hand motions like with physical magic?" she called out.

The magician shrugged. "Probably could, I guess, though the druids never do." He pointed at his chest. "Don't forget, the magic is within you and there is power in the created order.

This time he pointed to her. "Your task is to connect the two. Physical magic uses hand motions to help focus. The druids find touch to be the most important. This staff," he glanced down at the knotty piece of wood in his hand "is more than a decorative walking stick for an old man. It keeps me connected to the natural world. Most druids carry a similar object as a way to keep a hand on nature at all times. Clever, really. One day I may take you to the forest and the druids will help you find your own object. But for now, simply try to connect with the source itself." And with that the old man turned, and in moments was out of her sight.

Hannah pushed Sal out of her lap. "God, you're getting heavy given the little runt you were. Must be flies the size of cats out here."

She rolled up onto her knees. Hovering over the plant, she stared long and hard at it, wondering for the first time how one was supposed to connect with nature. Having lived her entire life in the city, she had spent little time with in such an environment. The park was the closest she had ever gotten, and even that paled in comparison to this spot by the river.

"OK, little guy," she said. "Why don't you open for me?"

Nothing happened, except that she felt a little awkward talking to a plant. Not for the first time, she was glad Parker wasn't here to make fun of her. She pictured their time spent together under a tree after a long day of work. If she could figure this out, maybe she and Parker would never have to steal again. She stared at the flower again, then shook her head.

"This is going to be harder than I thought."

She bent over and cupped her hands around the plant. Closing her eyes, she pushed all the thoughts out of her mind, as she had practiced within the tower. It was easier out here in the breeze.

Hours seemed to pass as she lost herself to the peace of this world. In those few instances where the thoughts tried to intrude again, it was but a small task to release them and sink back into calm.

When she finally opened her eyes, all Hannah noticed was the bud.

Instead of trying to command something to happen, she imagined a beautiful blossom in its place.

As she did, her eyes glowed red, and the bloom unfurled. She smiled, then plucked it gently and held it to her nose to breathe in the sweet fragrance.

It was as if she were smelling flowers for the first time.

She looked around, reveling in the peace and calm of the river. Then she stood up, grabbed Sal, and made her way down the path the magician had followed. It took only thirty steps before the birds heard her gripe. "Ow! Fine! But don't be asking for a ride, you can walk the whole way on those spindly little legs."

"Nicely done, Hannah," the magician said when she had returned to the tower. "I had half-expected you to be out there all night." He nodded to her hand. "Evidenced by that flower and your reptile companion, your connection with nature must be very strong. Most likely stronger than my own. So, you must meditate every day out there. You will only get stronger and the bond will be reciprocated. Nature will do your bidding, but it might also require something of you."

Hannah stooped and picked up Sal, letting Zeke's somewhat ominous words flow over her. "If it will help me get back at those bastards, I'm ready to pay it whatever the cost."

She looked up at the old man. There was a strange look in his eyes, something akin to sadness. He opened his mouth, then shut it again. Like he was trying to stifle a lecture.

Finally, he said, "Passion is good, Hannah. But for now, why don't you get some food and rest? We will continue tomorrow."

"Are you sure?"

He nodded. "I'm sure. Avenging wrongs can't be a full-time occupation, after all. Besides, I wouldn't be much of a teacher if I didn't give my student a break occasionally. Now, come inside and tell me more about the cons you and Parker used to pull. I have no desire to get pickpocketed by some kid from the Boulevard next time I'm in the city."

CHAPTER 13

⸻ ◆ ⸻

"Tell me, what do you know about mental magic?"

Ezekiel looked down at Hannah as he opened another room. Her training had been going well. Each day she spent time meditating by the river. Her progress there convinced Ezekiel that she would surpass him in nature magic one day.

Her work with physical magic was equally impressive, although she lacked any sort of finesse. For Hannah, it was all rage. But rage was as good a starting place as any.

Now, after weeks of training, Ezekiel had finally reached the decision to begin work on the third form.

"Not much. Only that it's what the mystics study," Hannah said confidently as they walked into the training room. This one, like the others, was mostly empty. There was a series of mirrors around the edges, all pointed toward the middle.

Hannah instinctively pushed her hair back as she saw her image. She knew others thought she was pretty; enough boys had said so since she was a kid. But just in the few days she had been at the tower studying magic something had changed. She could recognize a difference in herself. She looked more mature, more...something; she couldn't quite place it.

She was turning from a girl into a woman. Tapping into the power within was somehow changing her on the outside as well.

"Very good. And what do you know about the mystics?" he asked.

"Well, unlike druids, they actually come to Arcadia," Hannah said. "Though they don't stay long. No matter where I am within the city walls, I can usually find one of those freaks walking around. My mother always told me to stay away from them or they would make me do things for them, like rob the bank or something."

The old man stared at her a moment and then laughed, wiping at his eyes. "They probably could have, but they wouldn't. They are a gentle group at heart. And yes, their chosen path has made them an odd bunch. Or maybe it was their quirkiness that led them to the study. Regardless, despite the fear that Arcadians feel toward the mystics, they rarely use their power for violence." Ezekiel paused. "But it can be quite violent if you have the need."

Hannah nodded. A strange image came to her mind. "Your little demon trick in the alley?"

"Indeed. Mental magic. How did it work?"

She put one hand on her hip and raised the other into the air. "Hell if I know. I'm just the student, remember?"

"Sure, but you are a student with a brain. So..."

Hannah brought her hand down as she nibbled on her lip and thought about the question.

Over the days in the tower she had become more comfortable with Ezekiel, and she was glad of it. It was also obvious that he was impressed with her abilities.

Her powers were real and she must surpass many others or else she wouldn't still be learning from him. But when he asked these questions her body tightened up. She didn't want to be wrong, and she wanted to make him proud.

Finally, she said, "With physical magic, we manipulate the world outside of us. Nature magic communes with and influences the natural world; living matter and other things. I can only assume that mental magic can alter the way other people think. So, in the alley that day, I thought that you were actually some sort of deranged monster. Once I learned it was you, I thought that you could somehow transform, make yourself into a monster. But if it was mental magic…" she paused a moment, considering her next words carefully.

"Yes?" Sometimes patience wasn't Ezekiel's most prevalent attribute.

She looked at him. "You never changed at all. It was me and those douchers whose perception changed. You actually altered the way we thought."

He winked at her. "Excellent. And that is really the key to this form of magic. It is like nature magic, but a little more, well, *questionable*."

""Cause you're screwing with people's minds."

"Yes, you could say that. And as you can see, it is the form of magic with the greatest potential for evil. Thankfully, those mad for power tend to prefer the easy work of physical magic. Mental magic requires a patience that tends to weed out evil intentions, making mental magic the rarest of the magical arts and generally the cleanest."

"Can't imagine what those bastards in Arcadia would do if they had that kind of power," Hannah said. "They could really mess people up."

Ezekiel nodded. "Indeed. It is why I brought it to the mystics. Who else would I trust more than a group of people who were, by nature, recluses? Not to mention, their philosophy of life is bent toward detachment from our world for the sake of transcendence. They believe in a heaven that is right up here."

He tapped his temple. "If it were up to them, they would stay in their mountain temple in the Heights. They make their pilgrimages into Arcadia and other cities as a way to stay connected with other men and women. A way to keep their minds connected to non-mystics. And that is, of course, also why they all drink so much. Traveling into the minds of other humans can be a very disturbing thing. But getting into a human's mind is far harder than calling on a bird to land on your finger or moving a rock. The power of suggestion is potent, but you need to burrow through any walls that might be in place. I trained the mystics on how to also manipulate their own minds to keep others out."

"OK," Hannah said. "So they can make me see monsters. What else?"

"Like all the other arts, the sky's the limit. The best of them can do all kinds of things." Ezekiel started walking around the room, the mirrors reflecting him in the mirrors on the other side; it became an almost overpowering amount of Ezekiel for Hannah.

He started making gestures with his hands as he talked.

"They are illusionists, able to create worlds with their words. But they can also use their powers to subvert the will of others. Force the minds of others into their service. They can convince the best spies to spill sworn secrets and the bravest men to quake in fear. But most mystics are pacifists and use their gifts for these things in only the direst of times. They prefer to enjoy their lives, telling stories and brightening the world around them. They also can communicate telepathically and even project their consciousness to see far parts of the universe."

Hannah, who had closed her eyes to stop seeing Ezekiel in the mirrors, opened them wide. "Whoa. Mind travel? That's pretty bad-ass," she said. "So now what? Am I going to mess with your head?"

He stopped his pacing and looked at her. "Not a chance that I'm letting you inside my brain." He tapped his skull. "It's far too dangerous a place." He winked at Hannah. She smiled, but wondered how much of the comment was a joke. "You're going to work on yourself."

Her face scrunched, not understanding. "What good will that do? I don't want to brainwash myself."

Ezekiel smiled. "To know thyself is an honorable thing. You might just be surprised what a little self-brainwashing can do for you."

Ezekiel gave her basic instructions on how to focus and direct her powers toward her own mind. She was to stand in front of the mirror and persuade herself that her skin was completely blue—head to toe. He told her that mystics were the only magicians who actually utilized words, which most people thought of as spells, to focus the energy within.

"For this spell," he said, "you will repeat the words *ego sum hyacintho*."

The girl spoke the words over and over. "What does it mean?" she asked, once she had the words down.

"Doesn't matter," Ezekiel said. "Remember, magic doesn't work as most think. Like the hand motions, the words are only a tool to focus you. They could be gibberish. In fact, they are, until I tell you their meaning. But if I never told you, they would still work."

She looked at him. "You can be an Arcadia-sized ass sometimes, Z."

Ezekiel laughed. "Must come naturally, because I make no attempt at assery. And that phrase just means 'I am blue,' words from a tongue lost long before the Age of Madness. Now, enough questions. Time for work. Repeat the words, focusing on their texture and cadence. Let's see what your mind is capable of."

Ezekiel closed the door behind him, leaving Hannah alone with herself. She felt more than a little absurd—and naturally so. Saying the foreign words over and over while trying to convince herself she was blue made her feel like a fool. At one point, she wondered if Ezekiel was playing her— if the mental magic trick was some sort of magician hazing. But she tried as hard as she could to focus. The thought of scaring the hell out of Adrien's men made it worthwhile.

It took over two hours of practice, but finally she opened her eyes and the person staring back at her in the mirror looked exactly like Hannah, except for two slight differences. Her eyes had turned bright red, and her skin had taken on a light shade of blue.

At first, she thought it was some trick of lighting, or maybe the hours of intense concentration had broken her mind. But she moved closer to the light and examined her skin; there was no doubt that it was, in fact, blue.

She screamed in joy, and the old man came right in, as if he were waiting just outside the door.

"So, did you do it?" he asked her.

"See for yourself!" Hannah waved her hand in front of his face, her smile huge.

He raised an eyebrow. "You weren't enchanting *me*, Hannah. You were trying to convince yourself. Subverting the minds of others takes more than two hours of practice."

"Oh," Hannah said. She thought for a second. "Then yes, it worked. I'm as blue as the sky."

Ezekiel smiled, then his eyes flashed red. "You are certainly a little bluer, but I'd say you look more a sickly blue than sky blue."

Her eyebrows came together. "Hey, I thought you said you couldn't see it?"

"You weren't the only one who was practicing their mental magic. I peered into your mind and saw that you were only giving me a half-truth. And a half-assed half-truth at that." Despite his rebuke, his face looked gentler than ever. "Nice work."

Hannah beamed. "Turning myself blue is one thing. Reading minds, now that's a pretty cool trick."

Ezekiel held up his hand. "It's magic, Hannah. Tricks are what you and your friend Parker used to do for money. This is something entirely different. We," he gestured between the two of them, "create *magic*."

"Yeah, whatever. But if I got really good at this, how far could I take it? Could I disguise myself as another person? Could I just make myself look like your boy Adrien and walk through the front gates of the Academy?"

"Disguising yourself is one thing. Making yourself look exactly like another being is damn near impossible. Too many details. Too many people to influence. Remember, the entire ruse is a suggestion. You'd have to convince a helluva lot of people. I've tried and failed many times before. The demon in the alley is about the extent of my image magic. But there was this one magician—"

This time, she rolled her eyes. "Let me guess, your pupil?"

He shrugged. "Of course. And this pupil surpassed the Master in the mystic arts. And maybe you will do so as well one day. We'd better take a break for now. It's dangerous to continue until you regain some of your energy."

It wasn't until he mentioned resting that Hannah realized just how tired she was. The hours of repetitive practice exhausted her strength and the focus sapped her will. They left the room, and she reclined on a couch in the great hall with Sal curled up in her lap. Ezekiel brought out plates of meat and vegetables and placed a goblet of strong wine in her hand.

"Tonight we celebrate. You have taken steps in all three of the primary magical arts." He winked. "The Founder himself would say this is a great occasion."

The man was downright gleeful, and he took a large sip of his wine as if to prove the point. As Hannah picked up her glass, she looked into the deep red of the wine and an idea struck her.

"Zeke," she asked as he sat across from her, "the eyes of the magic users in Arcadia turn coal black when they do magic. But your eyes turn crimson. Today, when I convinced myself I had blue skin, my eyes were red as well. Why is that?"

Ezekiel took another large sip of his drink, but the smile never faded from his face. "You really are perceptive. Tell me, how many magic users in Irth can practice all three forms of magic? I told you before that it was rare, but I didn't tell you how rare. Can you guess?"

Hannah shook her head. Instead of answering, she stuffed her mouth full of a piece of cooked meat.

"I'll tell you. Now, let me see," Ezekiel said, raising his fingers as if he were doing some sort of advanced calculation, pointing to one hand, and counting on the other as he looked up to the ceiling. "As best as I can tell, there are only two who practice all the forms. Me," he looked at her as he lifted his glass and gestured to her, "and now *you*."

Hannah nearly choked on her food. She knew that Ezekiel would push her to do great things, but being in a category with her teacher was beyond her wildest dreams.

Ezekiel laughed when he saw her reaction. "Don't get a big head over it. You know virtually nothing in all three of them. A master of any would certainly wipe the floor with your inexperienced ass."

Hannah laughed at his vulgar tongue. It was something she seldom heard from the old man. "Why don't more do it?" she finally asked, cutting another bite.

"As I said before, there are risks associated with using magic, especially when you lack a teacher as experienced as I am. But when I was first starting out, I wasn't nearly as experienced as I am now. My students found it easier to focus on only one branch, the branch that came most naturally to them. And I allowed it, since it meant there was less of a threat to their well-being.

"Over time they became more and more entrenched in their disciplines, and it became nearly impossible to branch out. Then they separated themselves in terms of geography and culture? Why, I'm not at all surprised to see that my magical offspring have become such rigid specialists."

She shook her head and took a sip of her wine before continuing. "But that still doesn't answer my question about our red eyes."

"The power that is inside of us, that is in our blood, colors our eyes when we use it to tap into the Etheric. You and I, since we practice all three forms, have a purer connection to that realm. The color of our eyes reflects that. Our red eyes are as unique as our ability to use all three. But I imagine, once people see what you and I can accomplish and the possibilities, the old walls between these types of magic will break down.

"Combinations of magic are powerful and, perhaps more importantly, unpredictable. They allow for a creativity that can give you a distinct edge in all of your endeavors. In the alley, for example, I combined nature and physical magic together."

Hannah thought back to that day. "The lightning bolt."

"Precisely. My connection to nature allowed me to summon a storm, but it was my skill with physical magic that allowed me to channel that power into a precise attack. I was also doing mental magic, but it was a separate casting, not mixed in. Imagine when you master the three together. You'll be unstoppable."

"How do you know I will?" she asked.

"Because I saw you do it. Without even trying, without even knowing you had magic within, you combined all three."

She looked down at Sal, who was curled up at her feet. "You're talking about him."

The master magician nodded. "That's right. I have seen physical users turn glass into steel, and fields flourish at the behest of a druid. I've experienced mystics coloring the skies for miles. But to change a living thing, to transform it into a different living thing—that is a blend of magic I have never seen in all my years, Hannah. Your lizard isn't just a larger version of the newts common to this area. He is a fundamentally different creature.

"Nature magic allows us to shape life, to reawaken its potential. But you cannot create life where there was none previously. To steal from an old phrase, you can heal a tiger, but you cannot change its stripes. The mystics could do what you do, but only in the mind, only as an *illusion*. The change would not be permanent.

"Physical magic users can, of course, change things at a fundamental level and make that change permanent, but their power runs into a strict barrier when it comes to the living, organic world.

"When you transmogrified that creature, it's as if you pulled all three at once. And it's one of the reasons why I chose you. I won't bullshit you. This fight that I've pulled you into won't be easy. Adrien's forces of evil are great. To win, we will need to change the game. We will need new magic and new sources of strength, and even then it may not be enough. But I believe that with someone like you, with your heart, we may just be able to pull it off."

CHAPTER 14

—————◆—————

Adrien drummed his fingers on the arm of the overstuffed chair as he looked down on Arcadia. Just days before everything he'd created had seemed so powerful, indestructible. And now, with the return of the Founder, he felt uncertain for the first time.

For a week after his meeting with his old mentor he had fumed over the man's return, angry at everything including himself for not being more cautious. Hubris had gotten the better of him; he hadn't seen a need to prepare for Ezekiel's return.

But the old man *had* returned.

As the days since their encounter passed, time built perspective and Adrien's anger turned to fear. The old man's trick was telling. Ezekiel had learned much during his time away.

The illusion he had created to trick Adrien wasn't magic known to the people of Arcadia. Theirs was physical magic, comprised of the study of material things and their manipulation. They were masters of it, and they passed it on to the next generation through the Academy.

He knew that the study of particular arts wasn't exclusive to Arcadians, but went beyond their walls to the farthest reaches of Irth. Regions and communities were specialists in different types of magic, though they all gained power from the same Etheric source. But magic was a difficult maiden to serve.

Magicians were fortunate enough to have the capacities and faculties to manage the power within. The notion that one could work in other specialties had always been inconceivable to everyone except Ezekiel.

When Ezekiel left on his mission he had already been talented in all three arts, though he exceled only at physical magic. But the image that Adrien had conversed with—and ultimately tried to kill—on Queen's Boulevard was evidence of the fact that his teacher had been busy since he'd been gone.

Casting one's image wasn't part of the physical arts, but the psychic. While a Master Magician might easily pick up a few cheap tricks from another art, image-casting to the degree that Ezekiel had accomplished it was no small task. It would have taken someone with a high level of mastery in mental magic to pull off the ruse. And that was precisely what scared Adrien to death.

The Chancellor was strong and confident in his own mastery, even better than Ezekiel was. But in the face of one who could navigate multiple styles, maybe the physical wouldn't be enough. And if Ezekiel had spent the last decades honing these other crafts? The thought was terrifying.

But it also gave Adrien an idea.

"Doyle," Adrien shouted toward his closed door.

The door swung open, and his assistant strode into the room. Doyle glanced at the chair, wondering if he should sit, and then thought better of it. "What can I do for you, Chancellor?"

"The magician, has he been spotted today?" Adrien knew the futility of his question. Zeke would only be found if he wanted to be. And that would mean that the magician was ready for the fight.

"No, sir. Nothing. Our men have been on watch 24/7 and the specialists are still on the hunt, but there's nothing. No magician. No trail."

"We may be looking in the wrong place," Adrien said. "I need a crew, not a big one. Five or six should do. But they need to be men we can trust, who can handle themselves outside the city walls. Can you get such a group together?"

Doyle smiled, happy to be useful for once. "Of course, sir. I have a small band of resources in reserve for a task such as this. Stellan and his men. They are trained for special missions and remain off the official ledgers in the Capitol. You never know when you'll need a secret operation."

"Yes, very good, Doyle."

Adrien explained to Doyle what he surmised from his encounter with Ezekiel's image and explained that if Ezekiel had improved upon his skill with the mystic arts, then it was possible the teacher had been a student.

"Now," Adrien said, "the only ones capable of mental magic to that degree are the mystics. Which means that Ezekiel may have spent time with the bastards. There's a good chance that Ezekiel may have persuaded them to be of some, well, *assistance* toward his ends. And those monastic sons of bitches are just as idealistic as the old man."

"Yes, sir. They could be trouble." Doyle cleared his throat. "If I may be so bold, what if we launched something more aggressive on the Heights? Maybe it is time to test the machine?"

Adrien waved his hand. "Only a schoolboy runs in swinging, Doyle. We are looking for something just a bit more elegant. I need you to send the men to keep an eye on the navel-gazers and bring back some information. They can be rough, but I don't want them to start a war. You understand?"

"Completely."

"Can I trust this Stellan not to screw up?"

"I'd trust him with my life, sir."

Adrien nodded. "OK, but this mission is worth far more than your life, Doyle. You might be giving yourself a bit too much credit."

Doyle flushed. "Um, yes, sir. I'm sure I am."

Laughing, Adrien said, "I'm screwing with you, son. Now, get your ass out of here and get those men to work. I want a report in no more than ten days."

Doyle groveled just a bit more before he left.

Alone again with his thoughts, Adrien turned back to consider how in the name of the Matriarch he might be able to draw Ezekiel out into the open. Adrien knew the collective power within the Academy was great; far greater than what Ezekiel could have acquired even if he had studied for a hundred years. He was only one man, after all. And the old man couldn't know much at all about the magitech and machines they had created in his absence. But Ezekiel wasn't stupid either. If he were planning an assault, he would be looking for stronger allies than the mystics.

Then it struck him. "The girl!" the Chancellor said aloud into his lonely chamber.

Among the few reports he had of the man, the only one that resonated with Adrien was the girl from Queen's Boulevard the magician stepped in to save. The old man had even put three of Adrien's Hunters in the hospital. He wouldn't have shown his hand so soon unless it was important. Unless she was important. Something was there, but Adrien couldn't put his finger on it. There must have been something unusual about the girl.

As he looked at the finely crafted marble chess set across the room, he realized that she might just be the pawn. Figure out how to move her—or the ones that she loved—and he might coerce the magician to do exactly what he wanted.

He called Doyle back in and sent him off with another plan to put the girl from Queen Bitch Boulevard into jeopardy.

———•———

Hannah opened her eyes to end her meditation session. It had been an hour—at least she was pretty sure it had been—but it felt like five minutes. Hours of work centering herself at the beginning of each day was turning her into a freaking monk, but the results were uncanny.

She had always thought mastery of magic was about learning the right moves, or spells, or shaping the right magitech weapons. But the old man was right.

She made the fastest advances—and recovered most quickly—when she paid attention to her inner self. Holding a finger up to the old man, she placed her middle finger on the opposite wrist and waited for a pulse. The tiny thumping under her skin was steady and slow. Hannah was pretty sure that within another week she might be able to make the damn blood in her body stop pumping altogether.

Turning to Ezekiel, she said, "Still pumping, Zeke. But barely."

"Good. Nothing is more important than what is in here." He placed his finger on her chest over her heart. "Control that and you control everything."

Hannah nodded. "But before, you talked about unleashing passion. What about the day when my brother almost died? My heart was sure as hell racing then."

"It was. And you're one lucky son of a bitch that the power inside of you didn't burn you right up."

"Bitch. Not son of a bitch. Like the Matriarch."

She winked at the old man. They still hadn't talked about the Matriarch and the Patriarch much, though she knew he was a true believer. Hell, he was old enough that he might have known them.

There would be time for religion, but right now training took center stage. He made comments often enough and used their names, not in vain, during their work together.

But otherwise, he didn't become religiously intrusive—which was refreshing since she had expected him to be as aggressive as the Prophet. The one thing she did know was that, according to Ezekiel, the Prophet had it all wrong concerning the use of magic by the public. Magical arts weren't meant to be restricted to the wealthy. Anyone who could control it should be given a chance.

She followed Ezekiel down the steps leading from their tower toward the woods. It was nature magic day, there was no doubt about it. He wanted to make sure she didn't progress in one art faster than the others, so he had kept her on a careful schedule since her initial training.

One day for each art.

Her training sessions were measured by skills, not time. The man had a careful curriculum marked out, and he kept her within the boundaries he had defined. Ezekiel had told her that if one art developed faster than the others then there would be a chance that she wouldn't become a polymage, which was the primary goal.

The old man had learned much from the Oracle during his own training.

This particular lesson has been learned through negative experience. His physical magic skills were more advanced than the others. Ezekiel's magic default was nearly always physical, though he could call up the others with great intention. Hannah would be stronger than her master, if he had anything to say about it.

When it came to which art she would perform when the pressure was on, he wanted her answer to be "yes."

Every damned one of them.

"What's up today?" she asked as they neared the edge of the woods. "Talking with trees?"

"Nope."

"Water sculptures?"

"No."

"Bestiality?"

"Hannah, please!" The old man had his limits regarding her cruder nature. She loved pushing the boundaries. "None of the above. Your skills are coming along really quickly. It is time to take the next step into new magic."

Looking down at Sal, she knew Ezekiel was talking about something similar to the transformation of the lizard, but she couldn't imagine what.

She had known this time was coming, but she hadn't been looking forward to it. How the lizard was transformed into a…whatever he was remained a mystery, and if the old man wanted her to replicate the task, Hannah wasn't sure she was up for the challenge.

It's not like she hadn't considered it herself. She even tried, without Ezekiel knowing, transforming an ant into something different. The damn thing had just kept walking away.

They got to their spot by the river and sat on the rocks. She was happy to be sitting in the warmth of the sun. The days they spent in the training rooms of the tower wore on the girl. No matter how hot it got outside, the place was always cold, damp, and reeked of mildew.

Both of them watched the river. Meditation was progressing, but all the damned waiting for her mentor to speak was getting old.

"Yep. It's still right here," she quipped, looking at the River Wren. "Freaking love it. Want me to stop it or something?"

After more silence, the old man finally said, "I want you to change Sal."

She and Sal exchanged glances. His tongue lashed in and out of his mouth. Ezekiel had never called him by name before, which was odd. "The lizard?"

"He's not a lizard, Hannah. What once was, is no longer. You changed him. The entity you first encountered in the market is a different being now."

"Um, OK. What the hell do you want me to do to him?"

"That's not up to me. It's between the two of you. I don't have a connection with your friend. To me, he is just another creature. Once you bound yourself to Sal, the possibility of me connecting with him became, well, impossible, as far as I know. The two of you are connected through a solid covenant that will not easily be broken or subverted."

"All right." She looked down at Sal and inspected the spikes protruding from his vertebrae. Hannah wasn't sure, but she thought they had grown slightly since the day she took him in.

She imagined what else she might do to him. Make him grow? Change his color? Give him opposable thumbs? None of it seemed right. She locked eyes with the creature, trying to read his thoughts.

Then it came to her; the perfect image of what Sal was to become.

"I think I've got the picture in my mind. Now, what do I do?" she asked, keeping the image primary.

Ezekiel gave her a gentle smile. "I haven't the slightest. This is your magic, not mine. We're in new territory here."

"Not. Very. Helpful."

"Like all magic, it is a matter of focus. Focus on the image inside of you. Maybe that will work?"

She snorted. "OK, but if something goes wrong and *I* start growing spikes, please stop me."

Hannah closed her eyes and began. She pushed Ezekiel, the sound of the River Wren, and even Sal out of her mind as she found her center. Everything faded into the background, and all that remained was her and the power flowing through her body.

For a moment a doubt that she could make it happen crept in, but then she set aside the doubt as well. Hannah was a magician. Her mentor had told her that as far as he knew, she had done something no one else had ever accomplished. She reminded herself of this several times, building her confidence along the way.

Then she pushed that away too.

Once again, it was just her and the power. She opened her eyes and focused on Sal, sitting still at her feet. Their connection was strong, and he knew exactly what she was up to. He was a willing lump of clay. Ready and eager to be molded according to her plan.

Considering that transmogrification was something akin to physical magic, she brought her hands in front of her and started a series of complicated motions, none of which she had ever considered or practiced. But she fell into a routine with it, repeating the same motion again and again. As her digits and hands twisted faster and faster, she tried to push the energy under her skin toward her hands and out into the lizard, but it wouldn't budge. It was as if there were a barrier between her and Sal.

After what felt like hours, Hannah's arms, heavy as lead, dropped to her side. She slumped on the rock and looked up at Ezekiel.

"Nothing." She told him, wiping sweat out of her eyes. "It's not working."

He nodded, "No one said this would be easy, Hannah. Try again. Please. The fate of Arcadia may depend on it."

She nodded, then gritted her teeth and tried to refocus. She closed her eyes and pushed away failure and disappointment. Ezekiel's expectations came into her mind's eye, and she thrust them away.

Once empty, she chose the path of nature magic. She turned her palms upward toward the sky and entered into something like a trance. All her mental and emotional energy flowed. She tried to connect with the creature, begging his body to do precisely what she wanted him to do, but Sal was unresponsive.

Finally, exhausted, she bent over at the waist and rested on the rock. This time she didn't care what he thought, she just wanted to go away. To sleep for a year. Arcadia be damned. Let Adrien have it. Magic was too hard, and she was far too weak.

Ezekiel had made a terrible mistake choosing her.

"You can do this, Hannah," he said, more tersely than she had heard speak him before. "Damn it, you have to."

She fought back. "I can't! It's not in me. I didn't do this before. It just happened."

His reply was a whip crack. "Don't be a damned fool. Magic doesn't just happen. Magicians *are* magic. You *are* a magician. You *are* magic." The old man was nearly screaming in her ear, pushing her over the brink.

Hannah lashed out. "Leave me the hell alone, you freak. I'm just a bloody kid!"

His answer was unambiguous. "You're not a kid. You're a *magician*. You were made for this. Stop wasting your life."

Her anger flared. "I can't!"

"You can!" he shouted. And with the words came a crash of thunder. "Let it out!"

Lightning hit the water, the whiteness blinding her for a moment.

Hannah collapsed around Sal and covered him with her arms. All the fear and frustration she had been setting aside for hours came pouring out of her. But as those emotions washed over her, she felt something else too—Sal's presence, as if they were connected with each other.

There was no telling where her body ended and his began. "Please," she cried, picturing the animal's potential. "Do this. For me."

Her mind began to swim and she lost track of where she was. She vaguely thought she felt the world shaking and an intense heat, but she couldn't focus on that.

All she could feel was the animal twitching beneath her chest. Something jabbed at her stomach and chest and Hannah jumped, afraid she was hurting him. Looking down, she saw the skin on Sal's back begin to bulge like two balls were trying to push through. Sal looked at her. She could feel his pain, but also his desire to please her, to do her bidding.

Hannah sobbed as she saw the pain she was causing him. The reptile wanted nothing more than to end the torment—she could feel it—but he refused to give up. Sal screeched as finally his scales could hold it in no longer. The balls burst through his skin, but they weren't balls at all. Instead, something long and bony emerged on each side.

They pushed up and out of Sal's back as his cries continued to echo across the waters. Extending an arm's length on either side of him, they expanded into two glorious wings.

The last thing Hannah saw before losing consciousness was her pet lizard leaping from the ground, wings stretching toward the sky.

But I'm wrong, she thought as she hit the ground. He's not a lizard at all.

CHAPTER 15

---◆---

E zekiel cracked the door and checked on Hannah, the woman who had quickly become the finest pupil he had ever taught. He beamed with delight. The magician who had seen more of the paranormal than anyone else living on Irth had just witnessed the impossible. Hannah had just reached into the Etheric and pulled out power like Ezekiel had never before beheld.

As she unleashed her frustrations, the ground beneath her began to shake. The trees and grass around them leaned in as if she were calling out to all of them. Fire bubbled beneath her skin. And then, in the midst of that terrifying sight, something beautiful happened. Hannah's pet, the creature that was once nothing more than a common lizard, become something far more majestic.

Hannah had pulled an image from her mind and created something brand new. And now that thing was curled up on his mistress's legs. Sal continued to stretch his new wings, as if trying to convince himself they were real.

Nodding his head silently, Ezekiel whispered, "You are new magic, little creature."

The lizard flicked his tongue and nestled closer to the girl. The movement disturbed her, and she cracked open her eyes.

"Ezekiel," she moaned, "was it a dream?"

"It was completely real," he replied in a gentle hush. "And it was amazing. I've never seen anything like it in my considerably long life."

A tired smile washed over her face, and her eyes closed again. As Ezekiel stared at his sleeping student, he realized that what he said might not have been true. While he had never seen a creature change like that, he'd seen magicians expend all of their energy like Hannah had.

Perhaps that was the connection.

But it was a question that Ezekiel was unprepared to answer.

He needed help, and there was only one place he knew to get it.

Once he had conceived the idea, it took mere seconds to make up his mind.

"I need to take care of something important. Dire even. You stay here. Stay safe."

She opened her eyes, and Ezekiel was gone.

———◆———

Recovery from whatever the hell happened between Sal and her took a full day and a half. Hannah spent the entire time in bed, feeling as if she had the flu. Her body ached and her energy level was next to nothing. Casting had exhausted her before, but it was more like being worn out after a long day of hustling the streets with Parker.

This was something altogether different, and it scared her more than a little. She wondered what would happen if her body reacted like this in the heat of battle. She'd be a sitting duck, and the Hunters would have their way with her, or worse, Adrien would.

Either way, she'd need to talk with Ezekiel about how one defends oneself in an exhausted state.

Glancing over, she found a plate of food on the bedside table. She touched the meat to see if it was still warm. It was the third meal she had awoken to. Before she had dropped into slumber, the magician had told her that he had to go and attend to something important.

The food appearing by her bed was strange, but she had to admit it was nothing more unusual than any of the other shit she had experienced since taking up residence in the tower.

She reached down and scratched Sal's back. Her fingers struck his wings, and she sat up in surprise. Somehow she had forgotten the magic that had taken her energy away for the past thirty-six hours.

The creature stood and slowly moved his wings, clearly showing off the new accessories to her. The spikes running down his back had grown, and his scales reflected a darker green. But the wings! The wings were like nothing she had ever seen except in her imagination. They were long and thin, and yet Hannah could sense strength within them.

Hannah wondered how far they could take him.

"Looks good, you little creep," she said. "Learn to use them yet?"

In response, Sal waddled to the side of the bed and started to vigorously flap the wings. Hannah's hair blew back as his little body levitated over the surface of her bed. He hung a few feet in the air before tumbling back to the bed and then onto the floor. He looked up at her and flicked his tongue in and out.

Hannah could swear he was trying to smile.

"Not bad. Looks like we are both going to take some time getting used to our new powers."

She swung her legs over the side of the bed, grabbed the plate of food, and made her way out of the room and into the great hall.

The meal helped immensely, but she was still feeling woozy from her use of magic. She also knew it was time to get back to work. Arcadia wasn't going to save itself, and if she were going to have a hand in its redemption, she would need to be ready for the fight.

Today it was nature magic. Ezekiel was still nowhere to be found, but she didn't need him to practice her forms. She quickly made her way outside.

The air felt refreshing on her face, and it was invigorating to get outside the tower. She made her way to the river where the forest met the short band of grass between it and their home.

She reached at her usual spot. The place had changed somehow. The large tree that had loomed overhead seemed to lean in a little more today. And where Hannah usually sat was a ring of dead grass that looked like it had been burned.

Hannah thought for a moment about the power it had taken to transform Sal, and she wondered what else she was capable of.

Dropping into a cross-legged position, she closed her eyes and focused. An hour passed in a heartbeat, and she opened her eyes and felt for her pulse.

Slower than ever, she thought.

Taking a few minutes, she ran through some of the simpler spells she'd mastered during her first week under the tutelage of Ezekiel. Pleased to find that they still came easily and required little energy, she stood, deciding to try something a bit more intense.

Her mind wandered, trying to imagine what the next step would have been if the magician had been with her. The sun beat down on Hannah, and her body started to sweat under the folds of her cloak.

"Wish we had some shade," she said to Sal, who was flapping around in the grass practicing his own skills. He looked like an awkward toddler just learning to walk.

She couldn't help but laugh at his difficulty. The reptile looked at her and then curled into a tight ball in the grass. "Some shade," she repeated as she looked up at the cobalt blue sky. There wasn't a cloud in sight, and she knew exactly what she was going to try.

She held her hands out to her sides, palms up. She pictured a storm cloud rolling in overhead, but nothing happened. The other arts made some sense in how they worked.

Connecting outward with the physical aspects of nature— the trees, the river, and even Sal—made some sense to her, but she had no idea how to connect with the weather. Imagining herself raising up into the sky and spreading clouds overhead didn't work. She tried saying some simple words, thinking that mixing with mind magic might help. Nothing.

"Looks like you might need a staff," a voice said behind her.

"Zeke!" Hannah shouted with joy as she turned around. She hadn't expected to miss him as much as she had. "You're back."

"Indeed. And you're practicing. I'm glad to see it, but weather control is a significant leap from what you've done so far."

She smiled. "I look terrible with a sunburn. Just trying to protect my doll-like complexion." Hannah winked at her teacher. "Wasn't sure how long you'd be gone, and I didn't want to fall behind."

"Very wise. Discipline is the key to mastery. Keep it up. And it looks like little Sal there has been working on his own discipline."

She laughed. "Yeah, poor guy. Not sure he knows what happened to him."

"Well," Ezekiel said. "He knows about as much as you do, which is a good start. Your dragon will figure it out soon enough."

"Dragon?" She looked down at Sal, who looked back at her. Then his tongue whipped out and back in. "What the hell?"

The old man chuckled. "Look at him. You want to keep calling him a lizard. I guess that's fine, but we both know what we have here. And if Sal is to grow into what he now is, it is going to take you nurturing him. The first step is to admit and name his new nature."

"Holy shit. I have a dragon!" She crowed.

"Yes, you do."

She raised her eyebrows. "Kind of little for a dragon. Wait, does this mean they actually exist? I mean, other than Sal?"

The magician shrugged. "I don't think so. At least none that I've ever seen. But that's the power of your new magic. You have truly created something new, brought something to life that once existed only in dreams as far as I know. The mystics devote their lives to accomplishing only a shadow of what you have done with Sal here. You connected with him during his change. He'll do your bidding forever, I suspect."

She looked fondly at Sal. "And I his."

Ezekiel leaned on his staff. "Yes, it does go both ways. But remember that you are the magician, not him. Now, about that staff." Ezekiel's eyes cut to the trees, and Hannah could tell he was looking for the perfect limb.

"Hey, Zeke, any chance I can have a wand instead?"

"A wand?"

"Yeah, you know. Nothing screams 'old man' more than leaning on a staff. A wand is, well, kind of sexy. And if it is about focusing…"

Looking at his own staff, Ezekiel said, "I've had this since I was not much older than you."

"Let's not get all self-conscious about this, Z. No offense, really. I mean, I never expected you to have been very fashionable, but—"

Ezekiel held up his hand to stop Hannah before she had a chance to say anything else offensive. "We can discuss that another time. In fact, the druids will have better luck than you and me at creating a tool for you to connect to the natural world. Let's wait until we speak with them."

"I guess that's on the to-do list, right after 'blow shit up.'" She gave Ezekiel a winning grin. "Now, where the hell have you been?"

The old man's face darkened a little bit. Hannah could tell that something was bothering him. "Well do you want the truth, or do you want the *truth*?"

She laughed at him. "What the hell kind of wizard nonsense is that?"

"Trust me, young girl. You'll be speaking my brand of nonsense soon enough. But to answer your question, I've been traveling throughout Irth, and I've been sitting alone at the top of the tower. I've been everywhere without budging an inch."

Hannah paused for a second and squinted her eyes. It was a riddle, and she was determined to solve it. Finally, the answer clicked and she yelled with glee. "You've been astro-whatever-ing. Traveling with your mind!"

Ezekiel nodded, proud once again of his young protégé. "Top notch."

"But where did you go?" she asked. His face turned cold again.

"Might want to sit down for this one."

The two sat in the grass and took in the sunshine as Ezekiel told his story.

"While you've been training these last weeks, I have been quite active mentally. At first I spent my energy walking the streets of Arcadia, but this time from the safety of the tower. I've been gone from my city for nearly half a century, after all. And when I went there physically, well, I stumbled across you within the first hour, flashing rude gestures at large angry men."

Hannah nodded. She remembered it well.

"Naturally," Ezekiel continued, "I needed to get you away from the city. But once I had, I decided to return. *That* is the battleground, after all, and I mean to be prepared. So, I observed and assessed and planned. But preparing for battle means more than just knowing the arena. You need to know your enemy as well."

"Adrien," Hannah said between clenched teeth.

The man's name rang in her ears. While many in Arcadia elevated him to god-like status, the third person with the Matriarch and Patriarch, many others, including Hannah, despised the man.

The people of Queen's Boulevard were pretty evenly split. Half were enamored by the rhetoric of the Academy and the Capitol, dreaming of one day working hard enough to make it out of the Boulevard and up onto the hill. The other half realized that those in charge were working for their own ends, not for the common good.

Hannah and William were lucky. Wisdom was the foremost of her mother's abilities, and she had passed it along to her children from their earliest days. The highlights of the stories told by her mother had remained etched in Hannah's mind, and no matter how much her drunk father went on about the virtues of the authorities, he couldn't sway what she had already internalized.

"Tell me about Adrien. I want to know what happened. How he became like he is."

The old man nodded. "Interesting question. I also want to know the answer to that. I cannot say exactly what has gone on with my student since I left Arcadia, though I have gotten some information. But I will tell you what I know.

As the Age of Madness ended, a small band of us started working together, not only survive but also to pursue the cure.

"The days were exciting and we were filled with hope. In those dark days it was almost all we had. There was a group of about five of us who started to think seriously about the founding a new city. Of Arcadia.

"One night—I remember it was winter—we were huddled by a stove in a makeshift shelter. A boy about your brother's age came stumbling through the door. His hands and face were white with frostbite, and he looked like he hadn't eaten in a month. We did the best we could to nurse him back to health.

"The boy told us about the loss of his parents to some of the Mad, the 'zombies' as you call them. He'd been making it on his own for a long time and had no plan to do otherwise. Trust was not one of his virtues, and we couldn't blame him. He had seen the worst in people, and it was only because of the harsh winter that the boy named Adrien agreed to join us.

"Over the course of a few weeks not only did he come to trust us, but I started to see that the boy had abilities beyond what he knew. It wasn't unlike what I saw in you. So I offered to train him if he would agree to stay and help to build our dream. We were quite a pair. He was naturally gifted, I was naturally stubborn. Many I have taught believe I was born special. I wasn't; I just worked without ceasing and doggedly pursued my aims. Magic was no different."

"As people started to come to our burgeoning town, Adrien's gifts advanced quickly. He took the lead on magical construction, helping others understand how the gift of physical magic could be used to actually construct the city itself. It was an amazing sight to see.

"While he led that project, I worked with the refugees pouring in, helping many of them to hone the power within them and focus it on different aspects of building. There was nothing like magitech in those days, but I expect that even then Adrien may have been imagining what he could do if he could apply magic to inanimate objects. It's clever, really. Nothing I would have ever have thought of."

"Yeah," Hannah interjected. "Magitech is a hell of a thing, really. They're applying it to all sorts of stuff. Problem is, no one on my side of town can afford it."

The old man nodded. "That is indeed bad. But I fear that something worse is coming. Adrien has plans for magitech, something bigger and more dangerous than anything we can imagine."

"How do you know?"

Ezekiel smiled out of the corner of his lips. "Like I said, know thy enemy. I confronted my old protégé."

As Ezekiel explained his confrontation with Adrien, how he tricked him into revealing part of his plan and then attacking nothing but Ezekiel's shadow, Hannah went from surprised to downright impressed.

The old man was full of tricks.

"I don't know what," the old man continued, "and I don't know when. But Arcadia is going to need us. Irth is going to need us. So, I spent the last couple of days locked in my room, searching for answers outside the city. In the deepest corners of Irth."

"Well? Did you find any?"

Ezekiel sighed. "Yes, but not the ones I wanted. I have been searching for an old friend, someone who could help us, help you. But I can't find him."

The two sat for a while by the Wren, each lost in their own thoughts. Hannah marveled at the man's stories, realizing that if she stuck with him her life would never be the same.

The opportunity she had been given by the magician was literally beyond her wildest dreams, but also her wildest nightmares.

She wondered if it was worth it, worth giving up her old life, not that there was much to discard. But she missed her brother and Parker like crazy and decided she would find a way to see them sometime soon. Maybe Zeke would teach her that astral projection trick.

"How did you end up doing it, Hannah?"

"Doing what?" she asked. She was hardly listening and was afraid she'd missed something he said.

"Sal's wings. Have you thought more about it? I've never seen anything like it before. If we're going to have a fighting chance against Adrien and his forces, we're going to need every unfair advantage we can muster. Right now, you're all we've got."

Hannah laughed. "Better call in some reinforcements, 'cause I've got no freaking clue what I did to Sal in the marketplace or out here. It just happened. I tried the physical magic approach, which didn't work. Then I did the navel-gazing thing. Nothing."

"What was it, then?"

"It was you. You kept bitching and badgering me. I was frustrated and angry. Felt like I was going to explode, and then I just kind of did. It just happened."

Ezekiel stroked his beard and sighed. "Well, we know it has something to do with emotion, which is no surprise. All magic is connected to our emotional states, but we still don't understand the catalyst."

Hannah picked up a rock and looked at it, turning it over in her hands. "If it is what we need to take down those bastards ruling over Arcadia, I'll figure it out. I promise."

She tossed the rock out into the Wren.

CHAPTER 16

———— ◆ ————

Y ou've been sitting there for an hour and haven't said a damned thing. Can you really not hear me when you're out starwalking or whatever?" Hannah paced the floor, and Sal followed her every step. But the magician kept his eyes trained on an imaginary dot on the wall. "Well, that's good. I was afraid that maybe you had lost your marbles or just plain gone *bloody nuts.*"

Ezekiel didn't twitch.

"Oh," Hannah continued, "that's nice. Me? Yeah, I'm doing fine, except I am in lockdown in a three-bloody-room building with nothing but a freak of a lizard and a magician who likes to go monk three times a day to keep me company. Otherwise, things are just peachy."

The wizard remained silent.

Hannah had been training in the tower for what felt like an eternity, and she was going crazy from being cooped up in one place. Other than the fact that there was absolutely nothing to do, the wizard was a peculiar sort of company.

Ever since she turned Sal into a dragon Ezekiel had been spending more and more time sending his mind to roam Irth. He wouldn't say what he was looking for, beyond a few oh-so-ominous answers.

Meanwhile, Hannah was feeling a strange stirring in her gut. She could only guess it was the thing other people called *homesickness*.

She called it *missing*.

Although the girl would never call herself homesick for the squalor and the abuse of the Boulevard, there was plenty that she longed for.

William. Parker. Her bed. And even QBB itself. Everything that was familiar had been stripped from her. It was the first time she had been away from the place that had made up her entire existence.

Hannah leaned down and picked up Sal. He folded his wings in so she could hold him more easily. "At least I have you, little guy." The lizard's tongue flicked in and out, moistening her cheek.

"The lizard isn't your only friend," the magician's voice boomed across the room.

She turned. "Thank the Patriarch. I thought you'd died with your eyes open."

Ezekiel got up from the floor and plopped on a couch near Hannah. "Someday, child, you'll find that magic is one part learning, one part practice, and fifty parts mindset. During my time abroad, the greatest of the things I learned was how to focus my life toward the work of magic and restoration. You will do well to learn this sooner rather than later."

"My meditations are coming along," Hannah said a little sulkily.

The man laughed. "I'm not too old to remember what it is like to be your age. I was only a few years older than you when we set off to build Arcadia. That year, I knew everything. And then, two years later, I knew I was wrong. Life is an endless road of changing perspective. Some call this waffling, but I call it growing in wisdom. And among all the arts, nothing is greater."

"Ah… OK. Got it. Change your mind. Get wise. I'll write that in my little book."

Ezekiel's face grew soft. A smile spread across his lips. "You're a hopeless smartass, aren't you?"

"Yep," Hannah said with a smile to match. "Gonna take more than magic to change that."

The man stood, and the smile faded from his face. His lips grew tight and Hannah knew that something very serious was coming. She had learned that the magician loved life and enjoyed a joke or three, but when it came to the survival of the world, the old man was all business.

"I don't understand you," he said.

"Most don't."

"No, I mean your skills. Though they are rough, magic is trying to escape you. That's how we got this little guy here." He nodded toward Sal. "But you're able to express magical arts that are foreign to all the guilds of all the corners of Irth. I've spent hours in study, and it seems you might have some unnatural combination of all of the arts."

"Hell, as far as I know all magic is unnatural," she shrugged.

The magician laughed, which brought her some comfort. "On the contrary, there is nothing *more* natural than magic.

It's in each and every one of us. The question is whether someone is strong enough to bring it out. People like me who have been mentored in the arts are taught to bring it out in a way that doesn't blow their bodies into little bits all over the city streets.

"Imagine how annoyed people would be if they went out in their best clothes, only to have them splattered with blood by someone losing themselves to magic? Others will never manifest the magic whatsoever. But you are different, Hannah. You've done nothing to bring your magic to the fore, but it refuses to be bottled up. Just by being in the world, the magic created Sal, and there is no explanation for that."

Her mouth hung open as she thought of a wiseass comment to dispel the seriousness of the room.

But she had nothing.

Finally she said, "So what should I do?"

"That, my dear, is the question for the ages. If I had the answer, I would give it to you. But I know some people who might know."

"More friends of yours from the old days?"

Ezekiel nodded. "Something like that. I've been holding off on this awhile, but I'm afraid there is no other choice now. I need to go visit them."

Hannah squinted her eyes, suspicious of what was coming next. "OK, when do we leave?"

Ezekiel's face answered the question before his words. "I'm sorry, Hannah. I'm afraid you can't come with me."

"Why the hell not? I've been practicing every day like you said. I've been getting better. And if these people can help me, then I should go with you."

"It's not that simple. I have been reaching out with my mind, trying to connect with them, but there has been no answer. Which means one of two things. One explanation is that they have turned their back on me, which means that they have become as great a threat as Adrien. Maybe worse."

"I'm not afraid."

"I know you aren't, but I am. Because the other reason I may not have been able to contact my friends is that they're dead. Which means that there could be some danger I can't foresee. And you are too valuable for us to run in blind."

Hannah dropped her eyes. Despite all she had been through, it seemed that Ezekiel still saw her as a child to be protected. When would he learn that she was able to contribute? To use magic as he did to protect others?

Finally she looked at her teacher. "Fine. What do you need me to do?"

"I need you to stay here and keep practicing. My trip may take… Well, it may take a long time. But when I return, I need you to be as ready as possible. There is no telling what comes next, child. But whatever it may be, it will not be safe."

The magician disappeared without another word, leaving Hannah alone in the tower for real this time.

———— • ————

Parker kept his head down as he paced toward Queen Bitch Boulevard. His bag was heavy with his tools, and the coin sack bouncing on his hip was evidence of a good day on the streets.

But he knew it was only a fraction of the haul he could have pulled with Hannah. To say his thoughts turned to the girl wouldn't be quite right. She was always there, at least in the back of his mind. He couldn't help smiling, picturing her by his side.

Parker, like most of the guys in the quarter, thought she was good looking, but she had captured him with more than just her looks. Smart. Funny. Gifted. And if Will wasn't bullshitting him about her magic, then her gifts were deeper than he had ever imagined.

And the young boy seldom bullshitted.

"Half your take, prick," a gruff voice said.

Parker looked up into an ugly mug he didn't recognize manning the toll booth into Queen's Boulevard. "Who the hell are you?"

"Doesn't matter. What matters is who I work for. Now hand over the toll and be on your way, you little shit."

"Where's Jack?"

"I don't know and I don't care. He's probably back at your house shagging your ma. Now drop the coin and be on your way."

Parker felt his face flush. He knew the man was trying to start something. Probably got his jollies off throwing his weight around. Parker held his tongue and reached for his purse.

"Or he might be doing that sweet piece of ass you hang around with." A disgusting laugh rolled off the man's double chin. "Heard she has a thing for Capitol men, if you know what I mean. Nice of you to share her with the Hunters."

Without thinking, Parker swung the bag of coins at the man's thick face. But Horace's man was deceptively fast. He ducked the punch and pulled Parker's arm up behind him. The brute slammed him face-first against the wall. Rough brick bit at his face as pain shot through his already sore skull.

"I oughta turn you in for even thinking about it," the man breathed into Parker's ear. "But lucky for you, I don't feel like doing the paperwork. Now, let me lighten your load, and you can be on your way."

He gave Parker one more shove against the wall and yanked the bag of coins from his belt.

"You're a shit-eating pig," Parker spat at the man. He considered a second attempt, but the men who worked for Horace were ruthless, and he knew that pushing his luck would have terrible consequences for him, and maybe his mother. The filthy words about his mother and best friend rang in his ears. He spat at the man's feet.

The obese man snorted like a swine. "By the way, you can tell that piece of ass that the Hunters are looking for her. They've put a price on her head, as commanded by the Chancellor. Or you could always turn her in yourself. You probably need the money." The man shook Parker's bag before stuffing it in his pocket.

Son of a bitch will get his, Parker thought. He would devise a plan to right the wrong, but first, he needed to find Hannah and warn her about the price on her head.

———◆———

Her fingers twisted with increasing intensity and speed. They were a blur in front of her eyes, but she didn't notice. Stuck in a trance, Hannah was more connected with her body than she'd ever been.

The practice was paying off, at least in terms of her focus. Finally, folding the fingers of her hands into each other, she spun them out and fanned them toward the pile of papers across the room. The sheets pulled toward one another, but stopped just short of a pile.

"Shiiiiiit!" she screamed into the empty room.

Sal ran and slid under the chair, the only furniture in the room. Hannah slumped into the chair and patted her leg. The little dragon obeyed and jumped into his mistress's lap. His tongue lashed out and tickled her arm, aiming for comfort.

"Thanks, buddy. Guess I need to rest more. Those wings of yours cost me something, that's for certain."

Sal rubbed his smooth head on her arm, and she gave him a pat.

"Yeah. We'll be fine. Let's see if I can't get this down before you can fly over the tower. A little competition might do us some good."

She was glad Sal was there, especially since Ezekiel had left for whatever important mission he was on. The man was full of secrets, and from time to time she had a strange notion that he might not be exactly who he said he was. But the man offered something no one else ever had.

A way out of misery for her and for Arcadia.

"Let's go get something to eat. I'm—"

A scream outside interrupted her. She shot for the great hall and looked out the window in the direction of the cries for help. The distance was great, but from where she stood she could see a person in a tree and some sort of animal on all fours leaning against the trunk.

"Damn it. Sometimes I miss the filth of the city," she muttered.

Ezekiel had told her to be careful. She suspected he meant for her to stay in the tower, but the man was all about righting wrongs. If she couldn't help some wanderer by shooing off an animal, she sure wasn't going to take down the evil empire of Chancellor and Governor.

As she strode for the door, she grabbed the silver blade given to her by Karl and made her way to the edge of the woods.

Halfway over the grass, she thought she could make out what the man was shouting. Then she realized it was her name. The voice was familiar.

"Parker? What the hell?"

Joy mixed with fear for her friend. She couldn't understand why he was treed by some stray dog. She'd be sure to call him a sissy when it was all over.

"No, Hannah, go back," his voice wrapped around her and echoed off the tower. "*Run!*"

She ran, only toward him. None of this made sense.

Ten more strides and she saw the creature turn. That's when it struck her. It wasn't leaning on the tree; the thing stood on two legs. It tilted its head, sniffed the air, and let out a blood-chilling howl.

Lycanthrope, she thought. *Can't be. Those damned things don't exist.*

She'd heard the stories all her life, but like the tales of dragons and druids, she'd assumed they were also residents of make-believe. Lycanthropes were sinister creatures that were a mix between man and wolf. It was said that they were descendants of the werewolves that roamed the earth before the Age of Madness.

The creature looked like it was a Were turning back into a man, only to get caught in-between, frozen forever on two legs. Its long arms stretched toward its knees, culminating in razor-like claws.

Sniffing again, it took a step in her direction, then paused. Hannah held her arms up. She considered casting. But with the magic fails she just experienced in the tower, she doubted her ability to produce anything at all. She probably couldn't even give the thing a good paper cut.

"Easy…" she cooed, hoping the thing was more animal than man.

It tilted its head back to Parker, then returned to her.

"Guess we're the easy prey," she said to Sal, who had wedged himself between her legs. "Now's the time for you to learn fire-breathing. Think you can do that? Yeah, didn't think so."

Holding her hands up, she said, "We don't mean you any harm."

The lycanthrope let out a howl and bolted in her direction. Its humanoid form—man blended with wolf including slavering jaws and reaching claws—was terrifying.

"Shit," she yelled. Scooping up Sal, she made a break for the tower.

The lycanthrope was swift. There was no way she was going to make it before she was overtaken by the beast. She cursed herself for falling into this position again, but something told her Karl wasn't going to turn up this time. So she changed tactics.

She turned downhill, taking advantage of the slope that ran into the woods to the north. Maybe she could lose the killer animal. She fled through the trees and found a thick patch of underbrush.

"Come on, Sal," she panted.

Her heavy breathing mixed with the panting of the animal on her tail. Pushing through the thicket, she burst into the open and found herself stumbling into the Wren.

"Shit burger," she cursed, as she realized she had miscalculated her trajectory.

The beast cut through the thicket just behind her. His mouth was curled up in a snarl, baring yellow teeth made for shredding meat.

Hannah shifted Sal into her right arm and tossed him into the air in the direction of the closest tree. "Time to learn to fly, Sal."

Flapping his wings like a wounded bird, the tiny dragon made it to a branch just out of reach of the lycanthrope. Hannah exhaled, knowing that at least one of them would be safe. It suddenly struck her as odd that her end might come, not in an act of avenging the evils done in her city, but in the jaws of a storybook animal.

"Just you and me, you mangy shit." She pulled the knife from her belt as the beast crouched for attack.

It leaped, and Hannah willed whatever power she could gather through splayed fingers. The beast struck a wall of energy just before it reached the girl. It wasn't enough to stop it, but it did throw the creature off balance.

The lycanthrope spun, hair, legs, arms, and tail in every direction. Hannah ducked and the animal flew over her, only to land in the river. Unfortunately he landed in the shallow part. Hannah turned to face him. Running was futile. She knew the creature could outlast her if she did.

Spreading her legs to shoulder-width, she spun her arms across her chest and drew fire from deep within. As the lycanthrope pulled itself from the water, she launched two balls of flame at it. Sizzling filled the air, accompanied by the smell of burning hair. The thing screamed, but continued to advance. She didn't have much left. It bore down on her, and she raised the rearick's knife in defense.

The lycanthrope circled her, a predator with its prey. Before it could strike, a rock the size of its head slammed into the beast.

"What the hell are you doing?" Parker screamed as he broke through the thicket. "Get out of here."

"And let you have all the fun?"

"That's my girl." He grinned.

"I ain't nobody's girl," she called back. "But I'm about to make this thing my bitch."

She slashed at the dazed creature, slicing a line down the middle of its chest. Screams spread over the river. It swiped a clawed paw at her, gaining purchase on her shoulder. Lines of anguish followed the razor-sharp weapons of the lycanthrope. Hannah could feel warm blood flowing down her arm.

It took another swing. This time Hannah was expecting it. She ducked and rolled to safety. Parker volleyed rock after rock at the wolfman. His throwing arm was better than his juggling, and he landed several projectiles. Letting out something between an animal's roar and the battle cry of a warrior, it rushed Parker, batting away rocks as it charged.

Hannah pushed everything out of her mind and reached for a peaceful state. Then she let go, brought back the fear and let it swell under her skin. With eyes glowing brighter red than they ever had before, she screamed as she launched every ounce of power she could muster at the beast. Light shot from her fingers and struck the lycanthrope, flipping it ass over teakettle. It landed hard in the dirt at Parker's feet.

Her partner was ready.

He had raised a giant rock over his head. With perfect aim, Parker brought the rock down with all the force he could muster on the creature's skull. The sound of shattering bones and splattering brain filled Hannah's ears.

Parker, not wanting to chance it, brought the rock down over and over, spreading the lycanthrope's head all over the shore of the river. Finally, when there was nothing left of it, Parker collapsed on the sand at the water's edge.

"Parker," Hannah screamed as she ran in his direction. She pulled him into an embrace. Pulling back, she held his face in her hands. "Holy shit. You good?"

"I think I'm pretty good. But did I see you throwing fire-balls?"

Hannah couldn't help but laugh. "Not bad, right? Guess we made him *our* bitch."

CHAPTER 17

———◆———

It took several exhausting jumps for Ezekiel to head south toward the temple of the mystics. Transporting took a lot out of a magic user, and even one as skilled as Ezekiel couldn't cross too great a distance without taking breaks. But the long journey paid off, and after one final jump, Ezekiel appeared in the heart of the Heights, which were the large mountain range making up Irth's southern border.

Steadying himself with his staff, Ezekiel got his footing on the rocky ledge he had landed on. Once steady, he sat down on a rock. Just beyond the tree line, he could see the temple clearly while remaining obscured.

He had chosen the right spot. He had used this one years ago, the last time he had been to the Heights. Pulling his cloak around him, he took in the view.

The sun was dipping below the front range. Its peaks, still snowcapped despite the heat of the summer, were turning red, blue, and purple. The Matriarch and Patriarch were painting an amazing welcome in the sky for the old magician.

He gazed further into the distance and saw range after range spread out behind the first. Although he'd spent plenty of time in the Heights, the view never disappointed. With a landscape as majestic as this, it was no wonder that the mystics were the masters of mental magic and had all but perfected meditation. But their art was not without its effects on them.

Residents of the Heights, while physically present on Irth, weren't always fully there. They were known for their aloof nature and the way they softened the effects of their mental gymnastics with strong drink.

The jump had taken its toll, so he spent some time drawing strength as he focused on his heart rate. The monastery wasn't far, but it was better to go in strong. There was no telling what waited for him. After recovering sufficiently, he got to his feet and started the short rocky trek to the home of his old friends.

It had been decades since he'd last visited, but he remembered every turn of the path. Holding his breath, he made the final climb and then stood before the towering monastery of the Mystics of the Heights.

The building was large. Simple by design, it was built with a welcoming air. The pale walls were like a blank canvas for the mystics to paint upon. Ezekiel knew that beyond this first building lay a sprawling compound of gardens, homes, and places for training.

He nervously paused at the door. An image of Adrien rushed through his mind. One of his students had already fallen—the one he never expected to turn to self-aggrandizement and manipulation of the weak. The fear that the same may have happened with his pupil in the Heights struck him like a rearick's war hammer in the chest.

But he needed to know.

Pushing the fear out of his mind, he tapped the end of his staff on the tall oak doors and waited for a response. It didn't come quickly, but that wasn't a surprise.

Dwellers of the Heights had a different conception of time than the humans who dwelt in the cities and woodlands of Irth. Just as Ezekiel and Hannah could lose time in meditative states, so did the mystics. But their meditations had become an almost constant state of being. For them, meditation was as commonplace as eating or sleeping for the rest of the world.

Just as he moved to knock a second time, the door eased open. A man only a quarter of Ezekiel's age stood in simple robes much like his own, except that the younger man's covering was pristine, unworn by travel in the world beyond the monastery walls.

The man stepped aside and tilted his head towards the inside as an invitation to their hospitality. Ezekiel nodded, smiled, and stepped into a grand entry that lifted into a vaulted ceiling designed to draw the eye toward the heavens. He stood just inside the door and waited.

The man simply stared at the magician, and Ezekiel wondered if his host had taken a vow of silence, a practice not altogether uncommon for the mystics as they plumbed the depths of the human mind.

Finally, he said, "Ezekiel, you are most welcome to the home of the mystics of Irth. We have been expecting you." A serene smile spread across his lips, and Ezekiel wondered if he was the worse for drink.

Ezekiel, who was capable in mental magic to a certain extent, knew the dangers of the art. It had its own consequences on its users. Traveling the earth through astral projection and stepping into the minds of others wasn't an easy task, nor a clean one.

The community had turned to the strong drink they brewed in the bowels of the monastery to take the edge off the damage to their minds. He couldn't blame them, but it made for awkward interactions at times such as this.

"Thank you, brother. It has been a long time since I have come to the Heights. It looks as though the community has endured these years well."

The man nodded. "Few make the trip to the Heights. Anyone attempting the journey is not here for harm, but for help. It makes life on Irth a dream."

Ezekiel smiled and wondered if that dream would always last. "Indeed. I am here to talk with the Master. Unfortunately, not all of Irth experiences the peace of the Heights, and I am going to need some guidance from the one I trained years ago. Can you take me to him?"

"Follow me. I will talk with the Master and confirm a meeting, but I know you must be tired. I hear that jumping from the lowlands takes its toll even on one as talented as you. Let me show you your room. I will have one of the initiates bring food and drink."

"Just tea for me." Ezekiel knew that the elixir they made in the lower levels was the best in all the land, and he would be happy to imbibe after his meeting, but he needed to keep his head clear and his intuition sharp for the meeting to come. The strong alcohol was good for sleeping, but he had not come to the Heights for rest.

The man nodded and showed Ezekiel his room.

Alone in the chamber, he picked at the plate of food provided by a child no older than fourteen. The kid said nothing as he placed the tray on Ezekiel's table.

At his age, he had already entered training. The mystics started earlier than the Arcadians, which was one source of their power. Paired with the seclusion of their mountain paradise, the early education made the young ones powerful much sooner than their lowlands counterparts.

Ezekiel's energy returned as his stomach filled. Pouring a mug of piping hot tea, he slumped in a chair in front of the fireplace. Its flames danced, lulling him into deep thought.

The magician's mind dwelt on the edge between waking and sleeping as he thought of his newest student.

Hannah had something in her that was different than all the others. Maybe even different than Adrien. Ezekiel's advantage was his diligence.

Hers was her spirit.

There was something about her that made her energy more pure and powerful than his would ever be. He wished that he could talk with the Oracle about Hannah. Lilith would certainly untangle the mystery of the woman's power.

But there wasn't time for that journey, and he hoped that the Master Mystic might have some answers to his questions. They were not only powerful but knowledgeable people.

His mind passed from his newest pupil to his oldest. As a boy, Adrien had been different from the others. Ezekiel had attributed his morose attitude and cynical view to that fact that he was an orphan who did whatever it took to protect himself. Without a doubt, this had contributed to the adult Adrien became. But there was something that flowed inside him that had contributed as well.

It seemed that nature and nurture had created a monster, and with Ezekiel absent and unable to guide the young man, the monster overcame Adrien's better tendencies.

The magician cursed himself for leaving Arcadia in his hands. If he had only stayed, he might have been able to see the boy and the city to maturity.

The door squeaked open behind him and pulled him from his mental self-flagellation.

"Was the food appropriate?"

Ezekiel couldn't help but smile at the odd turn of phrase that the mystics used, but he followed the man's lead. "Most appropriate, as is the rest of your hospitality."

Nodding, the man stared at Ezekiel. The magician reminded himself that navigating this community took the utmost patience. Monastery life did not value efficiency. After what felt like an eternity, the man said, "The Master will see you now."

———— ◆ ————

Climbing the stairs to the Master's residence, Ezekiel felt the joy build in his heart. The Master had been his primary pupil during his stay in the Heights. Their work together had not only laid the foundation for a community of magic users who were arguably the most powerful in Irth, but also a friendship that Ezekiel knew transcended time and distance.

While there was much to be discussed regarding Adrien, Arcadia, and Ezekiel's newest student, he also yearned to catch up with the man he considered one of his dearest friends.

His escort opened the door for Ezekiel and stepped aside. The magician stepped across the threshold and looked around, hoping to find his friend. But instead of the big old jolly man with skin darker than the night, he looked into the eyes of a young woman no older than her mid-twenties, with a beauty that could start wars—or stop them. Her hair was dark, with hints of auburn.

She rose as Ezekiel entered.

"Master Ezekiel," she said through a perfectly white smile, "I have waited a long time for this day."

He froze for a moment as if he were one of the mystics. "You're—"

"A woman? Yes. Young? Yes."

"Not Selah," was his reply.

Her eyes cast to the floor. "Forgive me. I thought you knew of his demise. Your friend passed on to the next plane two years before now." Her speech was steady, its patterns like the lowland dialect but still marked with the mystics' idiosyncrasies. "His departure was swift and distinctly appropriate. I now hold his chair. Please, sit."

Ezekiel took a place by the fire adjacent to the woman. Apparently Hannah was not the only young woman who had special talents.

Some believed that the Age of Madness would be the great leveler. A catastrophe that would allow the world to emerge with people on equal footing, it would wipe away the differences of race, class, and gender.

But Arcadia had demonstrated that it hadn't come to pass. Rich men still held the mantles of power, but this woman and Ezekiel's new student might be indicators that the patriarchal society was passing. It was said that the Queen Bitch had also been unusual.

A woman who could rise in a male dominated world. One who could show the power, might, and justice of the fairer sex.

"My name is Julianne. And it is now my honor to lead the mystics in our pursuit of the greater peace."

Ezekiel nodded. "How did you—"

She smiled and held up a finger. "First, a toast. We must proceed with procedural appropriateness."

Picking up two goblets from the table between them, she handed one to Ezekiel. She raised her own, its crystal causing the flames from the fire to dance around the room. "To the Matriarch and the Patriarch."

Ezekiel raised his glass and clinked hers. The scent of the strong elixir hit his nose before its wetness covered his tongue. He sipped slowly and took in as little as possible without providing offense.

The magician's defenses were heightened in the absence of his old friend. One had to be cautious among the mystics. They were good people, but they had never minded burrowing into the heads of those around them.

None of them saw it as trespassing. Everyone, in their experience, was a book open for browsing.

When it came to telepathy, nothing primed a subject more than a pint or two of strong drink. He would need to stay sharp until he could trust her, or determine that she too had been turned, like Adrien, toward manipulation and self-service.

She licked her full lips and color rushed to her cheeks. Tilting her head, Julianne said, "Your defenses are strong, magician."

"Yes. Forgive me. I am not prone to allowing strangers to walk the halls of my mind."

"Understandable. Where you're from it is common for people to use magic for nefarious ends. We are not like the lowlanders, though. Entering one another's thoughts is a way to increase intimacy and speed familiarity."

"Yes. Well, we will take this slow. Forgive me. The world has shaped this old man into a creature of caution. Now about you?"

She nodded. "As you wish, Master Magician. As for me, I am too young to have known you when last you walked these halls. But your name is legend here. Almost as much as the Matriarch and the Patriarch. I was born in a small village north of Arcadia, but Master Selah heard of my gifts on one of his pilgrimages and brought me here. My parents were more than happy to be rid of their *freakish* daughter."

"I took to the temple quickly and was chosen as one of three to study directly under Master Selah. Succession was always on his mind; something he learned from you, no doubt. We were taught mindfulness and the arts from the earliest of ages. Much younger than most students. I wasn't meant to be in this room so soon, but Selah's transition came years earlier than any of us expected.

"On his way beyond, he chose me to take his place. As you can imagine, I and those around him were surprised. The calling has been a most challenging one, but with enough time alone and drink to soothe my mind, it has been utterly tolerable and appropriate."

Ezekiel grinned and sipped from the goblet again. He didn't want to be rude, not to mention that the finest drink in all Irth called out to him. With the second swallow, he felt the warmth in his belly move up to his face. "Indeed, there is a time to drink for all of us."

Julianne burst in laughter. "We mystics agree, but that time is always now. Granted, we have become experts at judging the extent of the effects of our little potion here, always mindful not to go too far. We have not forgotten the lessons of control you taught Selah, and that he passed down to us."

She paused to stare at the fire. Ezekiel put his defenses on high alert, concerned that she might be trying to burrow in. Then Julianne continued, "There will be time to become better acquainted, but for now, may I inquire as to what brought you back to our humble home here in the Heights?"

"Of course. I wish I had come only for personal reasons, but I have been driven here by events which have occurred below." Ezekiel's speech was already bending to match the woman's, a habit formed over years of moving among the different groups spread out over Irth.

Ezekiel went to some lengths to tell the story, as far as he knew it, of Adrien and his cruelty in Arcadia.

She listened intently while sipping from her goblet.

As Ezekiel's tale ended, Julianne stepped in. "Yes, Selah had long been suspicious of your former student; a position I share. Word comes back from the mystics who travel to Arcadia and to the further reaches of Irth. And, from time to time, I jump to places to take in the scene myself.

"Adrien's thirst for power has been well documented. It is, as far as we can tell, insatiable. But do not think that his obsession extends only within the walls of Arcadia. His desires go further, and these might be more troubling."

"Magitech?"

"Yes. Our own determinations are that the tools he imbues with magical power are being created as test pieces. He is looking forward to things greater than magic-powered carts and automatic doors. Something more global. Adrien desires to spread his philosophy of magic to every corner of Irth, and with it his power and influence."

The old man nodded. "Your people still go on pilgrimage, even with the threat of Adrien's power?"

Julianne drank from her goblet. "Some do, but fewer and fewer. It is a difficult thing. Our magic is at its best when we make the pilgrimage, but there are risks involved from the lowlanders. Adrien has soiled their minds. He uses a man named Jedidiah—they call him the Prophet—to spread disinformation about the use of magic. It is a most clever deceit, as he does it in your name."

Ezekiel remembered the old man in Capitol Park and how odd it was that the man was preaching about the Founder's return only to pervert Ezekiel's own position on the use of magic. Now it all made sense.

The man was a plant—part of the narrative about magic and power that Adrien was trying to spread. The student had been brilliant years ago and now seemed to be something of a mastermind.

"The bigger problem for us," Julianne continued, "is that pilgrimage is also a time for our people to look for others with the gift of the mystics—those with a propensity for the art of mental magic. In areas where Adrien's influence has spread more rapidly, we are distrusted at best and attacked at worst. No one wants to join us in the Heights. Our number is dwindling, and soon the art could cease to exist."

"Magical extinction."

"Of the most severe kind," she agreed.

Knowing that their time was nearly over for the evening, Ezekiel drank deeper of the liquor. He needed the alcohol to ease his heavy heart. "Julianne, this is why I have returned. Adrien is a threat to all of magic—to all of Irth—and he must be stopped. But I cannot do it alone, and the Matriarch knows I would muster little magical support from Arcadia. I need the aid of allies beyond its walls."

"I understand your proposition. But you need to remember that mystics are not accustomed to the martial affairs of our world. We are a people of peace. We traffic in the merciful side of justice."

The alcohol and the conversation swirled in the old man. He had heard the argument before; Selah was a man committed to the peaceful life. It was one of the reasons the mystics holed up in the Heights, which made sense in a time of civil rest.

"Julianne, mercy has its time and place. And it is the appropriate companion to the sword of wrath. But grace without wrath is impotent. It is time for you to help me stop this threat to Irth. Cutting off the monster's head will be an act of mercy for the oppressed beneath his heel."

She nodded again, and he trusted she was taking in his arguments. But he needed more than passive assent. He decided to play his final card.

"There's more," he said. "I have a new student, someone special, who has a unique gift that may be able to help us reclaim this land."

"What is his name?"

"Not his, hers. Hannah. And she has fed on the root of oppression and it has left a despicable taste in her mouth. She is ready to do whatever it takes to overthrow Adrien's growing empire and to restore Arcadia to what we first meant it to be. And if we dig up the root, we keep the tree from extending to the rest of the world. We can keep it out of the Heights."

He finished his wine and placed the goblet on a side table. "But if you continue to ignore the threat, if you hole yourselves up in the mountain fortress, they will come. Maybe not today or tomorrow, but one day they will come, and it will be your end."

CHAPTER 18

---◆---

Stellan had absorbed about as much as he could take of the bitching from Dirk and Dietrich, the two young guards assigned to him. They were not much more than kids, as annoying as they were inexperienced. He had been commissioned by Doyle, the Chancellor's lapdog, to journey to the Heights to gather information.

Apparently the leaders of Arcadia had suspicions that the mystics might be involved in subversive activities, and his task was to ask some questions. It would be an easy in-and-out. The mystics had their heads in the clouds and were an odd bunch, but at the end of the day they made the best beverage in all of Irth, so he certainly didn't mind spending a night in the mountain monastery.

At this point he'd need some of the strong elixir to get him through the journey with the numbnuts who had been sent along with him.

Dirk, the younger of the two guards accompanying Stellan, bitched, "How much farther is it? My feet are bloody killing me."

"If you keep complaining, it won't be your feet killing you," Stellan replied without looking back.

He'd climbed the mountain enough times to know they were close, but the elevation only got steeper from here. Looking over the cliff that fell away just feet to their right, he considered for a moment how easy it would be for the younger guards to have an accident.

"Stellan," Dietrich asked, "what exactly are we doing with these mind freaks?"

"*We* aren't doing anything. You're along for the ride. Keep your damned mouths shut. Chancellor Adrien wants some information about whether or not the people of the Heights are working with anyone who might be a threat to Arcadia."

Dirk spoke up again. "Who would be a threat to Arcadia? I mean, we're pretty much the most powerful city in all of Irth, right?"

"Yeah," the leader said. "And we want to keep it that way. One city working alone couldn't breach our walls, that is for sure. But I think that the Chancellor and Governor are worried about something a little more insidious. An attack from within. Not to mention that these people you guys call the mind freaks are powerful. Their discipline is strong. They're not to be underestimated."

Stellan shook his head and realized just how big of a mistake it was to have the two men along with him. His time in the Governor's Guard had given him enough experience to know that the mystics could pick apart a man's mind faster than a drunk can down a pint.

And they could, if they wanted to, do some serious damage once in there. He'd shared too much with the men, and the mystics could extract it all if they wanted. But he'd assumed the Chancellor and Governor were just being overly cautious, maybe even paranoid.

The mystics were pacifists and more interested in the life of the mind than foreign affairs. It would be an easy job. Go in, ask some questions, get out, after having plenty to drink, of course.

Rounding the last bend, Stellan finally saw their destination—the mystics' temple. He stopped and looked at the men. "Listen, keep your damn mouths shut. Remember what you learned about mental magic?" The two nodded in unison. "Good. Someone *will* try to get in your heads. It isn't an attack, it's just what they do. For them, stepping into another person's mind is just like shaking hands. Keep your mental defenses up, just like they taught you in the Academy."

They nodded their heads again like a pair of idiots. Stellan knew his advice would mean next to nothing. Even if they had learned to defend themselves, it was likely they had forgotten everything about it. The Academy was strict on who they let into their fold, but they became much more lax once students were inside. And unfortunately, the bottom tier of the graduating class was often assigned to the Guard.

The force was mostly for show in Arcadia. Standing at the city gate was the most grueling assignment many of them had, and it didn't take a Master Magician to let loads of potatoes in through the walls. Stellan's group was different.

They were the Guard no one knew about—the ones who actually kicked ass and took out true threats to Arcadia. But Doyle was adamant about things going quietly, so instead of a fully armed force, he was stuck with the imbecile twins. Luckily, Stellan himself was more than capable of handling whatever threat was waiting for him beyond those walls.

———— ♦ ————

Belly full and head on the edge of intoxication, Ezekiel sat back with a feeling of deep contentment. The mystics were good at many things, but hospitality was the greatest of these.

Julianne had ended their meeting and decided to introduce Ezekiel to the rest of their little community. He was a legend, after all. Now that dinner was finished, the conversations of pairs of people swirled around him. His journey back to Arcadia had been a bitter homecoming, so a night like this in the Heights was precisely what he needed. It was balm for his weary heart, and a reminder that there was goodness in the world of magic.

His eyes cut to Julianne, whose was gazing back at him. She gave a subtle nod, an indication that his words were still on her mind. Ezekiel could only hope that their conversation would not be lost on her.

Amidst such a happy community, it could be hard to think of war. But Ezekiel could tell that Julianne would do what it took to protect this group. They were her family.

He only hoped that this desire for peace would lead them into the fight and not away from it.

After the plates were cleared, a young mystic woman with the face of an angel stood at the head of the table. The room quieted and awaited the evening story. Ezekiel knew the tradition well. Narratives were a key part of their

RAYMOND, BARBANT, & ANDERLE

community, and the people made sure they would not lose the oral tradition by ritually including a story told by a different member each night after a meal.

The girl smiled and closed her eyes to gather her thoughts. When she opened them again, all color had drained from her pupils. She stared out at the crowd from eyes like white marbles.

Ezekiel knew the sign of magic.

While a physical magic user's eyes turned black as night, this mystic's eyes shined like stars. As she began her tale, cloudy images of what she was saying appeared on the table in front of her, acting out her words like a play.

"A long time ago, before the Age of Madness and even before the WWDE, there was a time of peace—at least, relative peace. But a young freckle-faced boy named Clark wouldn't have agreed."

As her words and magic painted the story of Clark and his exploits at school, the young mystic had the community leaning closer and hanging on every detail. The audience was drawn in by Clark's survival of what she called Middle School, a time that sounded worse than the Age of Madness itself.

Dodging bullies and mean teachers, the kid had to learn to survive. The story must have gone on for an hour, but to the enraptured crowd it felt more like minutes. She had them eating out of her hand. Then she got to the part about the gift.

"In those days, the days before Madness, and before our esteemed guest walked Irth," she smiled and nodded to Ezekiel "magicians were few and far between. But there were creatures called genies, or at least some believed they existed. Clark discovered one when he dug an old glass bottle

243

out of the ground on a beach on what was called Lake Ee-Ree. The boy placed the glass bottle between his legs and rubbed and rubbed and rubbed and rubbed."

"Sounds like Mathias on a cold and lonely night," a drunken mystic said from the back of the room.

The room burst into laughter.

The girl flushed, but continued her story. "Finally, in a puff of smoke,"—at that point a puff of smoke appeared in front of the listeners, and several jumped in surprise—"the genie emerged from the bottle. 'You have one wish, Clark,' the being from beyond said in a deep and majestic voice. Now the boy had a hard decision to make, as any of us would.

"Clark walked the beach, trying to come up with the thing that might serve him for the rest of his days. Money was fleeting. And he was too young to understand true love. So finally, after pacing a hundred miles on the beach, the boy knew what to ask for."

The image of Clark walking on the table stopped, and there was a pregnant pause.

The girl was good. Everyone in the room held their breath.

"Come on, then. What was it?" the same voice called out.

"There was only one thing Clark could ask for. He looked the genie in the eye and asked that he be granted the ability to perform magic. With a nod of his head the genie granted the gift, then left the boy alone with the power to shape the entire world."

Ezekiel scanned the room. All the eyes were still on her, waiting for more. It was as if she had slid a delicious dessert across the table, only to take it back.

"Well, what the hell did he do?" the man in the back of the room yelled out again.

"He did what any boy who knew the world wasn't quite right would do. First, he righted the wrongs of his school, then his city." As she told this part of the story, her images began to darken. "But after he had conquered all evil, when all the wrongs were righted, Clark used his power to take over the world. The same thing that any of us would do if we were left alone with unchecked power."

The wispy picture of Clark disappeared as the storyteller sat. The room applauded tentatively.

The other mystics were uncertain about the story, but Ezekiel understood it all too well. It was a morality tale about magic and the current state of Arcadia. While Clark and his genie were only a fiction, the warnings about the dangers of power were far too true. The young mystic was very good at mental magic.

After drink and food, Ezekiel had dropped his mental defenses, and he knew that the girl had made her way into his mind. She was clever, and her magic was strong. She told the exact story Ezekiel needed them to hear. The girl had sown the seeds, encouraging her community to come to the aid of Arcadia, to the aid of all Irth.

Julianne rose and thanked the girl for her story, though her words were measured. Turning to Ezekiel, she asked, "Would you be so kind, Master Magician, as to share a tale with us? There is nothing like foreign stories to invigorate our craft."

Ezekiel knew an invitation to share a story was not something that could be denied. He decided to follow the young mystic's lead and put his story to good use. He smoothed his beard as he stood. "Of course, Julianne. I'd be more than happy." He looked up at the ceiling, searching for the right one to tell at this moment. "First, let me say thank you to—"

"Zoe," the girl said.

"Zoe, yes. It means life, in an older tongue. Might your lovely and timely tale give us life? Gifts, the best of them, can be both a beautiful and sometimes a dangerous thing. It does not, of course, mean that we should stop giving them."

The group of mystics nodded in unison, and he knew that they were all walking through his mind. It was no secret what his commentary on the situation was.

"You will need to excuse me, as I am not a master of storytelling, but I will share a tale about a boy as well. Not one of fiction, but of autobiography. As many of you know, I was not born nor raised here, but rather, my roots are in a place that was, before the Age of Madness, called Siberia.

"It was a cold and desolate land, and the people reflected their landscape. My mother was hardened by the eternal winter, but my father, he was a different sort. A man of great dreams and visions, he inspired me to believe that the world could be different, that Madness could one day end, and that we, the human race, could flourish once more. But my story today is not about flourishing, but about fear. The man who raised me knew no fear, but my mother instilled in me the importance of self-preservation."

Ezekiel scanned the room. The eyes of the mystics were glassy from the effects of their strong ale, but they were all attentive nevertheless. They seldom heard the stories of an outsider in the great hall, and Ezekiel hoped to give them something to feast on.

His story was not only for entertainment, but like Zoe's, was meant to move them.

"When I was a child, my family wandered through the wilderness from town to town, fleeing the Mad. In those days there was never a moment of rest. Those who took a chance, who settled in, their days were always numbered. So it was my mother, of course, who kept us on the move. She believed that if we ever settled down, or even rested, the Mad would catch up with us and we would be lost."

Ezekiel took a sip from his glass. Placing it back on the table, he continued, "One night we came upon a young woman. She was starving, half-frozen, and for all we knew, she was more than half-dead. My father, being the idealist he was, wanted to help. It was always his way.

"But my mother was always more discriminating. Our family was more important to her than anything else on Irth. I was young then, and I can still remember the fight they had. There was heavy conversation, and even a shout or two. But, finally my father's ideals overcame my mother's reservations. She relented."

"We built a shelter right there in the woods, although the position was far from secure. My father built a huge fire, a risk no matter where we were. But the generous man thought that we could revive her. And we did. The fire worked, but it worked too well. It brought this woman back from the brink of death, and it led the Mad directly toward us."

Ezekiel's eyes went red, and he raised a hand in the same manner Zoe had. An image danced in front of the audience. Although stories about the Mad were common, the mystics still gasped either in surprise or sheer appreciation of Ezekiel's magic.

The spell produced a moving image of ragged, starving people lumbering through the woods. It was hard to even conceive of them as human, though they shared the form with those watching. Their eyes glowed stunning red in the night darkness. The Mad lacked all thought except their desire for human flesh.

247

"None of you were alive during those days," Ezekiel said. "And lucky for you that you never had to see them for real, although the same blood runs through your veins. The same blood that gave our Matriarch her strength, the same blood that gave us magic. But the blood had turned bad, transforming these humans into what the Lowlanders call zombies."

"My father was busy helping the sick woman. He was tending her wounds and rubbing the heat back into her feet and arms. Because of his deep care for her, he was totally unaware of the Mad advancing upon our shelter."

The magician's factual story was nevertheless more compelling than fiction, and held every ear in the room. He was admittedly not much of a storyteller, but sometimes narrative trumped skill.

He gave them all a nod and continued, not wanting the cliffhanger to last too long. "I sat there, only a child. But even then, I marveled at the differences in my parents. My father was driven by compassion, my mother by vigilance. She had agreed to let her husband help a stranger, but she never once let down her guard. And as he fought off the frozen death of a stranger, she, with a walking stick in one hand and a large knife in the other, fought off the Mad."

"The creatures were strong, but she was fast, moving at a speed I could not fathom. In the shadows of our camp, I watched as her staff whipped around smashing heads and taking out legs. I remember the knife, its blade grabbing the campfire lights, driving through the eye socket of one of the Mad. The twitching of its body will never leave me. Then it fell still. She engaged another one in hand-to-hand combat. She fought off its lumbering blows, and parried the monsters' attacks with her own offense. She was a true warrior."

"There was a moment when one broke through her defenses and ran toward us: me, my father, and the broken girl. My mother drove the knife into the throat of the Mad she was fighting and dashed for her loved ones. I was frozen. Useless. Just a child. But I knew that my life was about to end.

"As the zombie reached down for me, my mother dove and took out the inhuman by the legs. They struggled on the ground, and pulling a flaming brand from the campfire, my mother drove it through the zombie's torso. The thing screamed until it died." Ezekiel paused and looked around the room. "And that is just a little story about my childhood."

Ezekiel finished his glass and sat down. For a beat, the entire room was silent. All eyes were on him. He took it as an invitation and continued, "Young Zoe's story was about watchfulness against pride. About the evil that can spread when power goes unchecked. This is an important lesson. But my little story might tell us this: watchfulness takes many forms.

"Like my father, often we need to learn to love and care for those in need. But that cannot overshadow the gifts and drives of my mother, who understood that we must always be ready to defend those we love with fire and wrath."

Ezekiel ended his speech and he, too, received applause, though it was more tentative than that given to Zoe. His tale was grave, and he hoped it had watered the seeds that Zoe had planted. He wondered if it had any effect at all.

Exhausted by the alcohol and the use of magic, he excused himself from the company of the mystics and made his way to the bedchamber his hosts had provided.

As he settled into bed the room spun gently, a result of a bit too much ale and the intoxication of the stories. It was good to be in the Heights, and Ezekiel wished he could remain here forever, but he knew that he couldn't stay. Arcadia called him. Justice called him. As sleep came rushing in, he prayed to the Patriarch and Matriarch that his journey to the Heights wouldn't be for naught.

On the edge between waking and sleeping, a commotion from the great hall woke him with a start. The vigilance that his mother instilled in him told him to fear the worst.

Ezekiel jumped from his bed, as sober as a church mouse, and entered the hallway.

CHAPTER 19

———— ♦ ————

The sun caught the edge of the rearick's silver blade as Hannah wiped it clean of the lycanthrope's blood. Karl's gift had already been a blessing, but she couldn't help but wonder how much more blood it would spill before peace returned to Arcadia. Her body was still tingling from her first kill, though Parker was the one who finished the job. Sitting next to him on the steps of the tower made everything feel a bit more normal, even if her world had been turned upside down.

"So, I guess you're a magician now," Parker finally said, breaking the comfortable silence. "What have you guys been doing up here? Sacrificing goats and shit like that?"

"Glad to see you haven't gotten any funnier in my absence," Hannah said. "And there were no animal sacrifices. Mostly it's a matter of focus. Tapping into the power that was always there, in my blood. In everybody's blood, actually."

"Wait." Parker looked at his hands, twisting his fingers into signs. "I could do that shit?"

"Maybe. Ezekiel says that in the days just after the Age of Madness, people were running all over Irth trying to access the power within. The problem is that it takes willpower and a sharp mind to control it. So, you're probably out."

"Man," Parker said, "have I missed you." He jabbed her in the ribs with his elbow.

"Yeah, I'm pretty charming. It's wild, I'm learning so much from him about magic, its history, and how it all works. The crazy thing is that the Chancellor was Ezekiel's first student. The old man even left him in charge of Arcadia when he departed. That's when everything changed. Adrien limited the magic, telling certain people they couldn't practice. At first folks thought it was to protect the citizens, but soon it just became the way things were."

Parker nodded. "Which is why we all thought that magic was something you were born with, not something just anyone could develop."

"Exactly. The son of a bitch is controlling magic so he can maintain power and control over all of us. I mean, imagine what QBB would be like if we had been raised learning magic and could use it to make our quarter better. That's some messed-up shit.

"Here's something else that's fascinating: There are three forms of magic. In Arcadia, we practice physical magic. It's taught and passed down from teacher to pupil. There's also mental magic, which the mystics do, and the nature magic of the druids."

Parker laughed. "He told you there were druids? OK, the Founder might be a madman after all. No such thing as druids."

"And I would have said there were no such thing as lycanthropes if you asked me over breakfast. But I just saved your skinny ass from one."

"Point taken. And who saved who's skinny ass?"

Hannah smiled and ignored him. "What's crazy is that all of those different kinds of magic are all from the same power source inside everyone. It is learned in communities and mastered. I guess some people are better at different forms, and then the form shapes them, reinforcing the magic style they master."

"So, which one is the Founder teaching you?"

"All of them."

Parker looked at her sideways. "You're learning all three forms. How are you not blowing up?"

Hannah jabbed him in the ribs. "Because I'm a badass. Actually, he's trying to teach me a fourth. Zeke thinks it is somehow a combination of all three arts into one. It's how I created this guy." She nodded at Sal, asleep between her feet.

"Damn. That's pretty awesome. So are you going to create an army of dragons or something?"

Hannah looked down at the Sal. "I don't know. I don't think I'd be able to do that. I have a special connection with Sal, you know? I think it might have been a one-off thing, but Zeke is hopeful. Enough about me. How's my brother?" she asked, her stomach tightening into a knot as she mentioned him.

"William's better than ever. Healthy. Strong. He's started doing a bit of hustling; he decided it was time to be done as a panhandler."

"Oooh, good for him. With those big pouty eyes, he'll do just fine. And my—"

Parker saved her from naming her father. "He's fine. Still walking all over the freaking city trying to find work. Will told me about the spell he's under. Hasn't touched a drink since you've left."

"Well, if you didn't believe in magic before—"

"Yeah, right. Arcadia is also, well, different since you left. Everybody is on high alert. The Guards and Hunters are always on the street. They're turning houses over looking for you and the Founder and rounding up Unlawfuls along the way. Word is there's a pretty sizable sum on your heads. The Founder's bounty alone would be able to buy you a place in the nobles' quarter."

"Now I know why you're here!" She pulled the rearick's knife. "Don't get any ideas."

She laughed at her own joke, but inside she was hurting. To think that her actions had brought more severe treatment on the Boulevard made the power within her boil. Nothing drew her passion faster than the mistreatment of her people, but she knew that soon justice would be hers.

Hannah also knew that she wasn't ready. Adrien and his forces were more powerful than a single lycanthrope or a wild boar.

"Actually, I just came to warn you about the bounty," Parker continued. "I've been saving your ass for years. I figured a few miles of distance shouldn't change anything. And…"

Hannah's throat tightened as she readied herself for more bad news. "And what?"

"And, well, I missed you."

She could feel herself flush. Parker had always been the person she was closest to. She thought he was great, and not terrible to look at. But while she wasn't inexperienced with men, she'd never thought of him that way.

"But you're mostly here for the reward," she quipped, deflecting his comment.

"You got me." Parker cupped his hands around his mouth and yelled, "Come on out, boys, we got her."

They both laughed as if nothing had changed.

———————◆———————

Stellan's patience had worn thin. The mystic at the door was both spaced out from too many years of meditation and already half in the bag on their powerful drink.

He didn't mind the latter. In fact, after a day with the douche brothers, he was mostly jealous of the man's intoxication. Not to mention that if his gift was walking around in other people's twisted brains, he'd be half drunk all the time as well. But the man working door duty was obstinate bordering on downright rude.

"I'm not asking to see the Master, I am *telling* you to bring us to her. Not giving you an option here, spacebrain. We are on official Arcadia business by order of the Governor and the Chancellor."

He could feel the mystic push against his brain. The man wasn't strong enough to get through Stellan's defenses, but he had to remember to keep the wall in place. Anger had a way of weakening one's capacity to keep a mystic out.

"Yes, yes, yes. The Governor and Chancellor… I heard that. I just can't, not tonight. She isn't to be disturbed. Would not be prudent to go against what she desires."

The man's bloodshot eyes dashed back and forth from Stellan to the other two guards. He was suddenly nervous, and it struck Stellan why. The mystic was in their heads, and now knew more than he should.

"Damn it, boys, defenses," he shouted.

But it was too late. Dirk pulled his gun, a magitech weapon, and pointed it at the man. "Out of my head, freak. Now!"

"Holster your weapon, Dirk," Stellan commanded.

The tension was thicker than a morning fog on the River Wren.

"Get out," the kid screamed again.

The mystic's confusion increased. Alcohol dampened his ability to think clearly. He jerked his arms up in defense, but it looked more like he was moving to cast magic. And that's when Dirk blasted him with a thick blue beam of magitech energy.

———◆———

Ezekiel heard the blast and took the stairs two at a time, his robes flowing behind him. He slid around the corner and saw the mystic who had greeted him earlier unconscious, or perhaps dead, on the floor.

Three men were standing over him, one of them holding what Ezekiel could only surmise was one of the magitech weapons he'd heard so much about. A chill ran down his spine as he thought of what other perversions Adrien was creating within the walls of Arcadia.

The oldest, who was clearly the leader of the gang, looked up at Ezekiel. Recognition washed over the man's face. The guards had been issued descriptions and even drawings of the powerful old Unlawful running around. And that Unlawful was now within his sights.

The leader's eyes turned black. He drew a sword, and with a flick of his wrist, it burst into flames. The man was clearly well trained.

"Hurting the mystic was a mistake, friend," Ezekiel said. "Perhaps if you lay down your weapon and let me attend to him, you might find mercy in this place."

The large guard sneered. "You are the one who will be begging for mercy before we're through, old man." The he nodded to his partners and they both stepped forward, magitech weapons drawn.

Ezekiel sighed. "So be it."

The man on the left fired, and a ball of energy flew toward Ezekiel. But the old man could move faster than most expected. He sidestepped the blast and waved his hand upward. The marble tile underneath of the advancing guard came to life. Ezekiel closed his hand as if holding onto a rope, and a hand formed of tile reached from the floor and grabbed the guard's leg. Ezekiel pulled his hand down and the marble hand followed suit, pulling the guard into the floor.

"Dirk!" the other fool yelled as his partner vanished before his eyes. He turned his weapon on Ezekiel, but never had the chance to fire. Ezekiel waved his hand and the weapon exploded, releasing its energy in the face of the man who held it. The guard screamed in pain, then dropped to his knees.

Ezekiel had dispatched two guards in as many moments, but they were only pawns compared to the third. The man smiled, his black eyes lifeless. "Well, at least the rumors about your power are true. I will actually enjoy cutting you to pieces."

The soldier threw his arm forward, and a large copper urn sailed over his head. Ezekiel reached out a palm and pushed the missile aside, but it was only a distraction.

The guard had sprinted forward, his flaming sword swinging overhead. Ezekiel raised his staff just in time to parry the blow. Light flashed as their two weapons met.

———◆———

Stellan was surprised that the Unlawful's staff blocked his sword. He had expected his weapon to split both the stick and the old man in two. Clearly he was a powerful magic user, and he must have enchanted his staff to increase its strength.

No matter, thought Stellan, *I'll find my opening.*

Stellan hammered his sword at Ezekiel again and again, attacking from every angle. But each time the old man managed to block it, his staff and robes twirling in a tight dance. Before long their positions were reversed, and Stellan was the one forced to block the deadly rod of oak. The old man's eyes burned red, and the anger in his face was clear.

When the old man feinted high, Stellan fell forward. He raised his sword to block the crushing blow, leaving his lower half undefended.

The Unlawful took full advantage of the error and swung his staff low. It crashed into Stellan's knee, and he screamed in pain. But the guard kept his wits about him and slashed his sword outward, forcing the man back.

Stellan accepted the fact that this strange old man outmatched him in hand-to-hand combat, so he tried another tack. Before the Unlawful could move, Stellan dropped his sword and reached both hands outward. He pulled with all his strength, and a window high above the old man shattered, raining shards of razor-sharp glass.

The old man twirled an arm above his head and pushed his palm forward. The glass followed his command and recreated itself as a glass wall between the two magicians.

Stellan took the opportunity. He grabbed his sword from the ground and drove it forward. The wall shattered around his arm; it was worth a few cuts to finish the old man. But as he broke through the wall, instead of flesh and blood, his sword found only air. The old man was nowhere. Stellan had stabbed only a hollow reflection.

He looked left and right, then a sinking feeling hit his stomach. He turned around just in time to see the Unlawful's staff swing through the air. It cracked the side of Stellan's head and stars clouded his vision.

In a desperate attempt to save himself, Stellan swung his flaming sword upwards, but the old man was ready. He caught Stellan's hands in his own. A cold feeling spread across the man's flesh and slowly, from the hilt to the tip, the fire in Stellan's sword turned to ice.

When the ice reached the tip of the sword, the blade shattered, leaving nothing but a jagged piece of frozen steel sticking out of the hilt.

The old man twisted Stellan's arms and forced the broken sword through his chest. Stellan coughed up blood as he looked down at his chest. With his last breath, he raised his head.

The last thing he saw was Ezekiel's blood-red eyes.

CHAPTER 20

T he guard slumped to the ground, hands still grasping the blade sticking out of his chest. Ezekiel saw his black return to gray and knew the guard was dead. For a moment, Ezekiel thought of his mother and smiled. He was a helpless child no longer.

Ezekiel turned to look around the room and saw a magitech rifle aimed right at him. Apparently the guard who had taken the full extent of the blast earlier wasn't out of the fight.

Just as he was about to fire, he began to scream. The guard dropped the gun and began clawing at his face. He then ran forward blindly, screaming as he crashed into a wall. His head rebounded off the stone and he dropped unconscious to the ground.

Ezekiel looked up and saw Julianne standing in the doorway. Her eyes were white, and they held no warmth.

He smiled. "I thought you mystics were people of peace. How did you say it? 'Not accustomed to the martial affairs of this world.'"

Julianne's eyes regained their color, and she looked down at the unconscious guard. "It was only a simple illusion. Who knew he would react so badly? And just because we prefer not to fight, it doesn't mean we don't know how." She gave Ezekiel a wink.

A cough broke the moment, and Ezekiel stepped around the carnage to see the doorman who had been taken down by the magitech weapon. His eyes were wide and his body shaking; blood seeped from the man's stomach, and Ezekiel could smell burnt flesh.

Julianne reached down and touched the man's temple. She spoke a word of comfort and Ezekiel could see the fear and pain disappear.

But Ezekiel wasn't ready to let this man die, no matter how peaceful Julianne could make his passing. The fight had taken nearly all of Ezekiel's energy, but there was a bit left. Laying both hands on the man's torso, his eyes burned red. Ezekiel could feel the man's body responding, the wound working double-time to heal itself.

When Ezekiel had finished, the man was still unconscious but breathing steadily.

Her voice was next to him. "Thank you, Ezekiel."

Ezekiel slumped to the stone floor. "Don't thank me just yet. I just killed a man, one of the Governor's soldiers, on your doorstep. When that man doesn't come home, there's going to be hell to pay, and the devil himself will bring it to your doorstep. I may have just involved your temple in my war whether you wanted it or not." He looked up at her. "For that, I am so very sorry."

Julianne looked over at the dead man, a smile on her lips. "Oh, we are involved. But maybe Adrien doesn't have to know that just yet. Who says that his dead soldier won't be going home?"

Ezekiel looked over at the man he had killed and Julianne's plan suddenly became clear. "Do you think you can pull it off?"

"I was Selah's prize student, remember? Handpicked to replace him. I spend my days leading the mystics in prayer and meditation. My nights are spent exploring other worlds with my mind. I think I can handle a little mimicry for a few weeks. But fooling Adrien will depend on you."

Ezekiel cocked his head to the side. "What do you mean?"

"Adrien sent three men here," Julianne answered as she looked around and pointed. "One's dead," she turned to the one she had attacked, "and another's unconscious. But the third…" She looked down at him.

"Any chance you could dig him out of my floor?"

———•———

The plate of vegetables and wild pheasant gave off a fragrant smell. Parker drew in a deep breath, enjoying every moment. Food like this wasn't abundant in the quarter, and he had no clue when he had last eaten anything like it. "This is amazing!"

"Yeah, magic has its benefits."

"Wait. You…"

She loved fooling him, and this was no exception. "Leftovers. Zeke brings it in from somewhere." She shrugged. "Too many questions about magic and druids and history to get a question in about the food. And by the time we eat, I'm so exhausted I'd eat Sal if nothing else was around." The dragon scampered under the chair and hid from his mistress. She tried to look under the chair. "Hey! I'm just kidding, boy."

Parker thought about the dragon and the lycanthrope and all the other things he had assumed were just myths. "Little small for a dragon, don't you think?"

Hannah slapped his hand and let her fingertips linger on his knuckles for a moment. "Manners, Parker. He can hear you."

She laughed, but as she picked up her plate, pain like a jagged blade stabbed into her brain. The plate slid from her hand and shattered on the ground. "Shit!"

Parker jumped up, concern written clearly on his face. "Hannah! What is it?"

She held a finger in the air. Pushing out everything around her, Hannah attempted to control her mind, to remove the pain and assess what the hell was assaulting her.

Then it struck her. "It's William. He's in trouble."

"How the hell—" he started.

"He's in pain," she said through clenched teeth. "I can feel it. We have to go to Arcadia."

———— ◆ ————

Hannah and Parker kept silent as they trekked miles through the woods back to Arcadia. Darkness had surrounded them as they drew near the city walls.

Hannah created a flaming torch in her hand to light the way. She kept its power low. They didn't want to alert anyone to their presence, and she knew that if things got really bad she was going to need all the power she could muster.

"Gates will be closed," Parker said.

"I should be able to do something about that."

"You want to announce our entry by blowing down Arcadia's front door? Real subtle, Magic Girl. I thought you said you needed to be smart to control magic? I have a better idea; let's do this the old-fashioned way."

Parker led them around the southern wall of the city. Extinguishing her flame, Hannah stayed close to her friend, who knew the outside the walls like he knew the best places in the quarter to pull a con. They got to a spot where Parker crouched low. "Follow me," he whispered before disappearing into the darkness.

Hannah and Parker crawled through the drain pipe and under the city wall. Splashing through several inches of what Hannah told herself was water made the trip close to unbearable.

Worse, it smelled like a mix between cow feces and lycanthrope brains. She had to hold in dry heaves more than once. But she would crawl through worse if it meant helping her brother. Finally they popped out of the pipe on the edge of the Market Quarter.

"Piece of cake." Parker smiled.

"Funny, I didn't think of cake once down in that shithole."

He shrugged and led the way toward QBB.

Hannah noticed how quiet it was on the city streets. Normally people would gather, drink, and tell stories into the early morning hours in the market. You couldn't say unemployment was without its benefits. She mentioned the lack of people Parker, and he told her that after she and Ezekiel left and the Governor and the Chancellor had gotten serious about finding them, a curfew had been issued in the city. Breaking the curfew was punishable by jail time.

Hannah cursed them and the way they were ushering Arcadia into a deeper circle of hell. As they turned for Queen's Boulevard, they saw two men at the toll.

"Maybe it's Jack," Hannah said.

"Don't count on it. Jack doesn't work the toll anymore. In fact, I haven't seen him since you left. This new guy ain't so friendly, and I doubt his friend there is a barrel of rainbows either." Parker placed his hand on the small of Hannah's back and pulled her close. "You don't have time for this. If your magic head is right, William needs your help. Give me a minute with this guy, then you slide by."

"What are you going to do?"

"Well, when he sees me, I'm not going to have to do much of anything."

———◆———

Monte took a slug from his friend's bottle and winced as the homebrew burned its way down to his gut. "Shit, Hank, this sure ain't the mystics' elixir, but it'll do the job."

"Well," Hank said, "beggars can't be choosers. We don't all hold down a government job like you, you ungrateful twat. And they don't call me Wildman just for my work in the Pit."

The men laughed, passing the bottle back and forth. Monte's job had gotten a hell of a lot easier since the curfew had been set. Sure, there weren't as many tolls to skim, but he got paid to sit on his ass and do a whole lot of nothing. The streets were quiet at night, but if any shit hit the fan, he didn't hate the fact that Arcadia's best fighter was with him to handle a tussle.

"Hey, check this out," Hank said, backhanding Monte on the shoulder and nodding down the Boulevard.

A drunk with a jug swinging by his side stumbled down the alley. Piss drunk, the man started belting out the Arcadian anthem at the top of his lungs.

"Oh, this one's going to be fun," Monte said, getting up off his stool.

As the drunk got closer, Monte squinted, trying to bring the man's face into focus through the haze of his friend's booze.

"What the hell?" Hank shouted, suddenly recognizing Pitiable Parker from the Pit. But his recognition came too late. As Wildman's vulgar exclamation filled the alley, Parker swung the jug with precision. It shattered over the brawler's head, sending shards in every direction.

Monte cursed and dove for Parker, but the kid was too fast and Monte was too drunk. Parker ducked his giant arms and spun off down the Boulevard.

Getting to his feet and steadying himself, Monte picked Wildman Hank up off the ground. His friend's temple was leaking blood, shards of the jug still impaled in his face. "Let's get that son of a bitch."

The two friends raced down the dark streets after the kid from Queen's Boulevard with murder in their minds.

———————◆———————

Rather than teleporting the last leg of the journey, Ezekiel decided to walk. The last few days had taken more out of him than he expected, and he thought that stretching his legs would use less energy than another jumping spell. Nevertheless, he was exhausted when he finally arrived home.

He collapsed on the couch and exhaled. Reflecting on the meeting at the monastery, he was reminded just how precarious things were in Arcadia, and realized more than ever how many ramifications there would be on Irth if things didn't work according to his plan.

The fight with the Capitol Guard was a hitch he hadn't been expecting, but at least the arrival of the Chancellor's men had drawn Julianne into the fray.

Before Ezekiel left, he had dug the guard Dirk out of the floor and helped the mystics wipe his memory.

Julianne had appreciated that act.

Then he watched as Julianne took on an exact likeness of Stellan, the man Ezekiel killed. In a few days, she would lead the brainwashed guards back to Arcadia. So, now Julianne was on board. Time would tell if the other mystics decided to get involved in the fight against Adrien.

Unusually quiet, he thought. More often than not, his arrival would spark the appearance of his smart-ass little student.

He pushed himself off the couch and walked the halls of the tower looking for Hannah, but the place was empty. He stepped outside the front doors and scanned the edge of the forest.

Nothing, he thought. *Something isn't right.*

Returning to the great hall, he found two plates of food—one hardly eaten, the other smashed on the floor. Something was wrong, and the wizard feared the worst. She had company, and there had been some sort of conflict.

Ezekiel fastened his robe, grabbed his staff, and concentrated. His body had not yet rested from the last jump and his power was still low. Digging deep into his reserves, he concentrated on his pupil and jumped from the tower towards her.

———— ◆ ————

As Hannah raced toward her home, she smiled as she thought about Parker. Her friend was more than able to handle himself, especially at home on the Boulevard. She was lucky to have him. Although she didn't believe in the Matriarch or Patriarch, she nevertheless felt blessed by someone or something. For the first time ever she felt incredibly strong, like she had experienced abundance.

Her magic was far from mature, but the power inside her was present and just waited to be used to set things right.

Turning the corner toward her house, she was glad to see light in the windows. Something had psychically clued her into her brother's trouble, and now she was beginning to think that maybe it was just the power bubbling in her blood mixed with her imagination.

It wasn't exactly something she had learned from Ezekiel, after all. By the time she reached the door, she had convinced herself there was nothing wrong, and she was very glad for the chance to see her brother. It had been too long since she'd seen him.

Hell, she was even happy to be back in Arcadia.

Despite her haste, Hannah had the presence of mind to pause before entering the house, making sure that there were no prying eyes lurking outside. She then climbed the steps to her door.

The few weeks spent living in the ancient tower in the woods had changed her perception. Arcadia already looked smaller, as did her house. It was as if she had drunk a potion that made her grow. She turned the knob and pushed open the door.

As she opened her mouth to yell her brother's name, the smell struck her; something like the iron that made up Ezekiel's tower. But this was a bit different, and as she stepped farther in, her stomach began to roil.

Her house was covered in blood.

———— ◆ ————

Parker glanced over his shoulder just as Hannah cut down a side street toward her house. Their ruse had worked. Now he just had to keep those assholes busy to give his friend time to make it to Will. He slowed, letting the men advance on him. Their footsteps clattered on the cobblestones.

He knew that either of them would gladly rip his head off. Wildman Hank wanted vengeance for the humiliation Parker had put him through, and the toll master was just a cruel son of a bitch. In a fair fight, either of them would be able to do Parker serious harm. But there was nothing fair about fights in Arcadia, and he would use every trick he had against them.

Kicking over a bucket on the curb to make sure they still had a followed on him, Parker turned for Leroy's Pub. Leroy's was a dive, the kind of place where you could buy black-market booze that had a better chance of causing blindness than getting you drunk.

More importantly, he knew Leroy's had what he needed. With the men on his tail, he cut past the corner of the pub, climbed a stack of wooden crates and grabbed the bottom rail of the ladder that led to the roof. There were a hundred ways onto the roofs of Queen's Boulevard, and Parker knew them all. But he needed one that the clumsy, drunk men could follow.

Making it to the top of the pub, Parker ran to the opposite side and waited.

The men, in due time, scrambled over the edge and onto the roof. Monte, the toll master who'd spilled the beans about the government looking for Hannah, shouted, "Thought you gave us the slip, you little bastard? The Queen Bitch herself couldn't help you now."

When the men got close, Parker spun and jumped from Leroy's to the building adjacent. It was a three-foot gap and Parker cleared it easily. As his legs hit the flat rooftop he tucked into a roll and popped to his feet. Curses filled the night air behind him.

Glancing back, he saw the men standing on the edge, each trying to convince the other to go first. Finally, Wildman made the jump and Monte followed. Parker repeated the process several more times, the gap between the houses increasing as he moved on.

Growing up in the quarter, Parker knew the sequence of roofs like the back of his hand. It was the way the kids of the neighborhood would move around to avoid detection. But these two men had kept up with him so far.

All right, time to take it up a notch.

Parker took a running start. Sailing over the greatest gap yet, he nailed the next rooftop. This one had a pitched roof. He started to slide, his foot gaining purchase on a tile just before the edge.

"See you later, shitheads," he taunted. He could see on their faces that it had worked.

Monte the toll man went first. The brute pushed himself off the ledge of the roof, and Parker was actually impressed with his distance, but it wasn't enough. From where he was standing, he watched the overweight man hit the edge of the roof with the middle of his chest.

His hands groped desperately, but the tile didn't hold. He pulled part of the roof off with him as he slipped off the edge. With screams and a clatter, the man crashed into the alleyway below.

"Give it up. I could do this all day," Parker yelled to the Wildman.

Smiling, Hank shouted, "The chase will only make the kill more enjoyable, kid. I've been waiting for some payback."

Hank took three quick steps and leaped for the rooftop. Unlike his friend in a broken heap below, Hank was a fighter with better-than-average reflexes. He found his feet and scrambled up the pitched roof.

"Shit!" Parker yelled, feigning concern. He took off toward the other edge.

The rooftop chase that had begun at Leroy's would end on the other side of town. There was a place he and Hannah used to hang out to split their spoils when the weather was too bad for Capitol Park. But their lair didn't last; years of inclement weather and neglect made the condemned building so decrepit that it was dangerous to squat there even for a short time.

Parker ran across two more buildings, then lowered himself to another and cut away toward his target. Wildman Hank was on his heels. Parker was awestruck by the man's physical abilities. He was also seriously glad he wasn't in the ring with him again.

Slowing down a little, Parker prepared to make his last jump. He knew his aim had to be perfect. The jump from the last rooftop was short, but he also knew he had to hit the thin line of a brick wall that ran the length of the middle. It was almost dead center.

The brick below the surface of the failing structure was barely wide enough for a man to stand on. In the light of the moon, he could hardly discern the safe zone. Leaping, he kept his eyes on his landing spot, ready for the worst if he missed.

But he didn't. His feet stuck the landing. Regaining his balance, he turned to watch the night's main event. The abandoned house was at the edge of a block, and there was nowhere else to go. Seeing the kid waiting, Hank developed a shit-eating grin. Hunger for violence was plastered on his face as he made the simple jump, ready to take his reward. But Hank's smile was nothing compared to Parker's.

As Hank landed, his glee turned instantly to fear. The rooftop likely wouldn't have held Hannah's dragon, let alone a three-hundred-pound dipshit. The man disappeared into a hole of his own making with a mighty crash. Another crash sounded and Parker knew that he had fallen through the second floor as well.

Parker turned to climb down the building without even looking. The man was done for, and he hoped he wasn't too late to offer his friend some help.

CHAPTER 21

———◆———

Hannah had hated her father for as long as she could remember. Arnold wasn't an easy man to like and he didn't have many friends, if any at all.

The women who would occasionally stumble home with him from Lloyd's pub left early in the morning with more money than they came with.

And then there were the beatings. Hannah's memory stretched far enough back to recall him hitting her mother more than once, and he wasn't exactly gentle with her and William.

The man had been worthless at best, despicable at worst.

But when she saw his beaten and bloody body on the kitchen floor, a strange feeling of love washed over her. The kind of familial love that was often enough mixed with hate.

Hannah ran to his body and dropped to her knees. The back of his head had been bludgeoned, and she could clearly see the contents that were normally protected by his thick skull.

Anger and rage abated as fear took over.

"*William*!" she shouted, running to their bedroom.

The boy's body was crumpled next to her bed. Hannah dropped next to him, pulling him into her lap, and rocked his lifeless form gently. But then her brother twitched, and he looked up into his sister's deep brown eyes.

"You came," he said. The boy tried to smile. "You shouldn't have. They're looking for you."

"Shhh, quiet, Will. Be still. I need to get you help," she told him.

William ignored her, knowing his fate was sealed. "They came for information. Made me sit and watch as they beat Dad to death, then came for me."

Hannah put her fingers to his lips. "Shhhh… It's OK, Will. It's going to be OK."

He blinked, kissing the tips of her fingers as he continued. "They wanted you and the Founder. I told them to piss off."

The boy started coughing before he finally laughed, crunching as his stomach caused him pain. "Thought they would break me, but they couldn't. I told them nothing, Hannah."

The girl rocked her brother and wept into his hair. She cursed her so-called good fortune. She cursed Ezekiel. She cursed Adrien and the Governor. She cursed the Matriarch and Patriarch, just in case they existed.

"Hannah, you gave me *everything*," William whispered. "And this is what I can give you back. You always protected me. I'm glad I got the chance to protect you for once. I love you, Hannah. But now, you have to go."

"No, William, I won't leave you." She held her brother and sobbed uncontrollably, her tears dropping onto his face.

"*If it weren't for this bloody MAGIC!*" she screamed. And then realized that the thing she was cursing was exactly what she needed to call on.

She laid William's body flat and then leaned over him, placing her hands on his chest. Concentrating, she urged the power within herself to transfer to her brother.

Nothing happened.

Remembering that healing magic was the druids' art, she muttered in strange tongues, trying to convince the universe that her magic was strong enough to heal him.

But it wasn't strong enough; *she* wasn't strong enough. If she had only worked harder, listened more to Ezekiel, pushed herself to tap into the power, she could have done this.

She tried again, pushing on her brother's still chest, thinking she might just be able to physically force the energy out of her and into him.

Nothing happened.

And then she realized why she had failed. He was already gone.

———◆———

Hannah had no idea how long she had laid on the floor with her brother's dead body. She knew the right thing to do was to run.

But capture would only allow the ones responsible to get away with this and all the other atrocities they had committed. Hannah preferred death to living in the hellhole of Arcadia without her brother. But living would allow her to taste justice, and she would take her bloodlust all the way to the top. Her thirst for vengeance required it.

She would kill Adrien.

But first, she had to deal with the Hunters who slew William. Just then she heard her front door swing open. Her house's floorboards squeaked as large bodies moved across them. Without looking, she knew who it was.

She recognized their power.

"We're taking you to the boss," a man said.

She knew the voice. For as many days as she had remaining on Irth, she wouldn't forget it. She flowed off the floor and faced the man who had accosted her in the alley. The smile he had worn as he tore off her shirt was painted on his face. He looked exactly the same, except for his right hand. It was deformed as if it had been dipped in liquid metal. The smaller magic user stood behind him scowling.

"You did this." Her question was more of a statement. She knew the answer, but wanted the man's confession before she unleashed the power of the entire universe on him.

"I only wish I could have gotten the little shit to talk before I landed the last blow. But then again here you are, so same result." The man shrugged. "And without the wizard here to protect you, your time is up. The Chancellor demanded that we take you in in one piece. But I don't think he'd mind if we had a little fun. Torturing your family has me," he grinned, "all excited."

As the Hunter stepped toward her, Hannah didn't even try to control her emotion. She forgot every lesson Ezekiel had taught her in the tower. Instead, she let every emotion come to the surface. Her skin began to burn with power. She looked up at the Hunter, her eyes glowing a fiercer red than they ever had.

A gloating smile crossed her face as she saw fear in the man's eyes.

Her voice was malevolent; it sounded like two people were talking in unison as her energy radiated everywhere.

"Trust me. I'm not the one getting screwed tonight!"

———— ♦ ————

With his hands on his knees, Parker tried to catch his breath before going into Hannah's house. The place was quiet, so he assumed that she was caring for her brother. As he stepped toward the door, a rush of wind struck him from behind as Ezekiel appeared out of nowhere.

"You're him," Parker said in shock as he took in the haggard-looking old man.

"I am," he replied.

The old man stepped forward, then slumped to his knees. Teleporting took too much energy to use it as much as he had tonight, but Hannah needed him so he found the will. Now there was almost nothing left at all.

Parker ran over to him and leaned down. Hands shaking, Ezekiel accepted his help. He looked up at the young man Hannah had spoken so highly of.

Damage to his face showed that he was tough. The fact that he was still standing told him he was smart. Ezekiel knew Parker could be an asset, if not a key member of their team.

"Queen Bitch..." Parker uttered as the windows of Hannah's house started to flicker and strobe. Bright light shone through in blues and reds. Then a blinding white light burst, blowing the glass out of the windows. It sounded as if a lightning storm had rolled into town and collided with a hurricane. Parker heard high-pitched screaming from within the mass.

Parker took a step toward the house, but Ezekiel grabbed the tail of his cloak. "You can't," Ezekiel said. "It's too dangerous."

"But Hannah is in there!"

"I know. That magic is hers, but it is well beyond her means. She's losing control. If you go in there right now, you'll be obliterated."

Flames and beams of blue continued to fly, many of them jumping out of the windows, licking the sky.

"We have to try."

The old man, with surprising physical strength, pulled Parker down to his level. Inches from his face, Ezekiel spoke. "You go in there, you'll definitely be killed. Break whatever concentration she's maintaining and you could destroy her as well. She's still a novice. This power is beyond her. She can't control it."

Recognizing that the quarter was coming to life, Ezekiel thought about the earthquake that he felt when she transformed Sal. Fear filled him as he looked around. "She could take out the whole damned neighborhood."

Parker, uncertain how to proceed, decided to place his trust in this crazy old man. Hannah trusted the Founder, and that was good enough for him. "What do we do?"

"Help me up. I can't protect her, but maybe there is something we can do to save the rest of the quarter."

Ezekiel held his staff out, pointed above the roof of Hannah's house. The building looked like it was about to explode. With his free hand, he cupped a palm toward the dusty ground as if he were holding a ball. His eyes turned red, but only faintly.

The old man closed his eyes and started to chant in a foreign tongue. As the volume increased, so did the intensity.

His eyes flashed open and they were as bright red as any metalsmith's flame Parker had ever seen.

This was like no magic he had ever observed in Arcadia. The man's weight shifted onto Parker, who did all he could to keep the magician standing. Blue light streamed from the end of the staff, finding its apex directly over the house.

With a final word from Ezekiel, it wrapped down in every direction, forming a perfect cover over the structure. It was like an azure glass bowl had flipped over on flaming logs.

The magician's body went limp, but the shield around the house remained. Parker eased the man to the ground and watched as all hell continued to break loose inside the bubble.

As fire and energy continued to shoot from the house, they bounced off the blue forcefield keeping them within. Eventually it became too bright and Parker had to look away.

Finally the lights and flames died, and the neighborhood became deathly quiet. Parker held his breath, knowing that Hannah could have never lasted through whatever just happened inside. The blue shield slowly evaporated into the air.

"It is finished," the old man said, though Parker was unsure if it was a question.

Or an answer.

"Yes," was all he could say. They sat in the aftermath for a few minutes, Parker wondering what the hell he should do.

"Help me up," the old man said. "We need to find her."

Parker's stomach turned, because he knew they were going in to find her body. They stepped through the entrance, whose door was blown off its hinges. Blood and body parts and rubble littered the kitchen. His eyes scanned for some sign of his friend.

Nothing.

He wondered if the magic had completely disintegrated her. He walked down the hall, half-caring the magician along with him. Most of the roof had fallen in and they had to pick their way through the debris. Parker reached the back of the house and froze in the doorway to what was once Hannah's room.

That's when he saw her.

Hannah sat on the floor with William's broken body in her lap. Her hair was crusted with blood. Whether it was hers, Will's, or the enemy's, he'd never know. A dead guard with a hand of bronze lay in a corner. The skin had all but melted off the dead man's face.

Hannah lifted her head as the two men cautiously approached. Her eyes glowed red—brighter and deeper than even Ezekiel's had. But her face; her face was emotionless. She didn't even see Parker. As far as the girl was concerned, Ezekiel was the only one in the room.

Hannah spoke, her voice all the more chilling for its lack of feeling. "This? This is what *your* student has done, Ezekiel. He sent these men here to kill my family. To kill me. But I was stronger than they were."

Ezekiel looked down at the girl, sadness marking his weary face. "Hannah, I'm so sorry—"

She cut him off. She didn't need his pity.

"Teach me, Ezekiel. Teach me *everything*, *dammit*! Drive me till I fall exhausted to the ground, and I will get back up. I will never bend, I will never break, I won't yield. In the name of the Matriarch, in the name of the Queen Bitch, my queen, *I will not stop.* I swear on my brother's dead body that I will not rest until Adrien is destroyed. Even if I have to burn Arcadia to the ground to do it."

She turned back to view her brother's face, a faint red glow lighting it.

"I will see justice served."

EPILOGUE

A drien sat at his window sipping twenty-year-old elixir, the finest the mystics had to offer, as he watched Queen's Boulevard burn. The liquid bit at his throat as he swallowed. As the magical show died out, the world went black again beyond his spot at the Academy. The Boulevard was left in darkness, just as Ezekiel's student hoped it would remain.

"Cheers, old friend," he said, as he let the buzz take his mind.

Without knocking, Doyle burst through the door. "Chancellor, it's the Hunters."

"Yes," Adrien said. "They put on quite a show. Tell me they have good news."

"They're dead."

Adrien froze, the glass halfway to his mouth. His forehead just above his left eye began to twitch. He slowly got up from his chair and strode over to his loyal assistant.

The man began to stammer something, but Adrien slammed the glass across the man's temple before the words got out. Doyle stumbled back, blood dripping down his face and terror in his eyes. "No, please!" the man said as he pissed himself.

Directing his hand in Doyle's direction, Adrien began to crush the assistant's throat. Doyle's eyes pleaded with his master, but Adrien didn't see them. He saw nothing in his cold rage.

Once again his men had been killed. Once again his plans had been thwarted, and someone needed to pay.

Just before killing the man, Adrien released the pressure. His assistant gasped for breath and fell to the hardwood floor.

A thin smile formed on Adrien's lips. "We've been doing this the wrong way, Doyle." He extended a hand down to his assistant.

Doyle looked up at him in distrust. The Chancellor had always been erratic, but his loyalties had protected him from the ebb and flow of Adrien's wrath. Now he feared for his life. Nevertheless, he reached out a trembling hand and let his leader help him to his feet.

"I need you to set up a meeting, Doyle," Adrien said, as if they were in the middle of any ordinary appointment. "Gather the chief engineer, the Governor, and Jedidiah."

"Sir? Old Jed, the Prophet?"

Adrien paced the office. "That's right. This attack may have been precisely the push we needed to accelerate our plans. Tonight was a tragedy, but no tragedy shall be wasted, not while I'm in charge. Gather everyone tonight. We've waited long enough."

He paused a moment, speaking half to Doyle and half to himself, "*I've* waited long enough."

As Doyle scampered out of the room, Adrien poured himself another glass. He thought about Ezekiel, no longer afraid of the old man.

Once my weapon is complete, he thought, no magic of Ezekiel's, no force on Irth will be able to stop me. And then I will make him pay.

I'll make them all pay.

———◆———

AUTHOR NOTES:
LEE BARBANT

Written February 28, 2017

Thank you so much for reading Restriction (and for read-ing these notes!). It was a ton of fun to write, and I hope that you like it as much as I do.

When Chris and I first approached Michael about writ-ing in the Kurtherian Universe, we were thinking it would be about vampires or werewolves or secret government opera-tions. I even started rewatching my favorite vampire shows to prepare for it (everyone here watches True Blood, right?).

But then Michael completely flipped the script on us by mentioning a new direction he wanted to try… How far can the etheric take us?

Michael had this vision for a future world, where the Kurtherian nanocytes had taken over everyone but had also morphed in such a way as to give people access to *magic*. How would this influence culture? How would it influence our un-derstanding of the world? Could it create an age of magic?

Obviously, if you are going to have a magical world, you need magical schools to teach and train people in these dangerous arts (otherwise you're gonna have kids running around turning their siblings into toads or bar fights that end with blowing up the town.) A magical world would require a magical university.

But schools come with their own problems, political in-fighting and unequal access, just to name a couple. We figured that would hold true for magical schools too, right?

In some ways, Chris and I were the perfect match to try and figure this all out. We're both college educators, and our first series, *The Steel City Heroes*, focused on superheroes that work at universities in good old Pittsburgh, Pennsylvania.

But the Kurtherian world takes it to a whole new level. The stakes are higher, the world is more dangerous, and justice needs to be served with a large helping of whoopass.

It also comes with added benefits. I've always wanted to write a high fantasy universe with dragons and wizards and knights. But the stories that do that stuff best tend to have a well thought out history, with thousands of pages of historical addendums. That would take years to create, and I wanted to write about some freaking wizards *now*!

The Kurtherian world solves that problem.

If you've been a fan of Michael's works for years, then you know all about that backstory. Hopefully you saw in our book how Bethany Anne et al still have a strong influence on a world several hundred years later.

And, if Restriction is your first book in the Kurtherian universe, you're in luck! There's a whole body of literature supporting the Age of Magic. Want to know more about the Bitch and the Bastard? Check out the Kurtherian Gambit or the Dark Messiah. Want to know more about the mysterious Oracle, Lilith? Check out The Boris Chronicles. Curious about how we got from our world to the age of Irth? Start with Justin Sloan's Reclaiming Honor. We've got plenty more story to tell, but there's a whole world that has also come before it.

So thanks for reading. Tell your friends. Chat with me on Twittter (@lebarbant) or Facebook and get ready for book 2, Rebellion. Cause there are plenty of douche nuggets left to fight and Hannah has a long way to go before she gets her vengeance. Magic has a lot farther left to rise.

AUTHOR NOTES: CHRIS RAYMOND

Written February 28, 2017

Holy fireballs, that was fun!

I actually started writing my first book a little over two years ago. My daughter is a voracious reader and had wrapped up the Harry Potter series by the end of the third grade (yeah, she's wicked smart--pardon the dad brag). Then she read it again. And again. One of the challenges for Mrs. Raymond and I was trying to find stuff that she liked, was at her reading level, and that we were OK with her reading at her age (the second half of Harry's adventures were VERY borderline).

For fun, I decided I'd take a crack to write something for my little darling Simone. A short story turned into a book, which turned into a yet to be finished trilogy. Simone and her friends loved it, so I decided, what the hell, I'd post it on Amazon. (It's pulled now, but sign up for our list to get announcements of when the new and improved Arcanum Island series will be rereleased!!)

Little did I know that was the beginning of a writing career that I have fallen in love with!

I can't wait for Simone to read Hannah's story, but she'll need to wait a few more years.

So, how did I get from Middle Grade mysteries to foul-mouthed wizards?

Months ago, Lee and I started talking with Michael about the possibility of writing in the Kurtherian Gambit universe.

If we could revise history, we'd say that he begged us to contribute because of our prowess as writers and creative genius (not to mention our boyish good looks).

But... let's stick with reality for a minute.

We wanted in on TGK universe because Michael has shaped a kick ass world with tons of possibilities and a fan base that is ravenous, engaged, and interactive. And we are so glad he has taken us in as co-authors. We've learned a lot from him and from you all about what makes a story great.

I get to play a funny role in our triumvirate of authors. Lee and Michael sweat over the story arc and beats (detailed outline), shaping and reshaping the story into what it would become.

Me? I'm the word monkey who gets to take the first crack at writing their story ideas into a narrative. This means I get the fun rollercoaster ride of watching their ideas unfold as I type away at my keyboard as fast as possible.

The greatest thing about this work is that, like you, I get to hit all the twists and turns, the badass fight scenes, and the emotional highs and lows as I write them. And (hopefully) like you, I can't wait to see where the story goes from here.

As I write this author note, I'm actually about to finish up the words for Rise of Magic, Book 2. I'll tell you this: If you liked book one, you're going to love book two. It's the second step of a long pathway that will explore the Rise of Magic and of our favorite 19 year old...

Thanks so much for reading! As this is our first book in the Kurtherian Universe, we would LOVE it if you took a minute to leave a review. These are really important for visibility and to help other readers find our work.

And I'll see you back in Arcadia!

Cheers,
Chris

PS:

If you dug Lee and Chris's work, you can also find them collaborating on:

The Steel City Heroes Series

When monsters, magic, and mayhem descend upon the steel city, it's hard to tell the difference between the heroes and the villains-especially when they don't know themselves.

The Jack Carson Stories

On the run from a fate worse than death, with secret powers too dangerous to reveal, Jack Carson is not your average hero.

Sign up (www.subscribepage.com/smokeandsteelnews) to make sure you don't miss their new releases and giveaways!

AUTHOR NOTES: MICHAEL ANDERLE

Written March 16, 2017

SONOFABITCH!

Holy crap… First, before I forget, THANK YOU for reading these notes! However, they are going to go by SUPER fast because…

Well, I almost put the book up without writing them!

I mean, I have the file open right before I upload. I'm doing a last sanity check myself to see if anything was forgotten and I'm reading Lee's Author Notes, then Chris's Author Notes and then my page…

Completely blank.

Not. A. Damned. Word. On. It.

Yeah, that "blood drained from his face" description I write sometimes? Felt it happen to me just minutes ago and now I'm furiously writing down my Author Notes.

Which sucks, because really this book deserves a kick ass Author Notes from me to go into the back story that these to guys from Pittsburgh (or, at least they live there now) conned my gullible ass into …

Wait…wait…yeah, that isn't the truth (damn my dad and his 'never let the truth get in the way of a good story' preaching).

I have to fight the urge to lay it on thick.

Chris approached me some time before/during the Christmas break, and we agreed to chat when everyone got back into their respective towns in the new year. Partially, this new effort might have happened because I said a few things on their Podcast (Part-Time Writers Podcast - itunes.apple.com/us/podcast/part-time-writers-podcast/ id1092617862?mt=2 - One of my favorites even before they allowed me to speak on it).

Those two guys are just so damned honest, and funny. The honesty is something I treasure until it got turned in my direction.

Ouch…I say '*ouch*' again ;-)

It wasn't bad, but man, I know that if they don't like something, it will come out on their podcast, that's for damned sure.

Either way, they were looking at what to do in their second year of their Indie Publishing career, and I had recently challenged them to rethink their mountains. So, because of my stupidity (I mean, lucidity) of thought, they asked me and the rest is, now, history because we are in the 'Now.'

For those who have seen Spaceballs, you remember the scene when they are going through the Spaceballs - The VHS? "When are we? We are Now? When is Now? It's gone!" (Or something like that, I'm trying like crazy to publish fast, here!)

I'm both SUPER excited about this series and this age. It is (perhaps) the ultimate thought process to nanites. We have seen foreshadowing of this age all the way back in TKG 13 - My Ride is a Bitch (www.amazon.com/Ride-Bitch-Kurtherian-Gambit-Book-ebook/dp/B01M1MOZBS/). If you read the intro to TS Paul's Conjuring Quantico (think of it similar to a Marvel Scene at the end of the movie, AFTER the credits - www.amazon.com/Conjuring-Quantico-Federal-Witch-Book-ebook/dp/B01M1A6C8K/)…

Here is the part that is most pertinent, but go back and read the whole thing, because I place another hint at the end:

Why aren't witches real? Tom interrupted her thoughts.

What? She asked absentmindedly as she opened the app for communications.

Witches, why aren't they real? He asked again.

Bethany Anne stopped reading when she realized TOM's question had no context. Then, her eyes opened wide. *Oh shit, how the fuck is he getting stories again?*

They weren't near the kitchen crew (a requirement when the ship was built she had made damn sure was followed).

Bethany Anne thought back over the last few days, and nothing they had done together had anything to do with witches.

Wiccans? She asked. *It's a religion, I don't know if…*

No, not Wiccans, true magic using witches. Or Warlocks, Magic-Users and the rest.

Bethany Anne sat there, perplexed.

Why the hell would we have witches and warlocks? She finally asked.

Well, there is no reason that I can ascribe to that there can't be any.

———◆———

That was a MAJOR piece that started me down this path. However, if you go forward just a little further into I think Book 14, you can see me setup Bethany Anne with 'magic' when she melts the little pins the guys are wearing in the next book.

It ALL revolves around Arthur C. Clark's 3rd rule about, "any sufficiently advanced technology is indistinguishable from magic."

Then, we trace the next major beat in Justin Sloan's books with Valerie in New York (those that are messed up in their minds, but they aren't using drugs.)

Finally, we have items discussed in this book, and the major upheaval in humanity when the Kurtherian Technology goes WAY awry.

So, here we have it. The time is hundreds of years after Bethany Anne/Michael/Boris have left the planet…

That which is in our DNA, perhaps from eons ago, have manifested and Irth will never be the same.

I hope you enjoy this new age as much as we enjoy writing in it!

Michael Anderle

————◆————

If you haven't read The Kurtherian Gambit, I'll put a plug in here … It's pretty decent, if I say so myself ;-)

The Kurtherian Gambit - Death Becomes Her (Book 01)
www.amazon.com/Death-Becomes-Kurtherian-Gambit-Book-ebook/dp/B017I3NVP2

Also by
CM Raymond & LE Barbant

Steel City Heroes Saga

The Catalyst

The Crucible

The Casting

Jack Carson Stories

The Devil's Due

The Devil's Wager

THE DEVIL YOU KNOW
(COMING APRIL 2017)

Don't miss a single release by Barbant and Raymond. Sign up
for news and giveaways:
http://www.subscribepage.com/smokeandsteelnews

Come hang out on the Rise of Magic Facebook page:
http://www.facebook.com/TheAgeofMagic

Website:
www.smokeandsteel.com

Michael Anderle

Kurtherian Gambit Series
Titles Include:

First Arc

Death Becomes Her (01) - Queen Bitch (02) - Love Lost (03) - Bite This (04)
Never Forsaken (05) - Under My Heel (06) Kneel Or Die (07)

Second Arc

We Will Build (08) - It's Hell To Choose (09) - Release The Dogs of War (10)
Sued For Peace (11) - We Have Contact (12) - My Ride is a Bitch (13)
Don't Cross This Line (14)

Third Arc (Due 2017)

Never Submit (15) - Never Surrender (16) - Forever Defend (17)
Might Makes Right (18) - Ahead Full (19) - Capture Death (20)
Life Goes On (21)

New Series

The Second Dark Ages

The Dark Messiah (01)
The Darkest Night (02)

The Boris Chronicles
* With Paul C. Middleton *

Evacuation
Retaliation
Revelation
Restitution 2017

Reclaiming Honor
* With Justin Sloan *

Justice Is Calling (01)
Claimed By Honor (02)
Judgement Has Fallen (03)
Angel of Reckoning (04)

The Etheric Academy
* With TS Paul *

Alpha Class (01)
Alpha Class (02)
Alpha Class (03) Coming soon

TERRY HENRY "TH" WALTON CHRONICLES
* WITH CRAIG MARTELLE *

NOMAD FOUND (01)
NOMAD REDEEMED (02)
NOMAD UNLEASHED (03)
NOMAD SUPREME (04)
NOMAD'S FURY (05)
NOMAD'S JUSTICE (06)

TRIALS AND TRIBULATIONS
* WITH NATALIE GREY *

RISK BE DAMNED (01)
DAMNED TO HELL (02)
HELL'S WORST NIGHTMARE (03) COMING SOON

THE ASCENSION MYTH
* WITH ELL LEIGH CLARKE *

AWAKENED (01)
ACTIVATED (02)

THE RISE OF MAGIC
* WITH CM RAYMOND/LE BARBANT *

RESTRICTIONS (01)
REAWAKENING (02)
REBELLION (03
REVOLUTION (04) COMING SOON

THE HIDDEN MAGIC CHRONICLES
* WITH JUSTIN SLOAN *

SHADES OF LIGHT (01)

SHORT STORIES

FRANK KURNS STORIES OF THE UNKNOWNWORLD 01 (7.5)
You Don't Mess with John's Cousin

FRANK KURNS STORIES OF THE UNKNOWNWORLD 02 (9.5)
Bitch's Night Out

FRANK KURNS STORIES OF THE UNKNOWNWORLD
02 (13.25)
WITH NATALIE GREY
Bellatrix

ANTHOLOGIES
* AVAILABLE AT AUDIBLE.COM AND iTUNES *

THE KURTHERIAN GAMBIT
DEATH BECOMES HER - AVAILABLE NOW
QUEEN BITCH - AVAILABLE NOW
LOVE LOST - AVAILABLE NOW
BITE THIS - AVAILABLE NOW
NEVER FORSAKEN - AVAILABLE NOW
UNDER MY HEEL - AVAILABLE NOW

Reclaiming Honor Series
Justice Is Calling – Available Now
Claimed By Honor – Available Now
Judgment Has Fallen – Available Now
Angel of Reckoning – Coming Soon

Terry Henry "TH" Walton Chornicles
Nomad Found
Nomad Redeemed
Nomad Unleashed – Coming Soon

The Etheric Academy
Alpha Class
Alpha Class 2

Anthologies

Glimpse
Honor in Death
(Michael's First Few Days)

Beyond the Stars: At Galaxy's Edge
Tabitha's Vacation

MICHAEL ANDERLE SOCIAL

WEBSITE:
http://kurtherianbooks.com/

EMAIL LIST:
http://kurtherianbooks.com/email-list/

FACEBOOK HERE:
https://www.facebook.com/TheKurtherianGambitBooks/

CPSIA information can be obtained
at www.ICGtesting.com
Printed in the USA
LVHW112317021218
599033LV00001B/16/P